Were Tales:

A

Shapeshifter

Anthology

"Comprising poems and stories from some of the world's best in horror, *Were Tales* gives new form to the shapeshifter genre in a transcendent and transformative anthology. Eviscerating."
—Lee Murray, Bram Stoker Award-winning author of *Grotesque: Monster Stories.*

"With some of the genre's best poets and prose practitioners, *Were Tales: A Shapeshifter Anthology* is a verifiable midnight feast overflowing with the imaginative and the unforgettable! This one gets under the skin and remakes what it finds!"
—John Palisano, Bram Stoker Award-Winning author of *Ghost Heart*, President of The Horror Writers Association

"Evocative, engaging, and entertaining, the short stories and poems in Were Tales burst from the page like newborn, ravenous shapeshifters in search of fresh blood. A collection of tragic, thrilling tales that will have you locking your windows during the next full moon."
—Gaby Triana, bestselling author of gothic horror, MOON CHILD, and the Haunted Florida series

An Anthology Edited By
S.D. Vassallo and Steven M. Long

Were
Tales:
A
Shapeshifter
Anthology

BRIGIDS GATE PRESS
Bucyrus, Kansas
www.brigidsgatepress.com

Printed in the United States of America

Dedicated to everyone who enjoys tales of hairy deeds.

Content warnings are provided at
the end of this book.

Contents

Many thanks to Eric Guignard and Stephanie Ellis for their tips and words of advice regarding publishing, editing, and putting a manuscript together. Their advice was invaluable, to say the least.

A big thank you as well to the gang on Twitter: Max, Laurie, Cindy, Steph, Ellen, Kim, Steven, Tracy, Toni, George, and Wayne. You guys are a great bunch. Thanks for all your support!

Thank you to Jonathan Maberry for graciously allowing us to reprint one of his Sam Hunter stories in this anthology.

Most importantly, thank you to my wife and son, whose encouragement and support made the founding of Brigids Gate Press, and this, our first publication, a reality. I love both of you.

Foreword

by S.D. Vassallo

Ghosts. Vampires. Witches. Demons. All common creatures found in fantasy and horror fiction, and sometimes sci-fi. I couldn't begin to tell you how many stories I've read that featured one or more of those terrors. But as much as I enjoyed all those tales, none of them sparked my interest as much as what became my favorite monster: the werewolf.

Don't get me wrong; I love a good haunted house story as much as the next fan of horror fiction. Stories about demons and deals with the devil are favorites also. But give me a choice between any of those stories and a rousing tale of someone transforming into a nightmarish beast under the light of the full moon, and I know exactly what I'll be reading.

It's odd, really, that as much as I love that trope, it's also one of the harder to find. Mention vampires, and most people can rattle off several with no effort. Mention werewolves, though, and after *An American Werewolf in London* and *The Howling*, the average person will be left scratching their heads trying to come up with another title. Maybe *The Wolfman*. Fans of horror fiction will probably be able to name more. Still, in spite of how entrenched the werewolf is in our consciousness, there just aren't that many stories when compared to other tropes.

When my wife and I decided to fulfill our dreams of founding a small press, it didn't take long for me to decide that my first project would be an anthology of shapechanger stories. Though world folklore and legend are replete with stories of many different types of werecreatures, the majority of them are unfamiliar to readers, or at least nowhere near as well-known as werewolves. With that in mind, I decided to create an anthology of werecreature and shapeshifter stories, and in short order, *Were Tales* was born.

Within these pages, you will find a couple of stories featuring werewolves. You'll also encounter werebears, weretigers, and other shapeshifters including a wereskunk. Some tales are creepy, some scary, one or two are brutal, and there's some humor. There's at least one moment of sublime beauty too.

When I sat down to write this foreword, I had much that I wanted to talk about: stories I've read, movies I've seen, lore and legends of shapechangers that I learned about. If you're a reader like me, however, you're probably sitting there impatiently waiting to start reading the stories themselves. After all, that's why you're here, and that's why I assembled this anthology. I'll leave you to plunge into the collection and experience the tales for yourself. Enjoy!

Introduction

by Ronald Kelly

So, what can you say about shapeshifters and were-creatures—wolven or otherwise—that hasn't been said already?

After reading this collection, you'll know there is plenty.

First of all, you've got an old-school monster lover here. I grew up back during the big "monster craze" of the sixties and early seventies. The late-night "shock theaters" and "creature features", the Aurora monster models, those wonderfully detailed Don Post monster masks that you could never afford to buy on a kid's allowance, and the monthly issues of Forrest J. Ackerman's *Famous Monsters of Filmland* peeking gruesomely from the magazine rack at your local newsstand, nestled between Mom's *Ladies Home Journal* and Dad's *Mechanic's Illustrated.*

And, among those classic monsters that all of us know and love so well—Frankenstein's Monster, Count Dracula, the Mummy, the Creature from the Black Lagoon—it was the shapeshifters that intrigued me the most. First, there was the Wolfman. Poor, tormented Larry Talbot, bitten by Bela, the gypsy-turned-lycanthrope, and destined to sprout yak hair and a prosthetic underbite during the cycle of the full moon. Joining him were other cinematic lycanthropes: *The Werewolf of London, I Was a Teenage Werewolf, An American Werewolf in London, The Company of Wolves,* and *Teen Wolf,* just to name a few.

And the other changeling, brought about by science rather through supernatural means, was the dastardly Mister Hyde. That brutish other-self of the distinguished and studious Doctor Henry Jekyll. Robert Louis Stevenson's depiction of Hyde is more "human" in nature; more of an overbearing, self-serving asshole than an actual monster. The Universal Studios depiction was more horrifying and disturbing. Mister Hyde was civilized man regressed thousands of years backward in time, to his Neanderthal state. With each swallow of the serum, Jekyll grew even more hideous and murderous. Aggression gave way to cold-blooded barbarity, which, eventually, led to the good doctor's downfall.

A couple of other shapeshifter films that immediately come to mind are Paul Schrader's *Cat People* and John Carpenter's gross-out classic, *The Thing,* which have nothing whatsoever to do with lycanthropy or chemically-induced genetic regression. Of the pair, the alien Thing is the more severe. Its intentions are never truly clear and may not be of evil intent at all. It is simply a devourer, digester, and duplicator of that team of isolated men in the frozen wasteland of Antarctica. It is their own compassion—their love of a helpless dog—that allows the boogeyman to invade the compound; a human trait that the metamorphosizing extraterrestrial take's full advantage of.

Werecreatures and shapeshifters have always been prominent in literature. Beginning with the first known lycanthropic novel, Sutherland Menzies' *Hughes, the Wer-Wolf* in 1838, followed by classics like *The Werewolf of Paris, The Wolf's Hour, The Howling, Ravenous, Bestial, Wolf Hunt, Blood and Rain,* and *Cabal*—the list goes on and on. The shapeshifter tale has become a popular and well-used trope in the horror genre. I explored it myself, twice, during my tenure with Zebra Books back in the early 1990s. First, with *Something Out There* (originally titled *The Dark'Un)* in which a race of albino changelings and their overzealous protector, the dreaded Dark'Un, transform into everything from birds and animals to carbon-copy people and iconic pop-culture characters to prehistoric creatures. My other, more traditional shapeshifter offering, was *Moon of the Werewolf* (originally penned as *Undertaker's Moon*), in which a coven of Irish werewolves set up shop in a rural Tennessee town, posing as undertakers in order to discreetly feast upon human flesh without alerting the residents to their fiendish intentions.

Exactly what drives the fascination that we have for these transmutating creatures? What makes movie-goers love to watch hirsute beasts rend flesh and shatter bones for the tender marrow within? What makes horror readers hunger for books like Stephen King's *Cycle of the Werewolf* and Jonathan Janz's *Wolf Land*? Maybe it is traditional folklore or historic legend that piques your interest; the Epic of Gilgamesh, Lycaon of Greek mythology, or the Saga of the Volsungs from Nordic tales of old. Maybe it's the psychological aspect of true-life clinical lycanthropy. The Frenchmen Pierre Burgot and Michel Verden who, in 1521, murdered several children and were burned at the stake after claiming they had sworn allegiance to the Devil in exchange for an ointment that changed them into wolves. Or similar madmen of European decent, like Giles Garnier, who was known as the "Werewolf of Dole," or even Peter Stubbe, a wealthy, fifteenth-century farmer in Bedburg, Germany, who was said to have been executed in a particularly grisly manner after confessing to savagely slaughtering animals, men, women, and children, and devouring their remains.

The volume you hold carries on the tradition, and most admirably, I might add. Within the pages of *Were Tales: A Shapeshifter Anthology,* S.D. Vassallo has assembled stories to terrify and intrigue, to make the breath hitch in your chest at the howl of something in the night that is not quite 'dog-like' and cause you to walk just a little faster as you sense something stalking you from the shelter of the woods, just out of sight. You will find both old and new favorites here: Jonathan Maberry, Stephanie Ellis, Cynthia Pelayo, Laurel Hightower, Teresa Derwin, Catherine McCarthy, Gabino

Iglesias, Christina Sng, and the Sisters of Slaughter: Michelle Garza and Melissa Lason. Joining the pack are many rising stars of indie horror, each and every one contributing something delightfully bestial and memorably unsettling to the mix.

In its entirety, *Were Tales* is a wonderfully diverse tribute to our mutual love of ancient tales told by firelight and dark imaginings released from the printed page by the glow of the reading lamp. Here, physical form, mental restraint, and even the essence of the soul can transfigure and alter... can shed the fragile flesh of humanity and unleash the unthinkable... sometimes at will, but often quite involuntarily, with no grasp of control whatsoever.

Such tales unnerve us... frighten us... perhaps even bring us to the brink of terror itself.

And, being the kind that we are, we are the better for it.

Were-Mountain

by Cindy O'Quinn

it was normal as a child
       to visit the granny
after spending sunday mornings
       in the little church
listening to a pastor
       but never hearing his words
my thoughts were with the granny
       inside a cabin she built
with her own hands—much younger
       but a fine home she did build

no electricity
not even floors
nature's dirt nothing more
lizard shadows barely hidden
summer's heat blazed red yet cool
mountain herbs from a low ceiling hung
cures or curses for the old and young
glad for the visits from mom and me
i stood in silence and listened
savoring these lessons
heard every word
the granny shed
soon i learned
how to raise
the dead
secrets whispered

in darkness
eyes seeing through mist
the magic dust revealing all
as the granny spoke of the changed
ones from the mountain graveyard
who clawed their way out
on a blue hunter's moon
they came to her for answers
only she gave—one by one
she chose the animal
they became
on the next
full moon
raised
the granny's werecreatures and i remained
many full moons passed as we became
raccoons, rabbits, bears, and boars
but never the wolf
until the granny
was no more

More Afraid of You

by S.H. Cooper

He'd been looking for a spark.

Something to drive him. Motivate him. Reignite his passion.

He'd tried new locations, swapped out models, employed different techniques, but always with the same lackluster results. What was he doing wrong? Charles had been a professional photographer for decades, traveling the world to capture all forms of its beauty. Lately, though, all the lens reflected were shades of gray.

Where was the contrast and edges? Where was the life?

Sure, he'd experienced such lulls before, but he'd always been able to push through in a matter of days. This one had clung like half-melted saran wrap around his mind for months. Every attempt to rip it off had only made it clump and tangle more, until he felt like throwing his camera against the wall and giving up altogether.

Instead, he took a walk.

The boardwalk had always been a good place to clear his head. He liked to sit on one of the scattered benches and watch the crowds mill by, mentally maneuvering through how he might preserve the more notable moments. These exercises often helped him get back into the swing of things, but that day it just served to frustrate him more.

There were no bright-eyed children, their smiles painted with perfect innocence and promise, or elders whose deeply lined faces were roadmaps to history. Only screaming brats and cranky old people scowling at them.

Charles leaned forward, his elbows propped up on his knees and his chin resting in his upturned hands. Maybe *they* weren't the problem. Maybe it was him. Maybe he'd just lost his eye. The thought was a devastating one and he covered his face as if to hide from the very prospect.

When he could bring himself to straighten up again, he stretched his arms across the back of the bench and exhaled slowly, telling himself he was being overly dramatic over nothing. All he had to do was look around. Focus. Find the beauty in the chaos, same as he'd always done. His eyes, narrowed shrewdly, scanned the crowds.

And there she was.

Almost by some divine means, he saw her walking—no, gliding, her very air ethereal—through the streams of other people who had suddenly become faceless, background noise when placed next to her. Dark, silken curls piled atop her head, features an exotic, mysterious mix he couldn't place, flawless, olive-toned skin that seemed to glisten in the sun. She curved in all the right places, but none more sensual than the slight upturn of her red lips as she paused to look out over the water.

Charles was enraptured, drawn to her lithe form and effortless grace like he'd never known he could be.

Just looking at her from a distance was enough to send inspiration tearing through his artist's block. Oh, how he could envision her before his camera, bringing bursts of fresh color back to his work.

This woman was what he'd needed.

She was the key.

He had to have her.

Charles leapt from the bench, gaze transfixed on the woman, and hurried across the boardwalk.

"Excuse me," he said, a prepubescent squeak coming back to haunt him from his awkward teen years. But he wasn't that lanky, crater-faced kid anymore. He was successful, just on the border of wealthy. He'd worked with all sorts, been to more places than most people could ever dream of. He had no reason to become a blushing boy in front of this woman.

But when she lifted her eyes, deep green with flecks of gold, to his, sweat broke out across his palms and he stammered.

She smiled, polite, but awkward.

They're more afraid of you than you are of them, he recalled his father's sage advice when it came to approaching women and cleared his throat, shoulders squaring in a confident display.

"I'm going to cut right to it," he said, knowing brevity would be the key to his facade. "I'm a photographer and would love to have a session with you. Have you ever modeled?"

The woman's expression tightened, revealing her rejection before she spoke it.

"I'm legit," he added quickly. "I have references and everything!"

"Thank you," she said, and her voice was as smooth and rich as he'd expected, "but I'm not interested. Thanks."

"Wait, I—"

But she was already moving quickly away, letting the crowd close around her and swallow her up.

That can't be it, Charles thought with a desperation that surprised him. *I won't let it be.*

Over the next few days, he couldn't push the woman's image out of his head. The renewed passion she'd stirred in him left him breathless, craving even just a few seconds more in her presence. He couldn't say why, exactly, but every instinct within him screamed for her. He lost sleep, seeing her face every time he closed his eyes. Food lost flavor, music held no meaning, all of his prior photographs became worthless when he compared their subject to *her*.

She was art personified.

No matter how many more pictures he took, his collection would never be complete without her in it.

Even if it was for his eyes only.

It would be better that way, wouldn't it? Keeping his muse all to himself. Saving her for when the world grew pale again and he needed that delicious inspiration only she could give.

Yes.

Just for him.

He waited for her at the boardwalk the next weekend at the same time he'd seen her there before, but she never showed. He was sure if she had, he'd have seen her. Felt her. His muse.

No trouble. He could be patient if it meant seeing her again. So, he went again the next weekend, and the following and the following and the following, until a month had passed and he was beginning to fear she'd never return again, leaving him with nothing but her memory.

Charles was not a quitter, however, and 'No' wasn't a word he was accustomed to, so he deigned to wait as long as it took.

She'd be back. She had to be. The universe could never be so cruel as to give her to him only once.

In the end, his dogged determination paid off.

It was a late summer afternoon and he'd been seated on the same bench for hours, searching what seemed an endless sea of people for the only face that could ease his troubled heart.

And then, there she was.

As radiant as the first time he'd seen her.

It took every ounce of restraint not to jump up and run toward her. Only the whispered reminder, *they're more afraid of you than you are of them,* stayed him.

He couldn't scare her away. Not again, after so long.

No, he must take it slow, make it so she didn't even realize he was there. Photograph from afar to catch her at her most natural.

Her most beautiful.

His shutter clicked as he followed her progress through the lens.

He hadn't meant to do more than that, to trail her as she left the boardwalk. He hadn't intended to follow her by car, ensuring he remained an inconspicuous distance while she completed errands and met with friends to enjoy an early supper.

He certainly hadn't planned to follow her off the highway, down a quiet wooded lane, and park half a mile past the driveway she'd turned on to.

But he had, and as he sat there, pondering just how he'd found himself in his current situation, it dawned on him he'd never have this chance again. To capture her in her natural environment, all pretenses dropped.

The real her.

The thought of it made his chest constrict with painful need and he clenched his hands around the steering wheel. He would have it. Her private self would be his. He just had to wait for nightfall.

The heavens themselves were on his side, granting him a full moon to see by as he made his way toward her house, a grand stone mansion standing alone and surrounded by swaths of forest. It suited her exactly, stately and elegant in its solitude, and he lifted his camera to snap a picture before tiptoeing down the long drive.

The lights were on inside, giving him a clear view into the foyer and living room, both decorated with a minimalistic flair he found refreshing. Two more photos for his private series.

But she was absent.

Undeterred, he walked around the outside, to the rear of the house. The kitchen was dark, but a light shining from a door left just slightly ajar within it caught his eye.

The cellar? he wondered.

Could she have gone down there, perhaps to fetch a bottle of after-dinner wine? Oh, he'd very much like a photograph of her lying languidly across her sofa, a long-stemmed glass of red wine in hand.

His fingers curled tight around his camera in anticipation of what was to come.

Except it didn't.

He stood out there for what felt ages, waiting for her to emerge, but she stubbornly refused to show. He even checked around the front again to ensure she wasn't elsewhere in the house, but each room was empty and the upstairs windows remained unlit.

Was something wrong?

Cellars could be such dangerous places. The steep stairs, the rusty tools often left in them, the boxes of ill-placed junk just waiting to be tripped on. Terrible scenarios began to play across his mind, each worse than the last, turning his muse to a bruised and bleeding damsel in distress.

Charles couldn't allow that to happen.

He had almost convinced himself he could hear her crying out for help, for *him*, when he found an unlocked window in the adjoining dining room. He jimmied it open and, after carefully depositing his camera inside, pulled himself through.

The house smelled of sweet perfume and clean linens, and he inhaled the scent deeply before picking up his camera and creeping toward the kitchen.

As he'd suspected, the door he'd seen from outside opened to a set of wooden stairs leading down. The air that drifted up was damp and dank, sending a shiver across his shoulders as he pictured his muse lying helpless somewhere down there.

Still, he didn't call out.

He took to the steps one at a time, cringing each time one creaked beneath his weight. The closer he got to the bottom, the more aware he became of an unusual heat that had him tugging at his collar.

Heat lamps?

At least a dozen of them hung along the walls, bringing the cellar to a sweltering temperature.

Even stranger, the floor was covered in a thick layer of leaves and twigs, mimicking the woods outside.

And, as he stepped off the final stair, he saw *her*.

She was lying, nude, with her back to him, in the middle of the room upon a makeshift bed of large leaves. The light cast by the heat lamps bathed her bare skin in shades of red.

It was as if she'd laid herself out for him.

A gift.

His grin was broad, and he imagined her expression, nervous, but excited. Expectant. Of course she'd known he was coming. She must have.

They shared such a special connection after all.

Muse and artist.

He lifted his camera and lined up a shot.

A shudder ran down the length of her body.

"Don't be afraid," he murmured. "You're perfect."

She didn't respond, only shuddered again, this one rippling more violently from her head to her feet.

"Hey." He peered over the top of the camera. "Are you ok?"

No answer.

The ripping sound started off subtle, and Charles couldn't determine where it was coming from. Not until a thin line appeared up her back. Charles frowned and crouched beside her for a better look.

Yes, it was a line, only a hair's width, but going from the base of her spine to the nape of her neck.

"Hello?" he said, starting to reach for her.

Her body spasmed with a sharp convulsion, and the crack widened, the ripping sound coming from her sweat-dotted flesh's separation. He reeled back as she trembled and thrashed, all the while the rip in her skin widening in a snapping, wet cacophony.

Something moved beneath her skin, stretching and pushing against it.

Charles yelped and fell on to his backside as her supple flesh finally tore apart, and something began to wriggle free, leaving that flawless olive-toned skin discarded on the floor like a too-small dress.

The creature that emerged unfurled eight, long legs from a bulbous abdomen and stood, slowly stretching itself out to its full, monstrous height. The light that had seemed so sultry before now gleamed in a sinister crimson across its smooth, dark carapace.

Charles slapped a hand over his mouth to keep from screaming and started to scoot backwards, but the leaves crackled beneath him, betraying him.

His transformed muse whirled around, her many legs skittering across the underbrush. She reared back at the sight of him, flashing the red hourglass pattern on her stomach, large fangs bared, and then crouched low, stabbing at the ground with her two front feet.

Charles saw his own terror reflected back at him from eight eyes, each a deep green flecked with gold.

They're more afraid of you than you are of them.

That's what his father had always said. That's what Charles had believed. That it was the women who were truly afraid, that it was his place, his *right*, to approach them without fear. He was safe to do as he pleased.

It was that very notion that had brought him here to finally claim what he knew in his heart of hearts to be his.

But, as he'd known all along, she wasn't like other women.

He saw that so clearly now.

And in that moment, when she sprang forward, enveloping him in a tangled embrace of grasping limbs, pulling him toward her waiting fangs, there was no fear in her eyes, and Charles was the only one screaming.

The God of Viscera and Mud

by Shane Douglas Keene

what if a shapeshift is
not a transformation of flesh
but of emotion?
what if the mind of the
monster is reconfigured
before the
flesh has memory?
maybe
brain begets body,
body begets brain,
lifts it up out of the
weak state,
imagines your
transition into beast,
so real, your body
begins to
conform to the
monster,
the monster who was
always there made
vivid and
deadly.
the mind makes the
call, the demon
inside answers,
the love inside dies and
the lust is *everything*,

the need to devour,
to feast,
unleashes the brain's
desire to be
wolf or
bear or
cat or
mouse,
or, in this case, to
follow the path of
the pig, the feral
razorback with a taste
for meat made of man,
and the means to
rend it from
bare white bone,
needle tusks
not meeting much
resistance from the tender,
fragile flesh
of humanity.
slopping
fresh red
blood like
yesterday's
creamed corn,
wallowing and rolling,
rejoicing
and worshipping
the God of Viscera and
Mud

Refuge

by Kev Harrison

"So, when the Soviet soldier pointed his gun at your mother, what did you do?" Yara asks, polishing the glass entrance door of the bar.

"You wouldn't believe me if I told you," Johan says, grinning.

"Probably not. But tell me anyway. I love your old battle stories." She breathes onto the glass and wipes some more.

"I bit through the bastard's wrist. His hand hit the floor before his Kalashnikov."

Yara giggles musically. Johan loses focus for a moment, and he's back in his homeland across the water. The sound of raised Russian voices punctuated by the staccato rhythm of machine-gun fire. Yara's voice pulls him from his daydream.

"You're right, I don't believe. But that's when you ran away to Sweden, yes?"

"Across the Södra Kvarken. You don't want to row that crossing in winter, trust me, girl. Even if it is only thirty Ks."

Yara shivers. "No, thank you." She slings the cloth over her shoulder and glances through the window. "It's quiet. Shall I make us some lunch?"

Johan pats his belly and ambles across to join her at the window. The dark water of the river Ume below contrasts with the pale sky. The noon sun is already sinking towards the horizon. He pulls the girl who is the closest thing he's ever had to a child into a half hug. His gargantuan frame dwarfs her petite form.

"Great idea," he says.

***

Since she moved here from Aleppo—via Subotica on the border between Serbia and Hungary—Yara has teased him relentlessly about the stodgy, bland food they eat in the North. Occasionally she prepares tabouleh or kefta with goat's cheese and watches him eat his fill. Johan secretly knows, though, that she loves *palt*. Potato and flour dumplings filled with cubes of fried pork, served with a generous knob of butter and a spoonful of his homemade lingonberry jam. It's the first Swedish dish she's taken to preparing herself.

It's one thing to give someone a safe space. Quite another to provide a home.

They're eating in silence at one of the bar tables when music begins to bleed in from the street. As it moves closer, the doppler effect renders the first few bars of the national anthem strange, detuned. A garbled voice announces something inaudible over the tinny music before cutting out, leaving only a noisy van engine turning over.

Johan places his cutlery on the table, wiping away the smear of blood-red lingonberry jam from his lips and wispy white beard with a napkin. He stalks to the window at the prow of the boat.

"What is it?" Yara says. The engine cuts out, as if in response.

"Elections. They'd better not—"

The bell above the door jingles and two men enter, stamping snow from their boots. They each wear a suit, cut in silver-gray wool, hair shaved close to the scalp. One is slender, facial features all sharp angles, the other is a wall of muscle, what little neck he might have swallowed by his collar.

"Good afternoon," says the slim one. "I'm Anders and this is Niklas and we're hoping to ask for your votes." He grips a handful of leaflets emblazoned with a large national flag and the word *Patriot* in bold type.

Johan hurries to Yara's side, placing his bulk between her and the men. She gazes up at him and he hopes it isn't fear he sees in her eyes.

"I don't think so," he says.

Anders pulls the fan of flyers back and holds them to his chest defensively.

"Where's that accent from?" he says, making a face as though he's smelt something bad.

"I'm Finnish. Originally. Been here a *long* time now, though."

The two men eye one another, then Anders speaks again. "And you, my dear. What's your name?"

"Yara."

"Exotic," he says, licking his lips like a hungry dog. "Her accent's better than yours," he says, eyes returning to Johan. "She one of … you know?"

Johan clenches his teeth, pushes back against the anger that threatens to boil.

"I'm right here! One of what?!" Yara spits, face flushed. Johan places an enormous hand on her shoulder and squeezes gently.

"No matter, sweetheart. Don't want you getting flustered," Anders says. He places the leaflets down at the edge of the bar, beside coupons for tattoo parlors and boat tours. "I'll just leave these—"

"They'll be in the furnace if you do. Get out of my bar." Johan's voice is calm, but cold, serious.

Anders shoves the flyers back into his inside jacket pocket with a hand that shows faint signs of a quiver. The other man, Niklas, balls his fists, glaring at Johan.

"What are you waiting for? Get the fuck out!" Johan bellows and the pair disappear through the front door.

"Wow, I have *never* seen you look that pissed." Yara scoops up the empty plates and glasses and heads to the kitchen. "I'm making a coffee. You want one?" she calls as the kitchen door swings behind her. Johan is back at the table, eyes locked on the entrance.

"Johan. *Coffee*?" she applies more force to her voice this time, head poking through the serving hatch. He blinks and nods.

The espresso machine starts up, noisily building pressure. The bell above the front door chimes again and Johan leaps to his feet, sending the table and chair in front of him clattering to the floor.

Oskar, the beer delivery guy, stands wide-eyed in the doorway, holding his tablet to his chest.

"Johan, you okay, man?"

Johan unclenches his fists and wipes a large hand across his face.

"Sorry, Oskar. Nazis."

"Nazis? Oh, the *Patriots*? Yeah, I saw them on the way out. Did they…?"

"Don't worry about me. What have you got for us today?"

Oskar enters, taking his hat off, and hands the tablet over. Johan slips his glasses on and peruses the delivery note.

"I'll come down and give you a hand."

He follows Oskar out of the bar and down the covered boarding ramp to street level. The air is frigid, but the blood soon starts pumping as they load bottles, barrels, and pallets of cans into the hold. They swear like sailors, sharing jokes about how badly the local football team will do when the season begins in the spring. With the final pallet stowed, Oskar closes the delivery truck's doors and his voice takes on a serious tone.

"Listen, Johan, don't piss those guys off, eh?"

"Those politicians? Come on, you saw them. The skinny one I could break like a twig, even at my age. As for the brute, he's brainless. They don't scare me."

There's a long pause.

"Have you read what they've done further south? They're mixed up with skinheads. They've torched places, roughed people up. Just watch your step, *especially* after taking Yara in on the program."

Johan glances up at the kitchen window and sees her looking down, hard lines of concern scored too deeply into the face of one so young. He lowers his voice to something between a whisper and a hiss.

"If you knew what that girl's seen … I *will* not allow those shitheads to put her through … well, anything else."

"I'm only saying this as your friend, Johan. I'll see you next week, alright." Oskar offers a gloved hand and John shakes it firmly.

"I know. And thank you."

He slams the hold doors and shifts the bolts and padlocks into place. When he returns to the bar, Yara is picking up the table and chair he sent flying. She silently pours the old man a coffee and places it on the table, then scurries back behind the bar.

"Everything okay?" he says, stamping the cold from his feet.

"Of course. Don't forget your coffee."

"Look, Yara. I'm sorry if I frightened you."

She half-smiles. "I know you were trying to protect me. Thank you for that."

Johan sips his coffee and remembers things he's spent seven decades trying to forget.

***

The drive into work, downriver from the ancient-looking cottage which Johan built himself, is short. His boxy, retro Volvo clings to the road like it's glued down, despite the patches of snow and black ice. Yara watches the roadside forests of fir and pine, and the scattered snow drifts with her customary look of wonderment on her face.

They park at the usual spot on the edge of town and grab pastries and coffee at a small café on their way to work. Their passage is quiet, but for the sound of boots crunching through virgin snow and the occasional sip from a coffee cup. Then the boat comes into view.

"Fuckers!" he yells.

Graffiti is painted across the wooden gangway onto the boat. 'Moslems go home' it announces in badly spelt, angry, red spray paint.

"I'm not even Muslim. And so fucking what if I was!" Yara kicks out at a small pile of snow at the side of the road, the cloud of particles forming a rainbow in the mid-morning light. "Sorry for the language."

Johan rushes forward, rage surging through his veins.

"Paint's still wet! The bastards must be …" he lunges into the street, glancing around and scowling, brows low over his eyes. Yara dashes to catch up as quickly as she can without slipping on the icy ground.

"Johan, it's okay. I've dealt with worse before."

He turns his face to her and snarls, animal like.

"It's … not … okay!"

Yara steps back, hands held in front of her. "Johan, your teeth. And your eyes. What's …" His teeth seem to protrude from his hanging jaw, his eyes have a golden, almost yellow tint to them. Yara cowers, low to the ground, her eyes welling with tears, bottom lip quivering.

Johan buries his face in his gloves and shudders.

I cannot let her see this side of me. I cannot be this thing anymore.

He peels the gloves away and offers her the most genuine smile he can muster. He notices her hands trembling, gripping her thermal coffee cup tightly. A single tear traces a path down her cheek.

"Johan? Is it still you?"

He nods, eyes closed.

"Thank God. What happened to you there?"

"The force of the anger. It … does something to me. Let's get inside before our coffee gets cold. I'll clear this up later."

He ushers for her to go in, but she takes one more look into his eyes, now restored to the pale blue of the glacial ice they saw at Storglaciären the previous spring.

Yara sips her coffee before taking a hungry bite of her cinnamon pastry, then asks, "What happened out there, Johan?"

He puts his own pastry down, wiping his mouth with the back of a huge hand.

"I was angry. Anger isn't something I'm good with. Never have been."

"But I've seen anger. I've *felt* anger. That was … something else."

Johan's eyes flick down to the table, avoiding Yara's gaze.

"That's why I came here. I'd been fighting for so long. Always enraged. Always that snarling, animal version of myself." As he speaks, his thoughts drift to thirty-nine. To the Soviet invasion of Finland and the last time he tasted blood. Regaining his focus, he says, "When I wound up in this tiny art-town on the river … I knew it was a place I could … put all that behind me."

"How did you get the money to buy the boat?"

Johan shrugs. "I didn't. The old owner, Alf, gave me a job. A place to stay while I built the cottage. When he passed, I was the only one he had. Never married. No kids or siblings."

"He left you this place?" Yara's mouth curls upward into a smile of wonder as she takes in the scenery of the bar as though for the first time.

"He did. And life has been quiet. Nothing to get het up about. Until these so-called patriots."

She reaches across the table and places her hand on top of his. "Don't worry about them. A few skinheads in cheap suits are nothing to me. I'm an orthodox Christian. I survived IS warriors bombing my city. I'm not scared of them."

Johan sighs. "I made a promise to keep you safe when I took you in."

"And you're doing that. And teaching me life skills, like how to pour ale properly." She winks and Johan allows a grin onto his face. "Coffee is getting cold."

***

A quiet day has become a dead evening and Johan signals to Yara to start closing up. He lumbers to the prow of the boat and begins stacking chairs on tables, while Yara heads to the kitchen to kill the lights.

As she flicks the switches, plunging half the bar into darkness, the bell above the door rings.

"We're closing," Yara says, pushing through the kitchen door, then freezes.

The two men from the day before stand in the doorway, this time dressed in jeans and plain shirts under their heavy coats. Behind them, three large men in hoodies.

"The sign outside says you close at eleven. We need something to drink," says the heavyset one—Niklas.

"We've been campaigning all afternoon and evening. Thirsty work," Anders adds.

Yara glances in Johan's direction. He closes his eyes, nods. She hurries around the bar, taking four chairs from the biggest table and fetching another from the next one over.

"Here you go, gents, what can I get you?"

"Akvavit, of course. If the big Finn has it." Anders turns to face Johan, still in the darkened area at the front of the bar.

"After all these years in Sweden, I make my own. Let me grab a bottle. It's on the house … if dill is okay with you fellas?"

The three hooded men murmur affirmatively, and Anders gives a thumbs up.

"Yara, help me get the bottle and some glasses, will you?"

"There are plenty of glasses under the—"

"We'll get the good glasses for these boys. Come on now." Johan shoos her into the kitchen and through the hatch, and down into the hold.

"Do we have good glasses?" she says as they reach the bottom of the steps.

"Listen. I've got a bad feeling about this. I'm pretty sure they're here looking for trouble."

"And if they are I—"

"—will get the fuck out."

"Johan!"

"I told you. You're under my protection. Like it or not."

"Jo—"

"Stop!" He gently curls his fingers around her wrist. "Look, you're shaking. I don't know half of what you've been through, but I know it must have been horrific. If I give you a signal, you get out. Call the police, okay?" Yara lowers her eyes. "Now pass me those two bottles with the silver labels."

***

"We thought you'd got lost," Anders says, a sinister leer on his gaunt face.

"Just tracking down the right stuff," Johan says, waving the two bottles above his head. He places one on the table and opens the other. Yara lays out five short-stemmed shot glasses and Johan pours.

"Not going to join us?" Anders asks.

"The girl can't, can she," says Niklas, his barrel-chest thrumming with laughter.

27

Yara stomps across to the bar and comes back with two more glasses. Johan makes to protest, but she stops him dead with a look. He fills the two new glasses and lifts his own.

"Skål," Yara says, and drains the shot. The men return the exclamation and down their own, before glasses clink down on the table.

"Wow, maybe we'll make a local from this one after all?" Niklas says and places an arm around Yara's thighs, his meaty hand resting just below the curve of her behind.

Yara squirms, tries to pry his hand away.

"Get the fuck off," she says and slaps his face.

The men fall silent. The smiles have evaporated, leaving behind stony, harsh expressions.

In an instant, he's out of his chair and wrestling Yara to the ground. She groans and Johan lunges forward. Two pairs of hands lock around his shoulders and hold him back. One of the men in hoods gets to his feet and steps up. He punches Johan in the face and he falls backward, tables and chairs crumpling beneath him.

Johan crouches, hands over his bloody nose.

"Eyes on me," the letch on top of Yara says. "I'm going to teach you some manners."

She squeals and Johan looks up. The thug presses his body to Yara's, then runs his tongue up Yara's neck as she squirms and sobs.

Johan drops to his knees as the growl he thought he left behind starts rising from his gut. The hooded man glances round and Yara takes her chance, bringing her knee up sharply into his crotch. He howls, rolling off her, onto his side, hands between his legs. Yara scrambles to her feet and heads towards Johan. His body shakes, bones crunching and shifting beneath his skin.

"Stay back!" he screams in a bestial voice not his own. "That way!" he flicks his head toward the bar.

Yara's face streaked with tears, she backs away from Johan,

clearly terrified, but dashes toward the bar as he said. Her assailant bolts after her, but Johan reaches out a strong arm, stopping him dead in his tracks. He lifts the skinhead by the throat. The man must weigh a hundred and fifty kilos, yet his feet dangle above the floor.

The thug splutters, blood running down his neck as ivory claws extend from Johan's fingers and puncture his throat. Johan swipes with the other hand, leaving three deep slashes across the stricken man's face, his left eye dislodged from its socket, hanging by its pink, gelatinous nerve.

Johan throws him to the ground like a rag doll and rears back, roaring. His mandible cracks and crunches as it extends. A long stream of drool hangs from the terrifying mass of razor-sharp fangs. Thick fur begins to grow around his face and neck, dark brown with a V-shaped cowl of white over his face and the top of his head.

The next of the thugs picks up a chair and charges at Johan. He brings it down over his head. The chair legs buckle and splinter, but the bear simply shakes its head from side to side, as though irritated by an obnoxious insect.

The man cowers backward, hands raised. Johan pauses momentarily, before pouncing onto him, claws digging through his leather jacket and hoodie like they're made of paper. He rears up, then strikes with his claws, drilling them into the man's rib cage. The cracking of bone is sickening, and when he stands, his forepaws are slathered with thick, crimson liquid.

Niklas and the remaining hooded man bolt for the door, the jovial jingle of the bell entirely wrong amid the bloodbath. The bear snarls, scouring the scene until he finds Anders, cowering behind an upturned table.

He lurches toward him and the man whimpers, hands in front of his face.

"Please!" he shrieks. "We only wanted to scare you. Teach you— "

Johan smashes the table aside with his arm and the trembling man falls silent.

"Teach us *what*?" his roaring reply.

"Th-this used to be a good … Christian country. A *white* country, before—"

Johan pounces, pinning the man to the ground with one heavy paw, holding the other back, ready to strike.

"Johan, stop!" Yara's voice shudders with sobs. She's sitting on the floor, knees held up to her chin, rocking back and forth. "Enough bloodshed. You've made your point." She gestures to the two corpses bleeding out on the wooden floor.

Her eyes meet the bear's and, though they are the golden yellow hue of the animal, she feels that same connection with the father figure who has watched over her these past three years.

The huge bear backs up and the man shuffles away, shivering with terror. Johan begins to pad across toward Yara.

A metallic click sounds from behind him and he turns, launching himself. Anders is still taking aim with the small revolver as the wide jaws of the bear close around his face and clamp down. With a jerk to his left, Johan tears away the skin and much of the meat from Anders' face. Blood seeps from the raw death mask left behind.

Anders collapses forward, dropping the gun and screaming. His tongue visibly flails in what's left of his ruined mouth. Unable to listen to his death throes any longer, Johan leans in and snaps his neck, before collapsing to the ground, slumped on his belly.

As his breathing slows, adrenaline levels in his blood reducing, the fur, claws and prominent jaw retract, slowly restoring Johan to his human form. A wave of exhaustion from his transformation crashes over him. Through half-closed eyes, he sees Yara clamber unsteadily to her feet.

Hands still trembling, she takes a tentative step toward him.

"I'm not this anymore, Yara. I'm so sorry," Johan says with a rasping voice which still bears the hallmarks of his other self. "It was only to … protect you. I want you to feel safe here."

She kneels and puts her arms around his shoulders. "I know. And I do."

Skin in the Game
by Ruschelle Dillon

The beastly roar of the motor and unmuzzled exhaust no longer echoed through the Great Smoky Mountains National Park. It gurgled and sputtered for miles until the ancient 1972 Winnebago finally pulled over to the side of the road, belching plumes of white smoke. A long, lingering hiss rose from the pitted white hood. The old girl was dead. Carl, a thin slip of a man in his late forties, plucked a cigarette from the breast pocket of his button-up shirt. "Well, it looks like we're here," he said while fumbling in the pockets of his cut-off jeans and rummaging through fast-food bags and wrappers on the floor.

A staticky voice cut in and out from the FM radio.

"If you have information on any of the missing children, please contact your local police department or call the National Missing and Exploited Child hotline at 1-800-843-5678. In other news, police are still searching for a Gatlinburg family…"

Tired of listening to the tragedy and watching the comedy playing out from the passenger's seat, Carl's wife, Beth, switched off the radio and grabbed a lighter from a stash in the glove compartment.

"Is this what you're looking for?" she quizzed. An unamused mask painted her face. Behind the thick lenses of his glasses his hazel eyes grew comically wider.

"Ah, thank you. That's a nice one," he said, snatching the lighter from her freshly manicured fingers. "The news is so depressing."

From the driver's side window, a gray pickup truck hauling a thirty-two-foot camper slowed down as it passed them. A woman on the passenger side rolled down her window, seemingly to rubber neck, but the truck quickly sped up and continued through the tree-lined road when she noticed Beth glancing out the Winnebago window. As it began to crest the top of the hill, she pointed it out to her husband.

"There's that gray pickup and camper."

They had first encountered it a few rest-stops ago, then again at a busy gas station. Beth thought it odd they were on the exact same route, but maybe the woman had noticed them from previous rest stops and was thinking the same thing. Carl pulled himself up to the windshield as the brake lights from the trailer flickered.

"What pickup?"

Ignoring her husband's question, Beth stood up and raised her toned arms above her head as far as she could in the cab of the RV. Twisting her upper body from side to side, she peered into the tight living quarters at her two boys, Mark and Craig, who were too engrossed in their electronic devices to notice they were even at a stop. Beth pulled the hair tie off her wrist and wrapped it around her shoulder-length dirty blonde hair into a sloppy bun. Carl flicked a snake of ash out of the slightly cracked open window and began digging through a bag full of pamphlets and maps.

"As perceptive as ever. I'm going to get the boys."

"Don't forget to get all the trash," he said, his lips smacking together in a dismissive air kiss. Beth rolled her dark green eyes.

"When have I ever forgotten the trash?" she quipped, as she strolled through the dated orange-hued cabin, tossing potato chip bags and paper plates into a garbage bag. Tapping her sixteen-year-old's size fifteen sneaker for his attention, she pointed to his earbuds. Mark plucked them from his ears. "What?" was his sluggish reply, not really wanting an answer. Reaching above the driver's seat to the roomy bunk above, Beth gently tugged her eight-year-old's Hulk t-shirt until his eyes were no longer on his phone but on her.

"Okay boys, we're here. So let's clean up. Get any food out of the freezer, don't forget the fry pan, and get things ready for a campfire."

"I want to roast marshmallows this time!" Craig said as he hopped down from the overhead bunk.

Just as his mother expressed annoyance with Carl moments before, Mark rolled his green eyes at his brother's sugar-fueled excitement. Tucking his earbuds and phone into his pocket, he snatched the garbage bag from his mom, tossed in the frying pan from the stovetop and went up to the front of the RV with his father.

"Why, thank you, kind son, I love your enthusiasm," she said, feigning appreciation. Relieved from garbage duty, Beth rooted through a few cupboards until she found her quarry.

"Looks like you're in luck, Craig. Marshmallows. And not too stale either."

Grabbing the squishy sweets from his mother's hand, Craig shoved them in his backpack.

"Awesome," he purred, stuffing the pack with provisions from the RV.

Ash from Carl's cigarette snowed gray flakes across a map of the Smoky Mountains. He stared through the bug-encrusted windshield, and back again at the map.

"Well, I think we're—somewhere." Rolling the map, Carl stood up. Playfully swatting his oldest son's knee with it, he announced to his family, "Okay, let's camp."

Slinging tattered rucksacks on their backs, coolers and duffel bags in hand, the family dutifully followed one another from the downed Winnebago and along the road until they came upon an unmarked and slightly overgrown trail. Bored, Craig snapped a branch from a dying birch tree and immediately launched into an assault on the pokeweed growing along the trail. Beth saddled up next to her husband.

"Direction?"

Instead of answering, Carl started on the path. It wasn't until they were five minutes into the woods that he responded to his wife's question.

"This way," he said, unsure of his own answer. Beth rooted her legs in the dirt. Her youngest son, who was paying more attention to thrashing the bushes and low-hanging trees, ricocheted off her behind.

"Still can't read a map, can you?" she seethed. Her fingers clenched the belt loops of her jeans. Instead of pausing to engage in a doomed discussion, Carl kept walking. Glancing over his shoulder, he raised his hand beckoning them on. He smiled a nicotine-stained smile.

"It'll be fine. Come on," he rallied, lighting a fresh cigarette. "We can set up camp before it gets dark."

He whistled for Mark, who was more than happy to escape the sharp point of his brother's stick, and continued through the overgrown path, leaving his wife and youngest to bring up the rear. Beth swore under her breath but with daylight draining from the sky, it wasn't worth arguing with her better half. Instead, she nicked the stick from Craig, who was poking holes through a thick blanket of webbing suspended in the trees.

"Stop pissing off the spiders," she growled, flinging the stick through the dense shrubbery.

"Aww, Mom," Craig whined.

Beth clamped her hands on his thin shoulders and nudged her son to follow his brother and father. After fifteen minutes of uphill hiking, they came to a small clearing. The skeletal remains of a small firepit had been left among the weeds. It wouldn't take much to bring it back to life. Simultaneously, Carl and Mark dropped their packs.

"Looks like as good a place as any," Carl announced, surveying the area.

Beth and Craig tossed their packs next to the others, and like a well-oiled machine, each member of the family attended to a particular task, preparing the area and themselves for a night in the Smoky Mountains.

The fire blazed without much coaxing. Two small tents were staked under the canopy of pines and birch trees. Mark lugged two sizable logs to the fire's edge and the family sat tossing their trash from the RV into the flames and marinating themselves in the smoke. Everyone was transfixed on the fire as they fed it. The sound of the crackling wood had them in its thrall until Carl, hearing footsteps behind him, turned on his log and stared into the woods. The rest of his family did the same.

Beth glared at her husband as a man and woman, loaded with camping gear and a small child who looked to be around Craig's age, hiked into their campsite. It was the woman from the gray truck. Instead of walking through and extolling rhetorical pleasantries, the trio stopped.

The woman grabbed the child by the arm and pulled him close to her. Grinning with a set of large yellow teeth, the man, all six-foot-four of him, loomed over them. Dropping his backpack, he held his thick, meaty hands towards the fire to warm them.

"I see you found our old campsite," he said. The fire in his eyes burned brighter than the campfire flame.

Carl stood up; his head barely crested the stranger's neck. Mark stood up as well, following his father's lead. But in the barest of whispers, Mark heard his dad say, "ah-ah," and he slowly sat back down. Not wanting to fuel any provocation, he mirrored the man's off-putting smile and spoke soothingly, as if speaking to a pet or small child.

"I'm sorry. We had no way of knowing this was your spot. It looked a bit overgrown; we didn't think anyone had used it in a while. I hope this doesn't put a cramp in your camping," Carl said, apologetically.

The man let out a belly laugh.

"I'm just screwing with you. Ain't my camp. I couldn't help myself." His face cracked wider. "And look at you, boy. Just what were you thinking you were gonna try and do? Protect your family?" A deep gurgle percolated from his throat, producing a huge ball of phlegm which he spat in the fire. "Looking after your ole' man. Looks like he might need protecting. Like I said, I'm just screwing with you. My wife says I have a great sense of humor."

Beth stared at the man's wife, whose dirty fingers were digging into the meat of the boy's fragile looking arm. She could tell her grip was causing him pain but instead of crying out, he winced and kept his eyes downcast; not the behavior of a child his age to being hurt. His face was gaunt. His seven or eight-year-old cheeks were robbed of baby fat and his big brown eyes looked almost black from being sunken in. Addressing the child and not the mother, Beth reached in her pack and offered him a candy bar.

"Would you like something sweet?" she said, carefully choosing her words as to not offend the parents, who may have fallen on tough times. The boy's hands were tucked at his side, balled in tiny fists, but at the sight of the candy bar his fingers bloomed, almost daring to reach out. But he quickly thought better of it and coiled them back into his palms. The woman sucked in a quick breath of air through her nose.

"It'll just rot his teeth. But thank you," she said. Her voice was as gruff and raspy as she looked; dressed in a sweaty tank top, bearing mottled, sun-damaged cleavage paired with knee-torn jeans and sneakers. Beth could tell that neither the boy nor his parents had proper baths recently by the pungent pong of body odor wafting from them. Her comment about the child's oral hygiene was almost comical.

Craig's excitement at seeing a child his own age he could play with eclipsed the awkwardness going on with the adults around him. Rising from the log, he held out his hand just like his father taught him when properly introducing himself.

"Hi, my name is Craig. What's yours?"

The boy looked up at his mom before answering. She, in turn, looked to her husband who spoke for them both.

"Well, Craig, it's nice to meet you." He gripped the boy's hand and gave it a hearty shake. Carl, Mark and Beth watched warily. He continued, still only addressing Craig. "Now where are my manners? The boy, his name is Benji. They call me Gator on account of my purdy smile." He gnashed his teeth together, showing them off. "And that there is Mrs. Gator."

"Can Benji and I play?" Craig asked without missing a beat. "I mean, after you get your camp set up?"

Carl led his son back to his log, his eyes still focused on Gator.

"I'm sure these nice people have a million things to do before it gets too dark," said Carl. Craig lowered his chin to his chest. Mark pulled his brother onto the log beside him and shoved a new stick in his hand. Gator saddled closer to fire and ran one of his meat-hook-sized hands through his thinning, greasy, brown hair. The sweat from his pit stains ran the length of the button-down shirt. He waved the smoke around him as if he were anointing himself.

"There's nothing more important to me than family," he began. "Hell, I'm not ashamed to tell ya, the missus and I tried for years for kids. We got lucky a few times but, some of em just didn't make it. The good Lord finally smiled on us when he gave us Benji. We love the open road. Don't we, honey?" Mrs. Gator simply nodded. Her eyes focused on Beth's pink manicured nails, unconsciously hiding her ragged fingers in the folds of her son's shirt.

"We travel all over," Gator continued, not waiting for an answer, "communing with nature, ya know? Sometimes ya just need to get off the grid, live off the land and get back to your primitive roots."

Beth was unable to hold her tongue any longer. "I recognize you from a few rest-stops," she blurted out. "I saw you slow down next to us on the road before you sped off. It's almost as if you've been following us."

Gator stepped back from the fire and threw his bulky pack over his broad shoulders.

"Is that right?" he said, his tongue heavy with mendacity. "Well, I know we did stop at *one* rest stop. If it looked like we were following you, it's just coincidence. But I will admit, we have been through these woods before. There's a nice clearing right up ahead. Come on woman, let's leave these folks to enjoy *our* camp," he barked, slapping his thigh as if summoning a dog. Gator paused and stared over at Benji.

"Come to think of it, it might be nice for the boy here to have a playmate. Tomorrow is another day. Y'all have a good night," he cooed, ushering Mrs. Gator and Benji ahead of him. Craig ceased stoking the flames to wave at the boy, who feebly waved back.

"Come on, boy, you need to learn how to fix up camp." Gator snatched the boy away from his mother and lumbered through the brush. Benji's legs worked overtime to keep up with Gator.

Beth stood up, angry at how Gator manhandled his son. Gently, Carl lowered his hand in front of his wife, "ah-ah," he whispered, watching the spark ignite in Beth's eyes.

Mrs. Gator followed, but before disappearing into the brush, she turned to address Beth, "I love your nails."

Beth didn't respond. She just stood there and watched them melt into the greenery. No one said anything until the rustling of branches and the snapping of twigs was off in the distance.

"Can we roast marshmallows now?" Craig asked as he yanked his singed stick from the fire.

They roasted the sticky sweets in silence. The usual chirping of birds and the clicks and buzzing of insects were nonexistent. Throughout the evening, Mark kept his earbuds in his pocket and kept both ears out for Gator. He knew if the man with the yellow teeth came back to try and reclaim his camp, he was the fittest and the fastest. His dad could see the concern in his face as he positioned himself in the direction the Gator family took. Carl plopped down next to his son while Beth snuggled up to her youngest.

"I appreciate the assist with the uh, Gatorman," he said, his eyes focused on his wife and his eight-year-old. Mark chewed his top lip, unsure of how to phrase his thoughts without sounding rude.

"You and Mom are…"

"Old?" he chuckled. Mark put his head down. "I like to think we're well-seasoned. Don't worry, I still have some killer moves. See your brother over there? A special move I used on your mom," he said, elbowing his son.

"Gross, Dad," Mark shivered as he walked away from his father into his tent. Beth just shook her head as her husband snickered and puckered his lips, floating an air kiss from across the fire.

At around midnight, they all crawled into their tents. Mark tried to keep awake but fell asleep next to his brother an hour later. Beth and Carl attempted the same vigilance but eventually succumbed to the lull of four wheels battering the road and the soothing pops and cracks of the campfire. Craig, still wound-up from charred sugar, lay in the tent with his brother. Not wanting to wake him, Craig kept himself occupied scratching figures and designs in the dirt underneath him.

His play was interrupted as a small shadow crept across his tent. He propped himself up on one elbow watching for the shadow to morph into skin and bone. At the mouth of the tent, a familiar face bent down, a finger to his lips. It was Benji. Careful not to wake his brother, Craig slithered out from the tent. A wide smile cracked his face but before he could whisper anything, Benji slipped his hand in

Craig's. The boy grinned, a jack o' lantern grin with his front tooth missing, and quietly led his new friend into the woods.

Around three in the morning, needing to pee, Mark roused himself awake. Noticing he had more room in the tent to stretch out than usual, he reached out for his brother. Craig wasn't there.

He scurried from the small tent and into the wild. He stoked the dying fire before poking around the surrounding trees and bushes for his brother, who may have woken up just before him to relieve himself as well. Unsure of what to do next, he cupped his hands together and created a squealing sound that echoed in the darkness, hoping his brother would recognize it and respond back. It was something they would often do when they were separated by distance in the woods. He waited. No response. He called again, but this time, his parents answered by wriggling from their tent and joining him next to the awakening campfire.

Before Mark could voice his concern, a monstrous screech ripped through the night followed by a child's scream.

"Craig," Beth whispered, sinking her pink nails into her husband's wiry arm. Without further conversation, the trio ran through the brush and trees, hoping it wouldn't be too late.

The overgrown path led them approximately six-hundred feet away from their camp to the clearing Gator had mentioned. They stopped dead at the sight of both Mr. and Mrs. Gator, each brandishing a weapon; the husband a rifle and the wife a butcher knife. Both were hyper focused on Craig. Benji was crying, huddled as close to the fire as he could get. His knees drawn up to his chin, his arms wrapped around them. One of them was bleeding. As Beth and Carl emerged from the tree line, Gator changed the focus of his target.

"Stay right where you are. Don't move," he said, his voice no longer full of confidence, "before I blow that *thing* to hell…" he screamed, aiming the gun at Craig, who grinned, his lips stained with blood. "What the fuck is it? It ain't human!"

Both Beth and Carl shrugged their shoulders and took a few steps toward Gator. But instead of addressing Gator's question, Carl spoke to his son, standing in front of Benji, hiding his hands behind his back.

"Craig, we've talked about this. Did you show off to your new friend and scare him?"

"Yes," Craig replied, kicking up a plume full of dust. "But Benji said we could be best friends and play together all the time if I came to his camp with him."

"You were stalking us," Beth said as she wagged a lacquered pink finger at the Gators. "There was no coincidence. You were planning on kidnapping my son."

Mrs. Gator slunk closer to her husband, butcher knife poised to inflict damage.

"We'd have taken good care of him," she said.

Beth narrowed her eyes, clenching her jaw. But at the thought of these people attempting to kidnap her child, she threw her head back and laughed. Carl inched closer to Gator who was ping ponging his aim from Craig to his direction.

"Now to answer your question..." he said, staring at Gator. He called for his other son. "Mark, you want to help your 'old dad' out?"

Before Gator could spin around, from above his head a long black arm covered in course black hair snatched the gun, yanking him off his feet. He managed to squeeze the trigger, a bullet ripping through the treetops. Mrs. Gator screamed and froze in fear as Gator stumbled and fell backwards into the dirt. Towering over him was Mark, now a bipedal beast on muscular hooved legs. His lanky sixteen-year-old chest had swollen to resemble that of a brawny, onyx-skinned man with bulging arms. His fingers were the size of sausages, with razor-like claws at each tip. Two disturbingly long teeth curled from the lower jaw, jutting out from a wild boar-like creature.

Using his elbows and feet, Gator crawled like a crab on his back, away from Mark who shadowed him, lashing the would-be-kidnapper with ribbons of drool oozing from his mouth and snout. He lunged, and with one massive trotter to his belly, Gator was pinned to the ground, gasping for breath. Both Carl and the beast stood above him.

"I understand when you see my delicate frame, you think I am weak. But that's where you're mistaken. Neither I, nor my family, need protecting. Now, normally, since I am the alpha male of my drove, I would claim your skin for my own. Your flesh would keep us from getting hungry as we travel," Carl said as he lowered his glasses to the bridge of his nose. "How do you enjoy communing with nature now?"

Everyone except the Gators laughed.

"My wife thinks I'm funny as well," Carl continued. "And I am, but unfortunately for you, I'm not joking. And since my son has, well, exploded from his old skin, he can't walk among the humans. So, your skin will go to him. That's what a good father does." Carl patted his son's quivering hock.

"Go ahead, son. Try not to spoil the meat, okay?" he said.

Mark let out a deep guttural growl as Gator screamed in pain. Her husband's death throes shook Mrs. Gator from her stupor. With no one left to save her, she ran like a gladiator towards Beth, who was tending to a bite mark on Benji's hand. With an ear-deafening shriek, the once mild-mannered female jumped on Beth's back, stabbing her in the shoulder, tearing a gaping hole through her borrowed skin and exposing clumps of black fur. Giving herself some room, Beth's true self ripped and split the layers of dermas. Slivers of Beth littered the trees and curled up into blacked bits in the campfire, revealing a porcine beast as huge and menacing as her son. Yanking Mrs. Gator from her back, she levitated her by the neck and released an angry snort, slathering her with snot and mucus. The She-Beast flaunted her pink lacquered claws at her victim.

"Do you like them now?" she asked. The woman's eyes bugged out in response. Carl slapped the She-Beast on her haunches.

"She's not as pretty as the last skin, but I prefer your natural look," he said, winking. He realized Craig was sitting next to Benji, protecting and comforting him with his human arm draped around him while the other arm hung exposed. Thatched downy fur erupted through the elbow and rested at his side. A nurturing sight amid the carnage.

"Honey," Carl told his wife. "The boy might not be ready to see both his parents flayed, so you might want to move…"

"They're not my parents," Benji retorted.

"Well, I don't feel so bad about the flaying now,"

Craig's eyes beamed. "Can we keep him?"

"Seeing as you already decided to give the boy a nibble," Carl began, "if he survives the first transformation, we'll find him a nice, new skin. Speaking of new skin…" he said, pointing his cigarette at his progeny. "You're going to have to stay inside the new camper until we find you another. Or it's long sleeves and gloves for you for a while. How about you and your new brother go back to our camp and get the coolers and duffle bags, and don't forget the frying pan. We have a new RV to fill. Your camper has a freezer, right?"

Benji shrugged.

"Do you have marshmallows?" Craig asked. "The last camper we found had marshmallows, cell phones and everything!"

The clearing erupted in laughter.

Wastiger
by Baba Jide Low

I

Fuselage

We shall be in their rooms soon, to catapult them.

The reaping of cubs only happens once every century. Hungers rip through the entire Fuse but no one growls. We're too busy feeding, warm underground again.

We tear and suck at the underbellies of our Udds and push our claws beneath their pelts, for secret thrills. The Fuse trembles, collapsing the earth before it into sinkholes to eat, as it swims forward in a slow twisting grind that sends us all crashing into ourselves and our Udds, in a continuous rocking motion.

The Fuse is mechanical and organic, built after the carcasses of millipedes and caterpillars. We lay in the warm jelly of its gut, seats and beds carved out from the bent metal that emerges from the hull. The Udds are suspended above us, heavy in their strapless levitation. The rumbling of the Fuse continues as it chugs along beneath the city. We swing wildly. Our arms don't let go of the teat of our Udd.

They say the Udds birthed Gerty, the first weretiger. The Udds look like giant gelatinous tigers and keep us fed on a thick chewy roux that spills warm out of their teats.

They prevent us from being as reliant on flesh as our werewolf brothers, or on blood like our vampire cousins.

We end up needing only the warmth of the human body, to enhance our skills at *urr*, weretiger rune drawing which is the source of everything we are as a clan bound beyond time, traversing the Earth.

We should be in their rooms soon.

We drink from the teat of the Udd and our urr spells begin to awaken gradually. Runes drawn in spit on their walls and compound gates gaining a brighter strength. Their vulnerable minds tumble towards new depths of self-flagellation. Fingernails rip skin and toy with the wet apertures beneath. The Fuse continues its urr-seeking quest, crumbling a path underground towards the town of Gun-Eye.

Lust Rune

The boys waiting on us don't know they are waiting on us. They feel sick, as if with swamp fever. Trapped between heated walls under their father's roofs. They beg to be freed from their rooms, to be let out to breathe regular air again, but only feel themselves rejected, pierced, hidden from.

An ache as comes from a nail sinking into the soft arc of the foot, spreads from that unknown point at the base of the spine across their whole bodies. Becoming nothing but a many-tongued heat that eats into their bones, dredges up the tar of forgotten pain within the marrow, filling them with ekan so deep it makes them forget how to scream.

They are immobile, drenched in sweat as they groan low in agony, waiting for their deaths to come.

Transar

We only know how to claim the body of the cub eternally.

In their fever, the boys find themselves possessed of us. Here, in the narrow place between their skin and the pulp of open vascular systems beneath, we rush around mad as schoolgirls strumming harps, releasing clouds of unfettered ecstasy that cause the taut bodies of the boys to lift from the sternum into the air.

We push against the flesh like rubber, rising beneath the skin to show our feline heads, when the Exorcist is not looking at his Possessed's back, but into the Bible.

Urr thickens and begins to drip down the edges of the spit-drawn curves and lines and dots on their walls. It fills their rooms with the stench of rot and aged bone, growing fast lichen that blackens the windows and lightbulbs and walls.

The boys run up the walls to hide in plain sight, crouching in the corners of their ceiling to scream because their skull bones, they say, "It's vibrating like its gonna blow!" They can hear the Fuse as it rumbles closer and closer. They are screaming up in the corner of the ceiling and the Exorcist is passed out under his Bible and dead candles.

Their mothers try to talk to them, to walk through the smell to look at where they are terrified and trapped in the corners of the rooms, black fungus like an escaped trauma across the walls of the place. And the strength of our urr only grows. The black fungus thickening.

The boys growl and yelp in their up-corners, and their mothers run for psychiatry and its promise of straitjackets. All the bodies of all the boys who had gotten sick from our windswept spit clinging to their walls begin to tremble as the Fuse draws close, close enough they can smell us beneath the noisy rumble of the town outside.

They fall from ceiling to floor hard, alone in their rooms. The sunlight that manages to shine through the fungus-choked windows is a somber emerald.

Catapulting New Cubs

We catapult some of ourselves; five weretigers, barely two decades old in werelife, into the damp nest that the fungus that grew from our urr has turned the rooms of the once-human boys into, boys who were on the verge of becoming men.

The weretigers stand around their incoming-brother where he has fallen from up. Their bodies are firm, slick. Wet fur shimmers in the thin light that creeps through the fungus, which keeps growing, a slow smoke.

Sun-red eyes glow like lanterns in the dark of day.

Us weretigers begin a strange dance. Start-stop-start-stop. Calculated in the way it reduces our forms from standing in a circle across the room, into a tight ball of arms and backs above the collapsed boys in four slick motions.

Our weretiger shell with the boy within, collapses into a bubbling mess of melting orange, black, white, red, guts and fluid, until it disappears fast down an unseen drain.

After the boys are catapulted into the Fuse by the weretigers, the urr ceases to flow and the smell stops. Sunlight begins to melt through the black fungus.

There is a spurt, a ray of blood left on the floors of all the rooms, from the split moment when the boys left childhood and being human behind.

II

Theories on the Existence of a Wastiger

a. When Amukoko, the First Udd, birthed Gerty, it was said that they also birthed a twin, a shadow so deformed and unfit to live, it was discarded in the fire of the placenta after.

b. This twin, Gerty's shadow, is said to be the Wastiger.

c. The Wastiger comes out for the reaping and catapulting, at the same time as the Fuse filled with weretigers. It also charts a path beneath the Earth under which its ashes had been buried, post-birth. It moves at random, swimming and scattering through secret tunnels that it knows well. It is a cluster of bare organs; serpent's eyes, slippery flesh, forked tongues, dizzy snakes, big feline teeth and bees, wasps, roaches, centipedes, phlegm.

d. It lags behind the Fuse, waiting until the five weretigers are done from catapulting the cubs.

e. After the Fuse moves on, it moves into one of these emptied homes crudely, bursting through pipes and seeping up through floorboards, unequipped with the rune magics of its hale brothers.

f. Here, it stops before the point of the catapulting, where the blood spurt spans the floor like a hiding sword. Its tongues tease the blood, taste it.

g. Swallow.

h. A transmogrification occurs which no eye may recall, talk-less words describe.

i. Trailed by the attendants at the psych hospital and their solid steel gurney, the mother of the boy whose home the Wastiger decided to spill into, returns to the town of Gun-Eye, wrecked in body as well as in mind by the earlier ceiling-climbing antics of her feverish son. She pinches her palms as she approaches the room doors and screams when she sees the thing in her son's room.

j. It's her Aanu. He is lying still, somehow clean of all the wounds and striations of the days before. There's a long-dried bloodstain beneath him, but his eyes are open.

k. He is looking straight at her. Into her.

l. "Aanu, baby, how are you feeling?" She kneels and smiles at him. Relieved to see him so calm. The psych ward attendants stand behind her, feeling dumb. They try to hide the injections they hold like guns behind their backs, pushing them back into pockets.

m. She touches his forehead.

n. Cold as the maw of a long-dead goat.

o. Cold enough to cause sunlight to shrivel.

p. Cold, cold, cold, cold. Cold. Aanu's mother shivers and is unable to pull her hand away from her not-son's forehead.

q. The cold runs into her, through her skin, up into her spine and the nerves of her brain. She can feel it settle into her head like pins being set. She pulls her hand away as hard as she can but it doesn't budge. Her eyes roll back.

r. One of the ward attendants notices her discomfort and moves to see what is wrong. He touches her and his gloved hand sticks to her back.

s. The cold steals him from himself too. He grunts, growls in pain senselessly, as the sharp ice feeling bites deeper into the pulse of what he is. The heat of his skin swallowed into a bottomlessness, coated in spit from those screaming on their way down.

t. The thing that is not Aanu stands up. His mother's hand is still glued to his forehead, palm facing front. Her whole arm rises with his motion. Not-Aanu opens its mouth and the woman who birthed an image of him, and the man wearing gloves and a medical coat groaning behind her, slide into the toothless emptiness its jaws had separated to reveal.

u. The other psych ward attendant cannot move, seeing what he has just seen.

v. Not-Aanu walks to where the man stands at the door. His eyes trying hard not to fly out of his head. It tries to make a sound but all of its body collapses for a moment. The psych ward attendant sees the Wastiger's true form mere inches from his face. The skin of his head is overcome with an itching sensation, a filling of goosebumps so deep it makes him tear half his face with the tranquilizer needle before he can stop himself.

w. The house in Gun-Eye is now said to be empty. Nobody goes there to see or ask after what happened to Mama Aanu and her son, who were such good neighbors.

x. Past midnight, in the rainy months, someone sees Aanu walking in the garden again, mouth full of nothing.

The Butterfly Affect

by Linda D. Addison

The lycanthrope laid dying on the ground, hidden
in woodlands of central southern England,
having escaped the hunters, but not the
silver bullets deep in her chest,
sulfide in blood, bringing
inevitable death,
finally.
The male Purple Emperors, drawn to the quickly
decaying body, land in droves on the
cursed blood puddles ready to be
sipped by hungry *Apatura iris*.
Half die, unable to
survive the transformation,
half live, proboscis
become hardened, razor sharp
under full moonlight, purple-blue
iridescence brighter. They return to larger
females high in tree canopy, while below people wait.
Cameras
pointed up at trees
hung with carcasses of birds & rabbits,
bait for *His Majesty*. Imagine the surprise when
they land & pierce flesh. Muffled screams don't reach town,
as open mouths fill with winged insects, longing now for living flesh.
Homo sapiens hide behind locked doors,
praying the end of July
will bring the end
of the
Purple
Overlord.

The Skulk Legacy

by Alyson Faye

The black-draped carriage and horse pulled up outside Skulk Manor, and its new owner, a young man of no more than one and twenty years, stared out at his inheritance. He grabbed his carpet bag and stepped down, only to hear a whistling noise near his head, and instinctively he ducked. The bullet ricocheted off a nearby tree, the splinters covering the horse's mane. The animal tossed its head with nerves (Samuel empathized, for his own were none too steady) and the driver, a sullen, nearly mute local man, muttered an oath and tugged on the reins. Samuel had to roll in the dirt to avoid being crushed by the departing carriage wheels.

'Hey!' he shouted, but to no avail. He was alone, lying on his belly in the dirt, eyeing the bushes and greenery crowding around the drive.

Samuel waited a few more minutes, then crawled on his stomach, up the steps and over the threshold of his new home. A most ignominious arrival, but at least he was still in one piece.

Who the hell is shooting guns with so little care? And in my woods, too?

Samuel did not, as yet, seriously consider the possibility that the huntsman had been shooting at him. That idea would come later.

***

Samuel dusted himself down, and began to explore the rooms and multiple connecting corridors of Skulk Manor. His childhood memories of his late Aunt Harriet, were of a well-upholstered lady, in taffeta dresses, laden with diamonds, pouring tea from the

Chinoiserie service for him and his mama. It was, however, his aunt's eyes he recalled the most. The irises were a striking hue of amber— a trait he'd inherited, much to his mortification, as none of the rest of the family shared it.

"Quirk of genetics," his aunt had said, winking at her favorite nephew.

Samuel, six-years-old, buttoned up to the neck in a freshly-starched collar and squeezed tight into velvet knee pants, had nodded politely and gazed around the parlor and its contents in fascination. The room was overflowing with ornaments, armies of China dolls with painted dead eyes that followed you, a stuffed pike in a glass box, and hundreds of gaudy boxes holding heaven knew what secrets.

"Fairy dust," his aunt said, smiling. "Or rubies, blood stones from Arabia or perhaps the wings of butterflies."

"Nonsense and fiddlesticks," his mother retorted, clattering the teacup and frowning at the pike.

The visits to see his aunt had ceased soon after this, though Samuel had never elicited a full explanation as to the reason. Personally, he had sorely missed the silver sixpence his aunt had pressed into his palm and her whispered exhortation, heard only by himself, "Do not run with the crowd, Samuel, for *you* are not ordinary."

He had not understood her words, for he believed himself to be the most commonplace boy. His pater and mater, loving as they were, reinforced that impression. On their deathbeds, they had pleaded with him never to return to Skulk Manor. He had obeyed their wishes, until the letter from Simmonds, the family solicitors, had arrived three weeks earlier.

"Master Samuel Skulk, you are the sole inheritor of your late Aunt Harriet Skulk's estate which includes …" Samuel had gulped at the size of the bequest.

Samuel stood in the front parlor, listening intently. Had he heard footsteps outside the window? He no longer felt alone and, oddly, the hairs on his body were standing erect and his heart was pounding. He caught the flicker of a shadow, going past the terrace. *Intruders? Thinking the old house is empty?*

Samuel eyed the oil paintings covering the walls, the silver service set, the Italian-cut glassware and the many objets d'art littering the tables. There was plenty of loot for an enterprising thief. He felt vulnerable as he had no weapon, so he picked up the poker, tiptoed to the terrace's French windows, and peered out into the approaching dusk.

The lawns stretched away, fringed by shrubbery, providing many hiding places, and several stone statues, all with their faces staring at the house. Nothing moved. Then the bushes rustled below the terrace, and he lifted the poker in readiness. To his surprise and relief, a graceful fox trotted onto the lawn and, bushy tail erect, it headed to the stone fountain, where it rested its forepaws on the rim and dipped its red-furred head, supping at the frog spawn-laced waters. The animal appeared to have no fear and yet Samuel was certain it sensed his presence. The fox took its time, then, with a flick of the tail, sidled away into the bushes, pausing once and looking backwards at the house, maybe at him—he couldn't be sure.

Supper time and a drink, Samuel decided, and to choose a bed for the night. He ate a plain supper of bread, cheese, and cold meats, supplemented with a robust red wine he'd located in the pantry. Replete, Samuel carried his bag and took himself upstairs, counting off the bedrooms as he passed and selecting, not his late aunt's fussy boudoir, but instead a smaller room with only a single bed and chest of drawers.

"God bless you, aunty," he murmured as he fell asleep.

Outside, several pairs of eyes, both human and animal, watched the manor house. They would bide their time and wait, but not too long. Blood was what they wanted, some to spill it and one to claim their birthright.

Samuel slept deeply, unaware of any of these night watchers. He only stirred when he heard, through the layers of sleep, the brief yap of a fox, perhaps from somewhere deep inside the bowels of the mansion? He was too tired to get up and investigate.

***

The next morning Samuel rose and continued his exploration of his new home. He carried an unwieldy ring of keys and was working his way through them. At the end of one corridor, he unlocked a door bearing scratch marks, and, to his surprise, found a score of looking glasses of different sizes, stored with their faces to the wall and covered in quilts and blankets.

How odd, he thought. *I never would have guessed Aunt Harriet to have a phobia about her appearance.*

He locked the door and thought no more about this oddity. The rooms were providing a cornucopia of delights—ancient tomes, chests bursting with velvet and satin dresses from his aunt's younger partying days, reams of paper fans, Chinese vases, glass cases hosting fossils, rocks, and shells, maps, some hand-drawn in tarry ink, and, in his aunt's own room, a red leather-bound journal, filled with her graceful copperplate handwriting.

In the afternoon Samuel strolled around the gardens, but only as far as the woods. He paused, not keen to enter their glazy-darkened spaces. The memory of the misfired bullet hung over him. The shot had come from within these trees.

On his stroll back towards the house, he paused at the fountain, where a sad-faced maiden, frozen in stone, was eternally pouring water from an urn. His eye was caught by something glinting on the fountain's edge—at the very same spot he'd seen the fox drinking the previous evening.

Samuel looked around him—the same strange sensation of being watched prickling at his neck. He picked up the diamond earring from where it lay—almost as an offering. Whose was it?

"Hello? Anyone out there?" he called, feeling foolish.

Only the bushes rustled in reply.

***

After dinner, Samuel retired to the library and settled himself in a leather armchair with his aunt's journal. He was curious to learn more about her, since he knew nothing of how she'd lived her life here as a widow, with no surviving children of her own to visit her or bring her comfort and a brother and sister-in-law who refused to speak with her.

Were you lonely, Aunt Harriet? he wondered. *Were you afraid*?

He turned to the first page of the journal and read:

Dearest Samuel, you will be reading these words after my death, which will have been a violent one, a murder in fact. But one for which no one will ever stand trial.

Samuel sat up, rigid and tense. "No, Aunty, that's not right. You died in your bed, that's what they told me."

He read on.

Those ignorant, jealous bastards who live in the village will have caught up with me. Trapped me, no doubt tortured me and prevented me from turning back. I have evaded them for many years, but I am ageing, becoming slower, and there is always risk for our kind. We cannot resist the call of our blood, and of the   night. Not   when we have reached our full maturity, as you have so recently, my dear

57

Samuel. I wish I could be there at your side, sitting with you, explaining your destiny, but sadly I cannot. Skulk Manor is yours now and you must find a mate, procreate to maintain our line and pass on the house and the lands. They must not fall into the hands of those born of the full flesh.

Samuel took a deep gulp of the port. He was confused and worried. His aunt sounded completely mad and he couldn't understand half of what she was saying.

Who are "our kind"? Who are her torturers? And "those born of the full flesh"—what does that mean? He had so many questions and no one to ask.

There was more.

Your mate is here waiting for you.

She is a Volpe, brought over from Italy with much trouble, expense and in great secrecy. She will seek you out when you are ready. Now you must descend, my dearest Samuel, into the basement, through the hidden door next to the fireplace in the library, and drink of the liquor you find there. First you must prick a finger and drip your blood into the liquid. I know you will find these instructions most strange, but it is vital you follow them, else you will change and not understand and without knowledge, madness lies. Go now and do as I bid.

Samuel dropped the journal as though scorched by it and stumbled to the wooden panelling beside the ornate fireplace. He located a hooded acorn tucked into the seam of wood, pressed it and a door swung open, revealing a black space and releasing a wave of musty air. Worn stone steps descended into darkness, so, grabbing a lantern, Samuel edged downwards. He noticed—with alarm—

claw marks on the steps, and he prayed there was no ferocious creature lurking.

In the square room he found a decanter containing the liquor along with an empty goblet. He also found a painted mural covering the whole of one wall.

It depicted a rural scene, bucolic, peaceful, with a family of foxes—several cubs playing in front of their parents. The larger fox, the reynard, perched on watch atop the hillock above the den, whilst the vixen licked a cub's face. The sun shone on the auburn highlights of the foxes' fur, white clusters of sheep grazed in the mid-distance, and trees embraced the mural's boundaries.

Samuel eyed the goblet and the dark-colored liquid. He didn't like the look of it, nor did he want to pierce his finger with the conveniently placed silver penknife lying on the table, but he didn't wish to go mad either and end up in an asylum, as his poor cousin on his mater's side had done.

He picked up the penknife, closed his eyes, counted to five and sliced into his right thumb. "Ow!" He couldn't stop the exclamation popping out. He squeezed a few droplets of his blood into the empty goblet, wrapped his handkerchief around the wound then poured the noxious-smelling liquid into the cup. The smell reminded him of bad drains.

"Aunty, what the devil is this?" he addressed the mural. "This had better not poison me." But he remembered her whispering in his ear when he was six years old, "You are not ordinary, Samuel . . ." and the part of him which had believed her then still did.

He drank the liquid in one deep draft, tasting bile rise in his gullet in objection but fighting it down. His throat burned, his skin itched, and his lips were on fire. Samuel was now convinced he would expire here, in this underground chamber, and his corpse would not be found for years.

He slumped to the floor, pulling at his collar and shirt buttons, as waves of heat roared through his body and sweat trickled from him. He removed his outer layers, then his undergarments, until he lay naked on the stones. His sight was blurring, and he could feel his skin tightening, his legs shortening, his nose stretching. Something ticklish sprouted all over his body. His sense of smell became overwhelmingly acute, so he could smell the piss, sweat, the damp mold of the basement, the dust; he could even hear mice scurrying behind the walls.

How is this possible? Am I dying? Am I going mad?

Yet he felt no fear, nor horror; instead, he found his mind accepting the changes, even reveling in his heightened senses. The pain in his body became manageable, indeed began to lessen, and his vision was clearing.

When he looked down, he saw not hands but two paws, red-furred with claws, and he knew, without looking, there were two more at his rear. He lifted his behind and a bushy tail swished the air. If this was a hallucination it seemed very real and it also felt…right. He was at one with his new body and adrenaline coursed through him. His muscles responded lightning-fast. He was no longer two-legged, clumsy and slow, but fast, agile, and longing to explore the night. He knew, deep within him, there was another of his kind waiting for him.

The fox trotted up the stairs, leaving claw marks on them, into the library and through the house, seeking an exit. He found it through the coal door and emerged, soot-stained and moon-dappled, onto the terrace. He threw back his pointed head and barked, three short yaps, feeling his vocal cords vibrate.

An answering bark, repeated three times, came from the bushes, and a vixen ambled out, a white plume on her chest, with eyes as amber as his own and his aunt's. He knew her to be his promised mate. Samuel's heart rate soared; his blood roared at this first meeting with her. She bent her tufty head to his, and they nuzzled, smelling each other, memorizing each other's scents and pair-bonding.

An animal called out in the woods, an owl flitted between the branches, hunting, and Samuel tuned his vulpine hearing into the calls of the night, with animals scurrying about their business. It was time to join the hunt. He had a new role to play and a teacher at his side.

He was aware that in a buried, distant part of himself, Samuel Skulk was waiting to return, but mentally he closed the door on his human half and locked it away. The DNA of the fox dominated and his blood was up.

Together the two foxes, the reynard and the vixen, trotted into the woods, tails waving in sync, shoulder to shoulder. The greenery swallowed them in one gulp.

***

Dawn's gray light awoke Samuel the next morning. His head ached, his feet throbbed, and he did not at first know where he was. Then he recognized his bedroom, next to his confusion, taking in the blood stains on the bedding and feathers scattered on the carpet. His stomach was full, he noticed, and he did not want breakfast. He was also naked and cold, so he grabbed his Paisley dressing-robe and wrapped it around himself. Memories of the previous night flickered into his head as he stumbled down the stairs to the kitchen. There he found a coffee pot simmering on the stove, and a wood fire burning. Someone had been up already, but who?

He drank a cup of coffee fast, burning his mouth, but ate nothing. Sitting slumped at the kitchen table he recalled drinking the foul liquor, the mural, the garden, the vixen, the smells and sounds of the night, and going into the woods. After that it was blurry, but he knew something had happened, something awful but exciting. Something which had changed him forever.

"It's always the same," a voice spoke behind him. "The first hunt, the first kill. It's overwhelming, hard to remember the details. It will become easier."

Samuel turned and pushed his cup off the table to smash to the floor. A young woman stood near the door, her red hair falling down her back, a robe pulled around her slim body and a smile on her lips. She seemed completely at ease, and relaxed, as if at home.

"You—? I've seen you—at the fountain…no, you were a fox then…I heard you in the house at night…" He scrambled for her name, "Lucia," he announced in triumph.

She nodded in approval. "I am Lucia Volpe. Your aunt arranged for me to come here, before she died. I am your—"

Samuel finished the sentence, "My mate, my bride-to-be."

Lucia nodded and two locks of red hair swung beside her face. They caught the sunlight, glinting like a fox's fur. She walked over to Samuel and, bending down, kissed his cheek. He noticed her feral, earthy seductive scent and he remembered the chase, the damp mulch of the forest floor, the invaded nests of fleeing animals, the wetness of her nose, the power of her leaps, the grace of her body, the thrill of the kill, the taste of raw flesh and dead meat, the sharing of the food, the post-feast sleep curled up together, tails tucked in and the lovemaking that followed—oh God, yes, the lovemaking.

"You remember more?" Lucia stepped away, letting the robe fall from her body, standing naked before him and Samuel, entranced, rose to his feet.

"I do. I remember. Come to me."

She did as he bid.

***

Later that morning as they lay wrapped around each other,

62

entangled in the sheets, and in Lucia's long red hair, she turned to Samuel, "There is one more thing you must learn, if you are to keep your secret safe."

She took Samuel by the hand and together they walked, her tall and supple, matching him in height, both still naked, to the locked room of mirrors.

Puzzled, Samuel took out the key, and Lucia stepped ahead of him, her hair flowing like a cloak. She tugged the covers off and turned the unblinded looking glasses towards them.

"Look upon your true self." She indicated for her lover to step forwards.

Samuel took a tentative step, naturally expecting to see himself and, in a fashion, he did. His true self. Each looking glass reflected the face and body of a reynard—muscular, lithe, proud, with a thick auburn coat, sharp claws, and a white muzzle with cruel canines. Lucia stepped up to him and now there were two foxes, a couple, well-matched with their amber eyes.

"Now you have gone through 'la modifica.' Every mirror you pass will show your true reflection. You must be wary and stealthy, cunning as a fox," Lucia laughed, "and learn to avoid them."

Samuel raised his right hand and the reynard in the mirror raised his right forepaw. "I can't…this is beyond belief…"

Lucia shrugged. "Everything we are is beyond human belief, husband-of-my-heart, but we exist, we draw breath and we love. There are some who wish to harm us and many, many others who will never know of our existence."

Samuel remembered his aunt's diary entry. "You're speaking of Harriet's murderers? They are still at large, in the village?"

Lucia nodded. "I was there on that final night, close by, but hiding. Your aunt warned me to stay safe, so I could be here for you. Those men shot her, wounded her, cut off her—" Lucia sobbed, tears running down her face. "Her tail, then wore it as a trophy, and blooded themselves with her sangue. They are truly the monsters, not us."

"You would know them again?" asked Samuel, recalling the bullet which had greeted his own arrival. Lucia nodded, amber eyes glowing. "Well then, we must, my dear bride-to-be, throw a wedding party. A fantastical ball, and invite everyone from the village."

"What sport we will have." Her lips met his in a long kiss.

Hand in hand they left the mirror room and locked their secret away.

***

Lucia stood at the head of the staircase, her hand resting in her new husband's, wearing Harriet's diamonds, her auburn hair piled high. Later she would unpin it, let it hang loose.

A hundred or more pairs of eyes watched the newlywed couple descend; some with envy, some with genuine joy, but others with hate in their hearts.

The party wore on into the early hours. Finally, the dancers wearied, the drink took its toll, and pairs of lovers drifted away, leaving the hardened rag-tag to play cards, drink whiskey, and talk shop. Amongst these were the keenest hunters, a tough red-faced bunch whose own women were safely home in bed where they believed women should be at this time of night.

None of these men recalled seeing their host and hostess for a few hours, but no matter, the whiskey was the best Skulks' money could buy and it was free. The servants had retired for the night, when, from the garden, the men heard the sound of a woman, singing in Italian.

They were drawn out on to the terrace by her voice. They watched their hostess, Lucia Skulk, née Volpe, bathing naked in the fountain, her skin white as alabaster in the moonlight, her body lush with curves, her russet hair falling to the base of her spine.

The men, drunk and lusty, stumbled across the lawn, falling over their feet and laughing, whilst calling out lewd comments to their hostess. They gave no thought to the whereabouts of their absent host.

"May we j- join you?" asked one, as he pulled off his boots and landed on his backside.

"Time for a swim?" another laughed, tugging at his shirt buttons.

Lucia turned, as though surprised to see the group of men. But she was also unafraid, and bold, which, if they had been more sober, might have forewarned them.

"Of course, gentlemen," she said with a faint note of sarcasm. "Join me. It is time for our own private party."

The men guffawed, pulling at the rest of their clothing—so eager. A cloud flitted over the moon, leaving them in darkness, but not in silence. They heard a low growling from the bushes, a skittering, a padding of paws—more than one animal.

"Who's there?"

"What the hell?"

"Hey, watch out!"

The men lashed out in the darkness, thrashing about, hitting only each other. One toppled headfirst into the fountain, cracking his skull on the stone base and dying within seconds. The others were not so fortunate. Their attackers, both of them, rushed in low, but jumped high towards bare chests and faces, teeth bared, sharp canines ripping and tearing at juicy, fleshy cheeks, noses and eyes.

Blinded, one man lurched around, wailing, with arms outstretched. Another man tripped, landing face first, and heard his ear ripped off, whilst another felt his fingers tear, the cartilage snap, and smelt his own piss.

The men could hear animals' panting, broken by the occasional bark as their attackers worked in unison, supporting each other with lethal efficiency.

When the moon drifted out from behind the cloud cover, only a minute or two had passed, but the scene by the fountain had changed beyond recognition.

Five men's mutilated corpses lay strewn across the grass, their blood black in the moonlight. One lay toppled in the fountain, turning its waters pink, whilst ears, fingers and eyeballs were scattered around like grotesque party favors.

Near the bushes stood a pair of magnificent, muscled foxes, shoulder to shoulder, tails up and ears erect. The male tipped his snout to touch the vixen's face and she, in turn, nuzzled him. They held that stance for some time.

***

Later in bed during that long eventful night, now close to birthing a new dawn, Samuel turned to Lucia, kissed her bare shoulder and ran his hands down her body. She nuzzled into him. They drank a glass of red wine to the memory of Aunt Harriet, and to their own kind, scattered all over the world, hiding in plain sight—the Volpes.

Y Ceffyl Dŵr (The Water Horse)

by Catherine McCarthy

Welsh vocabulary:
ceffyl: horse
dŵr: water
gwrach: witch

Tied to the hitching post by a length of coarse rope, I kicked and fought until every scrap of strength was sapped. Lord Merrick's bay stallion snorted in alarm and stamped its hooves on the frozen ground at my noisy protest, but it too was tied and could not escape. The sound of my mother's screams pierced the brittle night air, the open window affording her no dignity.

"What have you done with my daughter?" she cried. "Don't hurt her, I beg you!"

I turned to face the candlelit window which transformed his bulky frame into a silhouette, watched him seize her by the throat and throw her onto the bed before both disappeared from view. A hard slap, a thud, then nothing more than the frantic squeak of bedsprings and his grunts.

I sensed the precise moment she died, for something in me changed, irrevocably. Concern for my own welfare snuffed in an instant, the ground beneath my feet seemed to disappear and I slumped within my bounds.

Silence. No whinny from the horse, no hoot of the owl, even my beating heart stilled. Then a voice, like wind blowing through reeds, "Hush now. Do as I say."

I opened my eyes and stared at the old woman who had appeared as if by magic. Branwen the gwrach. She lived in the woods and terrorized children with her reputation, but I had never feared her.

"My mother," I moaned. "She needs help."

The gwrach pressed a soiled, ice-cold finger to my lips. "It's too late to save your mother. You know that, child. I see it in your heart." I whimpered as she untied my hands, but my feet issued no protest as she led me deep into the woods.

The fire hissed and spat a warm welcome as we entered the little hut, and I gasped in surprise at the *tchack* of the jackdaw perched atop the drying rack in front of the fire. Its pale irises fixed on me and it bobbed its head in sympathy.

I shivered despite the warmth of the little room; the shock of events, I suppose. The gwrach took my hands in hers and rubbed them vigorously. Everything about her was gray: ashen skin, wild hair braided in two long coils like silver snakes, even her eyes were gray, yet her expression was one of kindness.

"Poor child," she said. "Tell old Branwen how this came to pass."

I spoke of the death of my father, of how Lord Merrick had always carried a torch for my mother and how shortly after father's death he began to plague her to marry him. Mother was of noble birth, and he lusted after her wealth and land as well as her body.

I explained how mother's heart still belonged to father despite his death and, besides, it did not take much wisdom to realize that whilst Lord Merrick might be titled, he was nothing more than a tyrant.

"You know what must be done, child," she said. "You cannot stay here. He will hunt you down and kill you, too."

I trembled from head to toe, teeth chattered in fear. "But where can I go? I am but twelve years old and not ready to live alone."

"Look at me," she said, tilting my chin in her direction. "I can help you, but not in the way you might imagine." She closed her eyes, and the lines on her face showed me what had to be done. Wrinkles formed narrow lanes which journeyed south through hills and valleys, leading eventually to a waterfall.

I shook my head, my stomach a viper's den. "I'm going nowhere until I have revenge. I'll not be satisfied until he's dead."

She nodded, shark-gray eyes narrowed like crescent moons. "And you shall have it," she said, "but you must be patient, child. Bide your time and vengeance shall be yours."

"You'll help me?"

"Indeed. I have two gifts to give you. The first will be familiar, the second is not what it seems. Now close your eyes."

I did as she asked and the jackdaw cawed its approval.

"Don't peep," she said. "I want you to feel her presence."

She pressed something into my hands, something warm that smelled of lilac blossom. I held my breath and explored the object with trembling fingers. A doll, made in my mother's own image by my father's hands. A mother in miniature. Tears gathered beneath my closed lids, desperate to escape, and my throat constricted.

"You can look now," Branwen said, and I did. Raven hair, each strand lovingly woven from the barbules of a crow's feather. Pale complexion, fabricated from the bleached skin of a foal, and piercing, painted eyes of celestial blue which captured the glint in mother's precisely. The paint would fade in time, as would my memories of her.

"But how—" The doll had sat on my bedroom windowsill. How could the gwrach have taken it?

She tutted. "You ask too many questions, and besides, I knew it was the most precious of all your possessions."

I stroked the doll's hair, stared into painted eyes which glistened with tears that mimicked my own. "Mother." As I spoke the word, the corners of the doll's mouth turned upwards in a smile.

"Now for the second gift," Branwen said, her hand hovering above a bowl of shiny red apples. "Anne manne miene mukke." She chose one and held it out to me, "Are you willing to accept?"

I nodded, though my heart plummeted with disappointment at the insignificance of the second gift. An apple? I would have preferred it to have been a dagger, so that I might stab him through the heart.

"You must journey south until you reach Cavern Cascade Falls at Ystrad Meurig. Remember the map on my face, for it will show you the way. When you reach your destination, you must stand beneath the stream and allow the water to return you to your former self."

"Former self?"

"Hush now, let me explain. You must not return home for ten years. By then you will have grown into a woman and that brute of a man will have forgotten your face. Only then will you be old enough and wise enough to wreak revenge."

"But how will I travel?"

What she said next shocked me to the core.

"But it's impossible! You're as crazy as they say you are!" The doll in my hands turned cold, the color in its lips faded to blue then parted as it spoke in a whisper. "Please, Rhiamon. Do as Branwen tells you."

Branwen grinned. "You see, nothing is impossible. Now pay attention."

The flesh of the apple stuck in my throat as I swallowed, but I had to get to the core. "It will summon the spirit of the Ceffyl Dŵr," she said. She handed me a glass of water to help the flesh on its journey, her eyes darting to and fro, eager to see the outcome. The core revealed three pips, each a dark promise. I held them in the palm of my hand and counted again, just to be sure.

"A little disappointing," Branwen said. "I had hoped for a few more, so be sure not to waste them. One will be needed to send you on your way and another to bring you home. The third you can choose to use as you wish, but take my advice and do so wisely."

My fingers trembled as I held the largest of the three seeds between my thumb and forefinger. "How am I to keep them safe for ten whole years? They're tiny."

The gwrach held out a hand, the lines of her palm mapped black with dirt. "Pass them here," she said. "I shall sew two into the hem of the doll's dress. Your mother's spirit will watch over them until you are ready to put them to use."

She hummed a whiny tune as she stitched, and when she finished sewing, she wrapped the doll in a linen cloth and bound it with hemp string before carefully laying it at the bottom of an old saddlebag.

"For the journey," she said, placing a handful of ripe plums on top. "Tide you over until you get used to the taste of grass." She gave a toothless chuckle then escorted me by the hand into the dusky woods.

We made our way to Dolgoch Falls with only the moon to guide us, and as we journeyed, she told me everything I needed to know.

Madness, sheer insanity. I stood in front of the waterfall, spray misting my skin and the roar of its voice in my ears. A faint sulfurous tang hung in the air from the wet limestone and quartz. Branwen took me by the wrist and pulled me closer to the falls.

"Be brave, Rhiamon, and never lose sight of your purpose."

I stuck out my tongue, encouraging my dry mouth to flood with mineral water, before swallowing the apple pip. Within moments my vision blurred, and Branwen's form misted behind the falls. An invisible hand shoved me to my knees. My neck snapped forward and every bone in my body stretched: spine, limbs, skull, as though I'd been placed on the rack. Arms became forelegs, ribcage the hull of a rowboat. My shrieks of agony were lost to the wind and the torrent of water. Pale skin, goose-pimpled from cold and fear, sprouted a glossy chestnut coat and my crowning glory became a coarse forelock and mane. I raised a hoof and stamped down hard, relishing the vibration that flowed through my body as bone struck rock. Tendons pulled and muscles flexed. A sense of power: formidable, majestic. I threw back my head in elation and neighed, rejoicing in my wondrous form. Bright-eyed and bushy-tailed, I galloped into the night.

I summoned the gwrach's face to mind: wrinkled roads and bony hills, furrowed lanes and dipping vales. Steaming breath left a ghost trail as I journeyed, one I knew he would not trace. Never before had I known such strength, such a potent sense of freedom.

I must have run a hundred furlongs before noticing that the saddlebag containing the precious doll, once fastened to my waist, was now strapped to my withers, though my woolen tunic had disappeared.

All through the night I ran, following the map inscribed on the gwrach's face. I did not think about my plight or even my mother's death. As the first rays of sun peeped between the hills of the Ystwyth Valley I slowed to a trot, sensing Cavern Cascade Falls close by. Ears forward, I followed the sound until I arrived at the pool beneath the falls.

Throat parched, I dipped my head to drink and for the first time caught sight of my reflection. Shock waves rippled along my spine. The reality of the transformation from human to equine was sublime. And yet some semblance of the girl remained: a jet-black mane of hair and fiery golden eyes that watched me admiring myself. I would grow into a beauty, just like mother.

I drank my fill then trotted nervously to the falls in order to wash away my disguise, half wishing I could remain in horse-form for a decade, until it was time to go home. But I could not. Branwen had warned me that to spend more than a day in my current form would mean I could never return to my human self.

The decade that followed did nothing to mend my bleeding heart. In fact, it only served to harden it. I had spent my formative years in splendor, wanting for nothing. I did not know hardship or what it meant to earn one's keep. I knew nothing of wile or cunning, little of how much power a young woman's looks wielded. But I soon learned. I had to. Begging for each crust, each opportunity to labor until my fingers bled, made me bitter as wormwood.

On occasion I would take out the doll cast in my mother's image and pour out my heart. At times I would feel anger, lay blame at her door for succumbing to Lord Merrick's vice, though deep down I knew she was not to blame. I convinced myself that she heard, that she condoned my behavior and gave justice to my evil thoughts.

At other times I felt sure I disappointed her, that she believed my malice an unjust excuse for how we had both been treated.

In the end, I chose to do as I saw fit, to use my beauty and power over men to my advantage as he had used brute force over us. In doing so I broke several hearts. Good practice, I told myself, for when I would break his.

I cannot say for certain whether it was the gwrach's magic or whether it had to do with the Ceffyl Dŵr, but as the years passed by my influence over others grew, exponentially so. I dabbled in magic, flirted with the supernatural, charmed those I encountered with more than guile and good looks.

Each year I marked the anniversary of my mother's death by brewing a tincture of wolfsbane and feeding it to whichever beau I happened to be courting at the time, and when the ten years were up, I unpicked the hem of the doll and popped out the second seed before closing the wound.

***

Homeward bound, I thrilled at every fence, delighted in every death-defying leap, eager to undertake the next stage of my life.

A little before sunset I reached Dolgoch Falls and spent an hour or so basking in twilight before once again allowing the torrent to resurrect me to human form.

Eager to visit Branwen, for I felt she deserved to hear of my return, I wended my way through the woods until I came upon the little hut hidden amongst the bracken. The chimney belched no smoke and the place was in darkness. I had hoped she might offer me a night's sojourn since I had nowhere else to go and no-one else to turn to for basic comfort.

When she did not answer, I opened the door and stepped into the gloom. A wisp of smoke from the candle suggested she had left moments earlier, as did the faint smell of pine and comfrey. The embers of the fire glowed red, but neither she nor the jackdaw were anywhere to be seen.

As I was about to leave, a note, scribbled on a sheet of linen and weighted to the table by a lump of quartz, caught my eye...

Rhiamon,
The time has come for me to move on. You are welcome to my humble abode, and remember, you have but one seed remaining. Use it wisely.
Branwen

I studied Lord Merrick secretly over the coming weeks until I learned the pattern of his coming and going. Each Thursday, he and two of his henchmen would ride out to visit his tenants, collecting rents and checking they met the agreed quota of land production as well as issuing threats if the agreement fell short. He was avaricious, covetous, his aspiration for wealth insatiable. He imposed levies on the use of the mill, tolls on roads and bridges, and expenses in the form of baptism and burial dues. My hatred of him festered like an untreated wound.

I had no doubt I could make him want me more than he had wanted any woman, even my mother. But I had grown cruel in my hatred, heartless and vindictive. I would do anything to gain the upper hand and so decided to craft a dress like no other, one with magical powers sewn into every seam: the gown of a seductress.

Weeks it took to make, every stitch a labor of love. I sat in the woods and sewed, imagining the power it would wield over the man who believed he could have anything he wanted, until eventually my task was complete.

With a gossamer touch, I stroked the breast of the newly-crafted gown. A thousand butterfly wings it had taken to fashion the garment, each one collected with a whisper of whimsy. Those whose colors were already fading, or whose wings were torn, I crushed in the palm of my hand, thrilling as the bright pigments transferred to my skin. But those which were unspoiled... now they were what I sought.

Each wing torn from the butterfly's thorax in one, swift rent. It was best that way. Far less damaging to the wing. I placed a few redundant, succulent heads and abdomens into the heart of a spider's web, watching with mild amusement as it pounced from its lair to suck upon the sweet juices. Others I discarded on the ground, before granting myself some moments of pleasure in watching their futile attempt to fly before giving up the ghost.

From the bodice of the gown, the azure eyes of the peacock butterfly judged my actions, its blood-red daubs reminding me of the pain I'd inflicted. The red and blue contrasted beautifully with the old gold of the gatekeepers' wings, regal almost. And for good measure, I'd even acquired a few purple emperors, rare in these parts. Those I'd meticulously sewn along the décolleté with the silken-thread of the orb-weaver and a needle fashioned from a wren's rib. Oh, how I longed to look upon the majestic image I must cast! Perhaps I should wander to the pool so that I might gaze upon myself.

Perched upon the fallen trunk of an alder, a pair of stag beetles—their antler-like jaws locked in a fight to the death over an elusive female—caught my attention. The larger of the stag beetles had wrestled its opponent to the ground and was off to claim its prize, who was no doubt waiting in the wings beneath some sliver of decaying bark. Its defeated rival limped off, head hung low in shame. Stone in hand, I put paid to its misery with one swift strike, the crunch of its armored shell a joy to my ears. A spatter of flaxen liquid spurted from the insect, threatening to stain the carefully-crafted butterfly gown. I'd need to be careful wandering the woods in this—it was fragile. Perhaps I should hide it away until I was ready to face him. He would be certain to fall in love with it—he liked pretty things.

As summer faded to autumn, I knew he was ready.

As Merrick and his men rode through the wood I stepped onto the path, causing Merrick's stallion to rear.

"Woah, boy!" he said, pulling up the horse.

For a fleeting moment his brow furrowed, but his expression soon changed to one of desire.

"Well, what have we here?" He dismounted and drew so close I smelled the whiskey on his breath. It was all I could do not to recoil as he placed a gloved hand on my forearm. With a lecherous grin he bid his men leave, saying he would catch up with them shortly once he had made certain I was unharmed. I knew by their laughter that they understood his intent.

Mesmerized by my appearance, he stood silent at first, drinking me in. "Where are you from?" he asked.

My heart raced with trepidation. "Hereabouts, sir, though I am only recently returned from the south." The charm was working, for he could not steal his eyes from me.

"Perhaps that is why I do not recognize you, though—" He paused, held firm my wrist and examined me from head to toe. "Something about you seems familiar."

My heart lurched, for I knew I resembled my mother. If he made the connection the situation would turn sour. I needed to think fast.

"You are mistaken, sir. Although I was born in these parts, my parents moved south when I was just a baby."

"That gown," he said, his fingers brazenly reaching out to stroke the front. "It's exquisite."

A surge of energy passed from wing to skin and I knew he was bewitched. "Thank you, sir. I am seamstress to Lady Cadwallader of Harlech." I fluttered my lashes, though there was no need.

We parted with words of promise.

"Meet me tonight by the witching tree and I shall give you the ride of your life," I said, bold as brass. I bit back the smirk that threatened to form and held out a hand for him to kiss. Little did he know the kind of ride I had in mind.

Returning to the hut, I unpicked the final apple pip from the hem of the doll's dress, ignoring the look of anguish upon my doll-mother's face, and made my way to Dolgoch Falls. As dusk fell, I stood one last time beneath the torrent, rejoicing in the pain and power of transformation.

Galloping towards the manor, it crossed my mind to turn in the opposite direction, away from this place of heartache, and choose to spend the rest of my days in equine form as a free spirit, though in doing so not only would I relinquish the opportunity for revenge but no doubt some man would do his utmost to try and tame me even then. Free will does not exist, neither for humans nor animals.

His stallion issued a loud protest as I stole into the stable block, but I hushed it with the promise of freedom before striking the stable door with my powerful hind legs. The stallion recognized a chance to escape and did so willingly, galloping into the night without so much as a nicker.

Soon after, Merrick came whistling through the stables, reeking of musk and cloves. His skin shone from shaving and his eyes glinted with lust. When he noticed his bay stallion missing, he called for the stable boy, issuing a harsh threat if the horse was not found by the time he returned home, then, without hesitation, he mounted my back.

As soon as we crossed the paddock and were out of earshot, I sped up. Try as he might to whoa me, he could not. I had promised him the ride of his life and would keep my word. Like a bolt of lightning I streaked across fields, keeping up the pace when we reached the woods. The harder he yanked at the reins, the faster I rode. Branches whipped our faces, snagged at his hair and tangled my mane. Dips and troughs posed no challenge, for I was fleet of foot. He was a skilled rider, but his talent was no match for my tenacity. Several times he cried out in anguish but apart from throwing himself to the ground there was little he could do. I smelled his fear and reared in triumph.

By the time we reached the waterfall he was spent, his face lacerated, body bruised. Adrenaline coursed through my veins, eyes wild and teeth bared. With a squeal of delight I reared, tossing him like a rag doll onto the rocks. He cried and begged for mercy as I stamped down hard. The crunch of bone as ribs snapped, a spurt of blood as his nose exploded beneath my hoof. And I did not let up, not until every bone in his body was broken. He lay whimpering, unable to move a muscle.

I needed him to witness my next act. Face to the waterfall, he saw me change, shock and disbelief evident on his face. In human form I stood before him, naked and dripping onto his wounds. His left shoulder popped as I gripped his arm and dragged him towards the clearing.

"My name is Rhiamon," I said. "My mother was Efa, Lady Efa."

The moon cast a beam on his face, highlighting his guilt, and I watched as the light in his eyes gradually dimmed then died.

His ribcage was shattered, the flesh around it torn, so it was not too difficult to remove his heart.

Like me, the hawthorn was a mistress of disguise. Delicate

blossoms with pink-tinged stamens veiled needle-sharp thorns, capable of taking out an eye. I hummed a merry tune as I nailed his heart to the trunk of the hawthorn with one of its own needles. Did it beat still, or did I imagine it? The tree thanked me for my gift with a shower of petals, white as snow.

I strode a few paces towards where he lay prone on the grass and bent over him, before moistening my hands in the dew and licking the blood, finger by finger.

Needle in hand, I carved my mother's initials, one on each of his corneas, before engraving the letter *R* upon his forehead. Calligraphy complete, I stood back to admire my handiwork. I was no artist, but it would suffice. "The evidence of your sins will be witnessed by those you encounter in the next world," I said, "and you will bear the mark of our names eternally."

As I approached the hut, I was surprised to see mother's doll watching my return from the window. I was certain I had left her on the bed. Head tilted to one side, she appeared downhearted. I washed his blood from my hands, scrubbed his flesh from beneath my nails before picking it up. The scent of lilac, her scent. I held her close and breathed her in. She whispered in my ear, faint and soft, "Enough now, Rhiamon." she said. "It is done. Take back your heart from the lake of ice and let it thaw."

The Forgotten Ones
by Tabatha Wood

Bound at the turn, at the break of all things,
Where dark tides inhale ragged shores,
A herald moon pinned to a blackened stage,
Hauls hope to the endless; the Changed.
Where old lives are held down by weed-wrapped hands,
Wound tight in the ropes of old fates,
Silver-tongued maidens, forlorn, lunar-cursed,
Sing to the vanishing stars.
Their song is a wrenching, surging need
To peel back slick, ribboned skins.
And all those who hear them are damned by their call,
Lured to their wretched embrace.
Here I stand with my sisters on cancer-gray sands,
Chewed up and spat out; bone-piled,
Enwrapped in fine robes of my second flesh,
Caught in the cold currents of time.
I may wear many faces; slit-eared or fin-tailed,
As I slip through the whispers of lore,
Yet my voice on the wind is the shriek of death;
The crushing despair of the soul.
And my blood bears the echoes of heart-sick loss,
Of mourning a life long before.
Reflections of everything I once was,
Now lost to the moon evermore.

From Mist to Sinew

by Michelle Garza and Melissa Lason

Eyes, ever watching, formed into white orbs amidst the smoke, like miniscule moons floating in the darkness beyond the fire, never blinking. They watched her, the little huntress on her horse, the weak girl who was more skeleton and skin than muscle and fat. It would eat her all the same. It had just fed and still it hankered for her flesh. They were both starving. The beast could feel the agony in the girl's gut from a great distance, hunger howling louder than the wolves the beast fought tooth and claw to devour. It took their spirits into itself, and when its stomach was empty it took on a bastardized version of their form to hunt and it was always hungry. It would take the spirit of the huntress, too. She would make it even more powerful. The girl was more akin to it than she'd ever realize, both feral animals tracking their prey to the edges of Hell.

The horse's legs moved in long, graceful strides, even in the snow it didn't falter. A locomotive of flesh and bone and tendon powering onward with white puffs of steam spewing from its nostrils as it covered the frosted ground. Its hide, scored with jagged scars down its flanks, was black as night but for white socks extending from its hooves to its knees. Those white markings were tinged red, blood-stained like the snow it fled over.

The girl sat upon the horse's back, doubled over, moving mechanically with its strides. Her stomach was empty, gnawing itself painfully. Her hands were frozen to the reins, raw and bloody. Her eyes rarely blinked, just stared forward towards the horizon where thin smoke danced and beckoned her to the warmth of a fire which birthed it into the gray sky.

The path before her was well-worn. She had traversed it countless times, back and forth, back and forth through the forest, by night and by day. Her hunt was endless, she always one step behind the beast. Her strength has waned by the day, her muscles became thin and useless. The only thing driving her was her need to end the nightmare. It would be over with once the beast was as dead as everything else in the forest.

She found no comfort or warmth to welcome her at the fire, only more blood-soaked snow. Her horse danced and stomped the defiled earth, displaying the remains of an unidentifiable person. A crimson skeleton, whose bright eyes were left lidless and staring into the approaching night, granted eternal rest after a savage death.

"It has killed again. I'll never make it through this season of the beast." She coughed and gagged. If her stomach wasn't so empty, she would have vomited onto her skittish horse.

Winter had become a ravenous monster, and not in a poetic sense, but a real creature, one of mist and sinew and teeth. It took as it wanted and spared very few. Only the strongest among them would survive it, that was no secret, and only those who became monsters themselves. The cracking of bones, the spilling of blood and innards, meant survival. There was nothing left to eat. Feeding silenced the hungry howling in one's gut, and the demons in one's mind. Meat and marrow, those were warm and enriching, nourishing to the hunters who partook. They, with blood on their hands and guilty souls, fought to emerge on the other side of the endless winter, in the springtime when flowers would bloom among the bones of those who were too weak to make it through. She refused to eat of the flesh of men, even when others followed the lead of the beast just to survive. Her stomach was hollow and her limbs trembled most of the time but still she would not feed as the creature fed. She felt the act only cursed the lands she grew up in even more than they already were. What good was survival if she became akin to the monster she sought to destroy? The forest had always been harsh and unforgiving, but it had changed now, something had come along and transformed it. She meant to find that something and kill it, even if it took her soul with it to the abyss.

"Come along." She spoke to the horse, leaving the body in the bloody snow.

The huntress and her horse ventured beyond the fire to the trees on the other side, her eyes scanning for footprints or droplets of blood. She found not a clue to guide her, like so many times before. It was as if the beast was no more than a swift, ravenous wind or a spirit. The trees hunched over her, their branches like fingers raking at her hair. It came loose, lack of food and nourishment let it come free from her scalp easily, leaving little pieces of herself on branches and twigs hanging like spider silk. The evening forest was silent and still. Her stomach growled loudly, the horse spooked at its sudden complaining, and she fought for a moment to get it to steady itself.

"Easy now."

She could feel her horse tensing, expecting to be taken down beneath her by the killer of the wood. It was a walking feast, after all, one of the last four-legged animals left alive in all of the forest. She patted its neck and tried to calm it, imparting to it the truth that the easiest prey to subdue was always bipedal, shivering with lack of fur, and prone to being ruled by emotion. Those of the human variety, they fell faster than the wild, hearty dwellers of the forest or the horse beneath her. The winter beast knew this all too well, as it had also devoured every stag, hare, fawn and bird, every bear, wolf, and cougar. Its hunger remained unsated no matter how much flesh it consumed, so its hunt was eternal, and so was hers.

The deeper they tread into the forest, the more the suffocating silence grew. Not a single bird fluttered or chirped, but the heavy stillness was something she had become accustomed to in the weeks of agonizing winter. Her gaze went to a well-worn path, one she followed almost daily when she was a small girl. In truth, she was only a few years beyond being a child. The harshness of the forest had matured her, yet she was still so young. An orphan in a brutal world, with nothing left to drive her but vengeance. In her mind, revenge would taste much sweeter than any morsel she could consume.

The path led to the old woman's cabin, the grandmother of the forest, who lived on the farthest edge of the trees. The grandmother was bent, and frail, and mostly ate the berries and vegetation around her instead of the flesh of animals. She was a kindly woman who always shared her fire and food with the girl from the time she was just old enough to venture alone up until a few weeks before the winter of the beast struck. She would dream on lonely nights the grandmother was her own mother, what else do motherless children dream of? The huntress hoped the white-haired old woman had survived the endless hunting of the creature, but she held little hope. She hadn't dared venture so far once the killing began, but after finding all of her neighbors dead and the corpse by the fire, fear gripped her for the old woman's safety.

It stalked her from the darkness, shrouded in a cloak of stillness, both headed in the same direction. Even beneath a heavy coat, the hunter girl's bones could be seen, jutting out at her collarbone, poking out at her wrists like spindly sticks forming a scarecrow. Her cheeks were hollow, her eyes sunken. The huntress had become the picture of starvation.

The horse, with its scarred hide, it would be a feast of blood and innards. The creature nearly had the stocking-legged horse once but the girl saved its life. If only it could taste the horse flesh again, the creature would wallow in it until it hollowed the horse out like a maggot beneath the moon, but only after it ate the girl on its back first. The beast's stomach rumbled and rolled under its pale, furry hide. One of them would need to feed soon.

It crept parallel to her, she on horseback, riding the well-trodden pathway, and it slinking through the dark brush, each seeking the grandmother's house. The forest was thick, and the pathway wound through switchbacks as it climbed a hill on the southern end of a clearing where the old woman's cabin stood. The horse and its rider crested the hill only steps behind the creature as it broke free of the reaching arms of the trees. Its cover was blown as it sprinted from the tree line towards the tiny wooden cabin. It didn't fear the girl on her horse, it only wished to make it to the grandmother's door before the huntress. Their game of hide and seek was nearly complete.

The horse shrieked at the emergence of the enemy. A white dash of movement from the dark forest startled the mare and its rider and sent the horse dancing and bucking. The horse kicked and reared, unwilling to come in contact with the claws of the winter beast again. Its hide bore the story of the night it was nearly devoured, and the skeletal girl on its back came to fend off the creature with a flaming torch. For a moment, she refused to move, even as her rider kicked her sides with her heels and cursed her for her cowardice. The creature with fur as white as winter snow was now far ahead of them. It bounded for the grandmother's cabin, one of the only humans left alive in the forest, or at least she hoped, besides a handful of men who were just as monstrous as the beast itself.

"Grandmother!" the huntress cried.

The horse settled a bit and began to obey its rider, who kicked it and urged it to gallop after the monster. She had never seen it as anything more than a blur of flesh and teeth. Even when it attacked her horse, it moved like flesh made of the wind, like mist forming into sinew then back again. She studied it as she gained ground on the beast sprinting towards the grandmother's cabin. It was more wolf than anything but had long human-like arms and hands. The huntress barely had the strength to fight anymore but fight it she would, especially if it meant to protect the old woman who could be the last kind soul alive in the dark forest. The grandmother, her dream-mother.

In a few hoof beats, clods of snowy soil flying up from the horse, they would be upon the beast. It sensed them and, in an instant, the beast of flesh and fur exploded into mist and shadow to fly over the rough terrain, leaving the huntress and her horse to power through the snow. Her anger rose as her hope faded. It would be at grandmother's door long before them. The sound of cracking wood echoed over the white, frosty ground, and she knew she was far too late.

The cabin windows were dark but for a faint flicker of firelight and the chimney belched a thin line of smoke into the dark sky, drifting over the face of the yellow moon. The door was broken in jagged shards of hanging wood, a menacing maw gaping to reveal the black throat of the dark house beyond it.

The huntress brought her horse to a halt, an easy task since the horse had slowed to a begrudging walk at the sight of the cabin. She climbed down from the saddle, her small stature accentuated against the height of her horse. She glanced down at her shadow on the snow, so small it made her bravery shrink. She had been riding for days uncounted, tall and valiant atop her mare, but now she remembered she was only a few summers beyond being a child. Her back and thighs hurt from riding for what felt like an eternity, youth usually triumphed over such aches and pains, but malnourishment was racking her small bones and muscles.

She pulled an ax from her saddle, her only inheritance from her father besides the hovel with a leaking roof he left behind when he was eaten by the winter beast. She had found him, his body torn to pieces, his head never recovered. It was far more than what her mother ever left her, twelve years and the woman had never even written a letter to either spit at or covet depending on the stage of depression the girl was experiencing. Her mother had left her nothing but a hole in her heart, she tried to fill with the old woman she hoped to defend.

"Robin," a voice called from beyond the broken door.

The little huntress felt a tug in her heart. Only the old woman would call her by her birth name, but the voice was labored. She hoped the grandmother had already bested the creature, struck it down as it burst through her door.

"Little Robin, have you come to visit? It's been so long."

"Grandmother?"

"Come in, child. You have nothing to fear, now."

She was a hunter, a role forced upon her in order to survive, but she was also a child. She felt a lonesome pull in her heart. It ached more than her empty stomach. Ever since her father died, she had to put every thought she had toward avenging him, to staying alive. Now, she longed to be warm, to be fed, to be held in loving arms.

"The monster is gone, Robin."

The huntress took a step toward the door, toward grandmother's voice.

"Come share my fire like we always used to."

Robin felt the chill of winter, brutal on her thin skin, gnawing at her growing bones. She quickened her pace.

"Good girl."

She breached the doorway to see the glow of a small fire and a figure in an old chair bathed in orange light. The frigid winter air was left beyond the threshold as she crossed the creaking floor, blinking her eyes to adjust them to the faint light, and the utter darkness surrounding grandmother.

"I never partook of flesh," grandmother said, "but in my age, and with this endless winter…something I kept shackled inside me became stronger than the mental chains I kept it bound up in."

The huntress remained silent but, for a moment her, mind was filled with memories of when the cabin was a bright place, filled with herbs and books. The grandmother always smiled at her as she read and told her stories, but now she didn't show her face to the child.

"Did you ever wonder why I made you go home long before the sun went down?"

The old woman stood and lifted the lid of the stew pot hanging over the warm glowing embers of the fire. She held a spoon out to the child, the little huntress. The girl opened her mouth wide but froze when she realized the spoon was empty. She glanced at the pot; it, too, had nothing inside. She noticed that the hand holding the wooden spoon had elongated fingers and gnarled fingernails.

"Oh, dear. The pot is empty. This winter has been exceptionally harsh. It has pushed many to do things they wouldn't normally do, and to do things they swore they never would again."

The old woman tossed the spoon aside.

"The cold made me weak, made me want to give up the fight and, one night, I became too old to combat it, to hold it inside with tinctures and charms. It promised me a youth I hadn't experienced in ages."

"I don't understand." The words were a lie, the things young souls tell themselves to guard against the pain of knowing the truth. Robin had shared a few awkward moments with the old woman shooing her down the mountain when dusk stained the sky. Her tender little heart always wondered why the old woman didn't want her around when darkness fell but she accepted the excuse the old woman wanted her home safe before the moon rose. She had no idea behind the kind face and gentle eyes of grandmother, something ancient and hungry hid.

"You always wanted me to be your mother, didn't you? Soon we shall be as one. You can be with me, always. We'll never be hungry again," Grandmother promised, leaning closer, revealing her twisted wolfish face to the girl.

The huntress felt a pang in her heart; the hunt was over. She should have lifted her axe but she let it fall to the floor; she was too weak, too overcome with the agony of both heart and body. The pain of being devoured would pale in comparison to living in a world without her dream-mother, the old woman on the farthest edge of the wood. She bowed her little head.

"Your spirit will be in me always, my little one. You will be my blood, my flesh, my child—until the end of time."

The Rattling Howl

by Sara Tantlinger

Misunderstood creature, calm temperament
unless provoked, unless humans come trampling
along, shaking the earth and wrecking habitats
in an attempt to steal you from the den where
you've burrowed beneath frozen ground
waiting for the Full Cold Moon; dark scales
ache for spring, for escape from this dormant
state of brumation, but there is nothing to fear,
not until the rattle becomes a howl.
They choose not to understand you
because seething in fear and adrenaline
makes it easier to hunt you, kill you, mount you
upon cruel walls of taxidermy -- and if only
all those skinned creatures could come back
flay the two-legged ones alive where they walk,
and they're walking toward you because you've
left the pit of snakes, different from the others.
You roam at midnight, ravenous and waiting
for them to disturb you, agitate the venom
until scales morph into fur, and fangs lengthen,
until the maraca shake of interlocked rings
on your tail vibrate, hissing out a warning melody
yet closer they approach because they do not know,
not until the rattle becomes a howl.
Glorious in your transformation, growing taller
than the humans who did not prepare for something
as strange as you: rattlesnake, monster, creature

unknown fiend merely surviving harsh winter,
you slither toward them and their screams echo
as they learn when the rattle becomes a howl,
your howl, escape is nothing but a distant memory.
And you, creature of the rattling howl, slide toxic
bites to sting them into paralysis, devour all
and grow strong beneath the fat moon because
when the rattle becomes a howl, it is too late,
and you have been so hungry for far too long.

Two Hearts Make a Half; or, Ghosts of a Rodeo Clown

by Eric J. Guignard

When a Rodeo Clown dies, he creates not one but three ghosts, a division of the self he maintained while alive: one part imprudent jester, one part steadfast defender of the bull rider, and one part testament to frailty of the human condition. Each of these parts goes on to become its own entity-spirit within the transcendental realm of mankind, being specters illimitable and omnipresent, yet bound forever to the reaction of their one-in-three development, the essence of their once-mortal self: jester, defender, or testament. But when Teddy "Dove" McGuinn died, his division produced an exceptional anomaly, a development as astounding as it is ironic … his being—what he'd *been*—divided not three ways, but instead *quartered*, forging an additional fourth ghost. And that ghost was of the beast Dove McGuinn had equal-parts loved and tormented, for this fragment of his soul turned into the haunting creature known as …

The Were-Bull.

Listen close, and you may hear far-away echoes of its thundering hooves or the bellow of its indignant rage. Feel the whispered exhalation on your cheek of heated breath from its ringed nose. Look hard enough into the shimmering grass fields, when the sun hits dappled crests just so, and you may even see the ghostly glimmer of the were-bull, a foreleg lifting half-cocked as if to charge, reddened eyes, glowing, watching, intent. Lost. Adrift. Alone.

Though surely majestic, the were-bull is a cursed creature, a shadow of its once functioning, vibrant human form. Is it punishment? Karmic justice? Such reflective comprehension is no longer capable for this one-quarter of Dove McGuinn-turned bull-ghost, so it must wander confused and abstract, like nuzzling mist on a cold, dim day.

Until transformation.

The fourth quarter of the lunar cycle (as akin to this fourth quarter of himself), sees the were-bull corporealize! Now you need not listen close, for the bellow of its indignant rage turns chillingly real, a noise equally resonant as it is terrifying, for transformation into any new form is a painful process for all were-creatures.

One week a month, the were-bull exists in living form, in all appearance a massive, prominent example of the *Bos taurus* species, swaths of rippling muscle, gleaming black hair, horns the length of sabers, and just as deadly. But imbued, still, with the human psyche—albeit a quarter—of the consciousness of he who used to mock the bull, chase the bull, ride the bull, provoke the bull. What Dove knows is only that he is broken now, confused, somehow cast adrift in cosmic anthropomorphism. He has tried to communicate before, has brayed sounds constructed to mean, "Help me," and "Where am I," but instead causes only fear or laughter from any human who hears them. In fury or disgust, he charges them. They flee in terror. A sense of gloating floats up into his consciousness, of pride. He may be a monster, but he, at the least, is formidable.

It is not long before he finds himself shunning mankind anyway; grazing deeper and deeper into rich, wild prairies, away from the commerce and troubles of mortals' living. Grazing and brooding, until the fourth lunar quarter waxes away, and he dissipates back into the spectral.

Such is the cycle that perpetuates. One week a month. Twelve times a year. One hundred twenty transformations a decade. Two decades elapse. More.

It is thereafter at one of those shape-shiftings, as the moon wanes gibbous, that Dove is seen metamorphosing in the meadowed vales of Pawnee National Grassland, a hundred miles northeast of the Denver Coliseum, where he used to work the circuit of the National Western Stock Show. Finding his voice once again returned, the were-bull roars across the night, a cry of pain and wariness, a searching, repeated call for other splintered fragments of himself or others of his kind …

***

It's night. Dark but for the moon and the fireflies flitting across the plains. A dashboard clock reading midnight. The flickering smolder of a Marlboro Red dangling from the corner of Rod Reams's mouth as he sits in his 4x4 Silverado. Rod "The Bod" to the ladies of line dancing, the mini-dress-wearing, high boot Scootin' Boogie aficionados of Denver's rodeo cowmen (they ain't boys in Denver).

Rod's just staring out the windshield, not really looking at anything, but just thinking. Thinking and smoking. He's got a Sig Sauer P226 in his lap; the clip two bullets light. The body of his whore girlfriend is outside on the cold ground, wrapped in a tarp. Coupla shovels are out there, too, a pickaxe, a chainsaw. A fifty-pound bag of quicklime. He's heard that's urban myth, the quicklime will dissolve a body in the earth, but hell, why not toss it in anyway? It's gotta help, and Rod's all about maximizing his odds. *Play the long game*, he thinks, as he smokes and stares out that windshield to the prairie, a wind-ruffled realm of shifting grass and shooting stars.

Suddenly, a roar sounds, and Rod almost shits himself. The cigarette falls from his mouth to land and burn a smoldering hole in the leather upholstery. The sound is a fucking building collapsing.

Or an Abrams tank fighting for traction on a gravel road. A grizzly with its nuts twisted off. The roar comes again—pained, angry, beseeching in its timbre. Rod knows he ain't in any position to ask for a benevolent favor right now, but goddamn!—he prays whatever that thing is goes far away.

A third roar sounds and (ain't karma the bitch she's always said to be) it's instead gotten closer. Or louder. Or both … Rod's nerves light up. He was already on edge, but this heightened sense is like the icy tingle of silence before the chute gates open up, before the shot and shout of the announcer over the P.A., the moment that somehow spans an eternity, when the bronc is already rising up, and he cinches tighter the flank strap circling the beast, all before they shoot out into the ring; that's the sense Rod is feeling, but a hundredfold, and if it wasn't for cheating-filthy-whore-Brenda outside, he'd drive off right now, but instead he's got a grave to dig, and upon further reflection, he's a *man*, and hell-no he ain't gonna be scared off by some animal.

He gets out of the truck, steps over the tarp, and walks toward the bellowing sound, a Maglite in one hand, the Sig Sauer in the other. He tops a knoll of wheatgrass, and as a frayed shroud of silvery cloud floats away, he sees—there under the moonlight—a giant creature emerging from the air. Rod flicks off the Maglite just in time, while sucking in a breath so sharp the back of his throat prickles. He's heard the legend—every kid growing up in Denver has—and even known some folks claiming sightings, though most of them, Rod wouldn't give a piss for their claims.

But it's here now, in his sight—bigger than he'd imagined, more hideous too, though unarguably imposing, majestic, in the way a hunter may espy a monster-fanged 20-point buck across the range.

The Were-Bull.

His gasp is some word combination of "Shit," "Christ," and "Holy-fuck-me."

He takes two steps back, more a reflex than any reaction to get hidden, his mind reeling with a whole slideshow of outcomes based on what he should do next.

His first thought is to kill it and hang its head in his trophy room. But the Sig Sauer feels small suddenly … how many shots would it take to down that beast? A solemn certainty tells him way, way more than he's got, if it's even possible to do at all.

But going beyond that—using that big brain of his—he thinks, shit, this, *this* is the were-bull … Rod's been breaking broncos since his teens, riding bulls before he could drive. Always someone else's stock though, and that dream of owning his own show, his own ranch, had day by day slipped through his fingers, like cupping your hands in feed, and watching each grain slip away over your palm. That image is the golden-cascade of bad choices, missed opportunities … 'til now. He could catch the were-bull, showcase it, ride it in front of a hundred-thousand roaring, cheering fans.

The long game just got longer.

He fumbles out his cell phone, *prays* for reception here in the boonies. One service bar hovers, flickers. Rod dials his little brother. The call goes through. "Bobby," he says, panting and whispering at the same time, "get your ass out here."

"Where you at?"

"Pawnee. I'll text you my coordinates."

"At this hour? What'cha doin' there?"

Rod falters, stutters. "All right, first, there was a problem, and I was going to take care of it myself, but you're gonna see something when you get here, so don't get mad or nothin', but that *thing* I said might happen someday with Brenda, well …"

"God, no," Bobby says, his voice so small.

"I warned her!"

"You was drunk, you said that!"

"I was drunk again, it happened."

"Rod, you—"

"Right now, that don't matter! Why I'm calling you is our lives just hit stratosphere-rich, if I can count on you. 'Cause I honest-to-God just found us *the were-bull*!"

Bobby's silent. Rod thinks the reception dropped, then a crackle sounds, and the remnants of a sputtered reply, "I can't believe—"

"God's truth," Rod interrupts. "It's real. Bring the tranq guns, rope, prods, everything you got. And the cattle hauler. You get down here, we're gettin' this sum-bitch."

"All right, I'm puttin' on my boots." The call drops. Rod texts his GPS location while watching the were-bull paw at the ground, swish its tail, rear back on hindlegs and arch a massive back.

Rod scrolls his phone to camera setting, takes a picture. That big brain of his must've forgot there'd be a photo flash like lightning. For a hair's-second, the world goes bright, but the were-bull is still black. Rod's heart drops about twenty feet. The were-bull's head snaps to him, there's a snuffling sound, a tensing of its enormous body.

Rod knows what that tensing means. He turns and runs.

***

The quarter left of "human" Dove McGuinn is torn further, weakened in the way that something already shattered will be additionally compromised: the after-effects leave compound fractures, rent edges, irrecoverable lack of emotional underpinning. The rodeo clown-part of him sees a man in fear, running for his life, and that part of Dove seeks to protect the man, to throw up a floppy hat and goofy grin, or find a steel barrel to roll around in, call off the bull with flashing lights and taunts … but such a flimsy revenant of thought, so weakened and confused already by vivisection of the soul, and in conflict with the mythical beast he's become, has little hope of allaying the monster bull's natural instincts.

It was the man's fault, his sudden motion, the flapping of his clothes and jerky movements—like any cat drawn to a fleeing mouse—is what induces the bull's impulse to charge, engorges the syntax of the brain to hunt him down. Dove has chased other men before as the were-bull, enjoyed it even in a toying way, but this is different somehow; this fleeing man doesn't feel like a target of capering fun, but rather a mark—a *bull's eye*—for blind rage.

The were-bull gallops, gains on the man rapidly—in only moments he will strike, he will lower his head and slam the man head-on, with force not unlike an artillery cannon's discharge at point-blank range.

The man spins, there's terror in his wide eyes. Dove sees the man is holding a gun, recognizes what that means, and tries to stop the drive of the bull, tries to turn away, but the were-bull-part of him is determined and continues on, and the man fires the gun, again and again.

Dove feels the bullets strike—every one a hit. Pain detonates across his breast, his shoulder, his dewlap. A shot furrows his nose and pierces his neck. A shot shatters a carpal joint. A shot drills through his skull. A bull is color blind; it's a misnomer they're drawn to the color red, but nonetheless, it is Dove's memory of pain that colors the world shrieking, explosive red. His legs teeter, collapse, he plows face-first into the ground, the acceleration of his charge propelling him several yards more, to end in a broken mass at the man's feet, and the man's clicking, now-empty gun.

The were-bull's vision flickers in and out, matching the convulsing waves of agony.

The torn muscles, shattered bones, frayed nerves … as Dove lies there under a clouding black, he feels them begin to repair themselves.

"Holy fucking shit," Rod gasps. *"Holy fucking shit!"* he repeats with emphasis.

He's still twenty yards away from his truck; there's no way he would have made it there in time. Even if he did, that creature would have demolished the vehicle. Rod's life most definitely had flashed before his eyes, and it was not a pleasant view.

Plan A, at the least: Rod can hang this bastard's head in his trophy room. And he was wrong, he supposed—the Sig Sauer *had* worked just fine. Never doubt the power of German arms manufacturing.

He takes another long searching look at the downed were-bull, then makes his way to the truck. To the chainsaw there. That's what he's going to use next.

On *two* corpses, now.

Moonlight plays funny tricks on a landscape at night, especially with a wind; it moves shadows around, distorts objects, causes things to appear and disappear. Rod knows this, *thinks* this, when he sees the tarp that was covering Brenda is gone, blown away or vanished—that part doesn't matter so much. What's of more concern is that Brenda's gone, too.

"No," Rod whispers. "Shit no, no, no." This night is getting well and truly screwed, and visions of his long game are shortening drastically.

He left the Maglite behind in his mad flight, dropped his cell phone too, he realizes. He just cannot believe it … Thank God, he'd at least called his little brother. Bobby can help him find these things, clear away any other evidence, but first, of most pressing importance, where the hell did Brenda go? The bitch whore was dead … he'd shot her twice. He's never killed anyone before though, didn't even think to check for a pulse, just assumed she was gone. *I'm a fuckin' mess*, he realizes. And the Sig Sauer—what the fuck? Who survives two headshots from that?

Then Rod hears a moaning, a shuffling. A scrabbling in the dirt. A sob, a whisper, some plea.

Oh, she's right over there, doing a sort-of worm crawl through the prairie grass, pulling herself along on torn elbows, dragging unmoving legs. All is not lost.

He'd loved Brenda once. Thought she was "the one." She'd been smart, sassy—but not too much. She gave what he asked for, anything. But then she'd two-timed him. All that fire and love he'd shared, that part of himself he'd given her, fervor and devotion, and secrets and dreams he'd never told anyone else. But it wasn't good enough for her, he—Rod Reams—wasn't good enough for the whore. He'd thought before she was seeing someone else, but she'd been sneaky, he could never prove it, 'til tonight, he'd come home early from the bars, and seen someone leaving, someone getting their ass out fast through the bedroom window … but not Brenda, no, she'd had nowhere else to go …

"You got nowhere else to go," Rod tells her as he hefts up one of the shovels and brings it down clanging on the back of her neck. Her worm-crawl stops. Rod hits her again and again, just to be sure. And then he hits her a few more times.

***

Dove wakes. The were-bull wakes. He is whole again, in physical terms, regrown, repaired in body. The bullets pushed out by healed flesh have plunked into the soft dirt he lays upon.

When he opens his eyes, the first thing he sees is murder.

The man he'd chased, who'd shot him, brings a shovel down onto a prone young woman. Her neck snaps at a horrifying angle. Her head splits apart with a sickening crunch. The rage the were-bull had earlier felt seeps entirely into Dove.

100

He begins to rise, then stops, frozen by the sight of something incomprehensible … something he himself experienced, but never witnessed.

The woman's soul.

It rises up, visible to Dove, but not to the man who is still slamming down the shovel on her flesh, screaming obscenities, shrieking with rage and regret and fear.

The woman's soul, it begins as an ethereal thing, an unwinding exhalation growing in the night, something so insubstantial, yet a vast vale of shining eternity that glows and spreads, expanding, evolving, *dividing*.

Dove understands so much now, memories locked away find escape to uplift him. The woman's soul is a cloud, morphing by divergent pressures, billowing upward, and outward, and within itself, a thousand faces, a million faces, every face of every moment of her life, in love, in dread, in wonder, in lament. The face of a child looking into dewdrops at the curve of a rainbow beyond. The face of a woman staring into the eyes of another, seeing the refection of herself, dimmed, distorted, honest … faces yet to come. Faces never to be.

It is too much. Nothing as such can be contained in only one afterlife. The spreading realm of her existence begins to divide, first into two great clouds, then into three. Dove knows nothing of her life, who she'd been, what she'd done, only that she is ascending onto three separate paths, to three separate planes.

Dove had become the separate selves of jester, defender, and testament. And then the were-bull. What she would become would be yet one more inexorable mystery of the universe to him.

Yet there, there, even as Dove watches, as the madman continues beating her mangled corpse, there, feeling unable to behold more, the woman, her soul, spirit, the dividing cloud, it does not stop at three parts …

A fourth tears away, like parting veils of mist. A quartered part of her sinks back down to the ground, mere feet from her killer.

The cloud begins to form, to solidify into a shape, large, risen on four legs. Skeletal bones appear of their own accord, encasing organs, supporting muscles. There is a bovine head, a swishing tail …

The man has stopped with the beating, he's standing there, frozen in some terror, some recognition …

The forming creature lets out an anguished *mooo*, something of pain and confusion, that Dove understands well, that Dove has been searching for, pleading for, for all of his abhorrent existence.

The man raises his shovel once again, and advances on the were-cow. He does not realize the were-bull has revived … until the were-bull charges with a shriek that is as human as it is beastly.

***

Headlights stab through the darkness.

Bobby Reams drives his Ram Diesel Laramie, 370 HP, and a tow package that could pull half of Colorado; the trailer he's hauling is a 53-foot steel box, reinforced with iron girders at every seam. He's gonna need it if what his brother said was true.

Bobby's got a .450 Marlin hunting rifle, and a .458 Lott, manufactured for the sole purpose of bringing down the largest game ever known on the face of the planet. The borecartridge of each could punch a fist-sized hole through a hemi engine at a quarter-mile away. Hell, he even brought his FN M4A1 automatic machine gun, and 2,000 rounds of ammunition. Can't be too careful these days.

What Bobby's thinking though, what he's really wondering about, is who's he going to use it on? The were-bull, if his brother isn't full of shit, and this isn't a set-up, and if tranq guns and traps don't work, is the obvious choice.

Or is he gonna use them on his brother? His miserable, shithead brother, who was never good enough to lick the mud off Brenda Turner's boots?

Rod never treated her right, never deserved someone like her … and *how* had Brenda fallen for him in the first place? Rod was handsome, she'd said, and charming. Rod could be funny, vibrant in a stuffy room, and he was confident; loud and brash to a fault, but *compelling* … that was all true about his brother, but still … after a couple months, she'd seen the real side of Rod, the pettiness, the ugly, condescending speeches. The drinking, the explosive outbursts; the controlling demands, the insults. He'd never harmed her before though, and Brenda kept believing he'd turn it around, act better to her. He didn't.

Bobby knew, too, this was his own fault. No one should mess around with a brother's girlfriend, but it had just happened, one night, him and her ran into each other, and Brenda with that smile, like an ode to moonlight, melancholy and sublime. The upturn of her eyes when she laughed so easily, so honestly. Her fingertips, just a brush was all it took—softly across the back of his hand. The smooth, sun-touched skin … and then the touches intensified …

And Bobby wasn't any great catch either—he'd be the first to admit it. Brenda didn't need either of the Reams brothers, rodeo men-hustlers that they were. She'd been raised on a farm among cows, and had built a greater career from it, a name in the cattle industry, devoted to livestock breeding programs at the university, even quoted in magazines for her dairy work, her involvement and passion for domestic ungulates.

Bobby's headlights pick out Rod's truck and the tire tracks of crushed grass leading from it. Then he sees the blood. Everywhere. Literally. Blood on the truck's fender, blood on the wheel wells, blood splattered and soaking over a shovel and across the ground, where he sees some misshapen lumps; one of them looks like an upturned hand, broken fingers splayed toward the sky, and the other lump, imagination be damned if that's not a head. A man's crushed head.

Bobby drives in a little closer, and sees there's two bodies. One he recognizes by the floral dress she'd been wearing ... the other body, there ain't much left—and what remains is scattered over a couple dozen feet—but he knows it's his brother out there, mutilated and ravaged. Bobby feels sick, fearful too, wondering what could have done that. He turns the steering wheel a bit, flicks the beams from low to high, and sees ... *it ... them ...*

Massive and monstrous. Nightmarish, the were-bull most certainly. But there, too, is a second creature, and just as large, but without the horns. A cow. The two beasts are staring into each other's eyes, muzzles nuzzling in communion, something more than harmony passing between them. The two creatures, they look up, slowly, straight into the beams of Bobby's truck. Maybe it's a trick of the light, or a wistful fancy, but for a moment he swears that cow has a smile like moonlight.

The were-bull, it exhales a breath of steam, paws at the ground in challenge to the newcomer.

But maybe it's not Bobby he's pawing at, since Bobby glances movement at the edge of the beams, a third creature that's materialized, something also monstrous and deformed, writhing on the cold, dry ground. Something with eyes on wavering tentacle stalks, and a skirt of slimy fringe; something culled straight from his vegetable garden, but the size of a log; something that strikes him with impossible familial association, and maybe Bobby can still smell a hint of Marlboro coming off it... He has no other name but to call that other thing out there a *were-slug*.

Bobby Reams doesn't know what went down here, but he no longer wants anything to do with it. He silently wishes Brenda all the happiness she deserved in life, and he speeds away as fast as he can.

Just Deserts

by Beverley Lee

The forest was silent as it began.

The sound of the creatures came closer, heavy feet trampling tender shoots. She heard the cries of small things dying.

Run, her father had said as her brothers and sisters scattered like raindrops, scrabbling for safety.

Afternoon sunlight speared through the dense green canopy of the forest and the earth steamed its fury like the breath of a dragon.

She ran through the fallen leaves, legs burning with exertion as she made for the small moss-coated pagoda standing under the shelter of a stand of red-barked cypresses.

This was her home and the place she felt safe, sleeping with her siblings curled up tight against her.

But the creatures still came. The shadow of one passed over her as she cowered beside a small rock.

"There. Take that one. And that one." The creature spoke in a tongue she did not understand back then. His words were just harsh, guttural sounds.

Sapling trees were pulled from the rich loam of the earth. She heard their roots screaming in pain as they were placed into sacking and loaded onto the backs of mules.

She wanted to ask the mule why but his eyes held no light.

Afraid to move she waited. From the corner of her eye, she saw the pagoda topple. Its roof broke in two as it hit the ground and the tremor raced along to her feet.

Terrified beyond reason she ran for the palm tree set in a patch of shadow. Maybe she could hide amongst the fan of bright green fronds.

And there she stayed, fear erupting along every limb. She made herself still as her father had said she must if a predator came.

And these were the ultimate predators. They paid no heed to what they destroyed, their only thought to uproot and cleave and kill.

As the sun began to sink below the treetops the creature who was in charge mopped his face with a piece of cloth. His hand clasped the back of his neck as he turned around. His eyes narrowed as he surveyed the forest.

His gaze came to rest on the small palm tree.

"Take that one too."

A bird screeched high in the trees and she wished for feathers and wings. Wished for everything to be as it was. But she knew that she was lost.

***

She thought often of the day her life was torn apart. Many would say she should let it go, why taint her present with the misdeeds of the past. She could do nothing to change them.

But in the dead of night, she still remembered the fear of being torn from her family. Remembered the scent of the strange creatures rampaging through the undergrowth, destroying the peace and tranquility of the forest.

The irony of what her mother had named her was not lost on Hikari. It meant light or sunlight, but Hikari was always happiest in the dark.

She hid in the shelter of the palm tree for a very long time. The floor beneath her moved violently. Sometimes she heard the heavy feet of the men as they came down to check their cargo but they never disturbed the sacking through which she peered in terror.

They reached their destination and the stolen plants from another land were loaded onto another form of transport that bumped and creaked.

The sacking fell away a little. Now she could see buildings much larger than the small pagoda. Everywhere were strange scents and people. So many people.

The shock of it all made her feel queasy. Her legs throbbed in pain, the fluids in her round stomach burning. She closed her eyes, felt her skin stretch and twist.

Hikari thought she was dying. The pain strung along every nerve ending. Each time she opened her eyes something seemed wrong. What she *was* seemed wrong.

At last, the torture subsided and she curled into a small ball as exhaustion cloaked her body.

She slept.

When her eyes flickered open again it was to meet those of a woman. Her large hat threw a shadow over Hikari and for a moment Hikari imagined she was back in the dappled shade of the forest.

"You poor mite," the woman cooed. She reached out a hand and Hikari shrank away. Humans were dangerous. It was a lesson her father had drummed into her daily.

"Bring a blanket," the woman said to someone Hikari couldn't see. Of course, back then she did not understand the sounds of this strange language but to tell her tale she has done her best to insert the right words.

Hikari looked down upon her limbs. A gasp of shock left her lips. They were clothed in skin like the woman's. She had odd stalks at the end of her arms that she could move.

That was her first Change, brought on by the trauma she had gone through, far too early for her species.

But what she had been, lived within her bones. She never forgot it. One day she would let it loose and avenge all she had lost.

***

And that was how she came to live under the guidance of Miss Priscilla Leonard. They thought she was a stowaway, had run from a place that gave her no favors.

Hikari grew to be beautiful. Her long black hair shone like silk. Her skin was porcelain fair. She let Priscilla fuss over her appearance, dress her in silks and satins.

Men noticed her as she strolled in the park and inside, she smiled.

Soon. Soon she would be ready.

"May we go to the grand opening of the Palm House?" Hikari asked over breakfast. Slanted sunlight striped the floor. She could feel the heat from it on the back of her neck.

Like the heat of the forest. Her vision dimmed for a second as her skin itched.

Priscilla looked at her from over the top of wire-framed spectacles.

"Are you sure the heat won't be too much? I've heard dreadful stories of how young women could faint right away beneath the glass."

Hikari nibbled on the edge of a piece of toast to stop her smile from spreading too widely.

"Will Mr. Dawson be there?" Hikari asked. "I should like to ask him about the great lands he travelled to bring such beautiful specimens home."

"Indeed, he will. The Palm House is his pride and joy. But don't go bothering him with your girlish questions. Young ladies must know their place."

Hikari bobbed her head. She brought a linen napkin to her lips so Priscilla would not see the way her teeth were bared.

The evening of the grand opening arrived. Hikari dressed in red silk, and after a tussle with Priscilla, who deemed that black gloves were for funerals, she finally got her way. Priscilla coiled Hikari's hair onto the top of her head and secured the weight of it with two silver clasps in the shape of palm fronds.

"You are exquisite, my dear," Priscilla said, securing the last pin. "As beautiful as any bloom."

But Priscilla could only see the exterior shell. Inside, Hikari's blood began to burn. This was the night she would set eyes on the man who had stolen away her family and her birthright.

Of course, he would not recognize her, not in this form or her other. But Hikari had a plan.

The carriage dropped them at Kew, and as she alighted to a warm and balmy evening, the smile of a crescent moon hung in the dusk-heavy sky.

She walked with Priscilla, nodding to various acquaintances as they passed.

As they neared the Palm House, Hikari swept her fan over her face, both to keep away a scattering of midges and to hide the fever in her eyes.

A gasp of amazement fell from Priscilla's lips.

The great glass dome of the Palm House rose into the evening sky, the pathway to it lined with lanterns.

They made their way towards it. The pulse in Hikari's throat quickened. From within came the scent of warm earth and green. A special kind of green. For one long moment she was back in the forest with her brothers and sisters, running through the undergrowth and climbing trees.

"Come, come, my dears!" A rotund man with a handlebar moustache beckoned them in. "See the wonders of distant lands right here on your doorstep."

Priscilla looked down her nose at him and muttered something with the word *circus* in it.

Blessed heat enveloped Hikari as she stepped through the doors.

Trees towered above them. Trees with names that did not belong in this land, ones with strange-shaped leaves made for catching water, shrubs with exotic flowers. Hikari wanted to weep for them, but at least they had each other.

They took the pathway to the left along the tiled floor. A metal latticework edged the rows and Hikari could sense water flowing beneath it.

Priscilla glanced her way and patted her arm.

And then a voice she knew boomed out from above. At the top of a circular metal staircase the man who had destroyed her life was holding court, surrounded by a group of men. Congratulations sang on the air and the man accepted them all greedily. His face was pink and bloated with exertion, his brow shiny with sweat.

"May I have a glass of water?" Hikari asked softly, holding the back of her hand to her brow. Priscilla rushed off to find one, no doubt horrified that her ward might faint.

Hikari wandered to the bottom of the staircase.

And there it was, the palm tree that had saved her life. Larger now, of course, but she still recognized the markings on the bark, could still see the space she had cowered into. She ran her fingers through the fronds, imagined the forest sun caressing them.

She placed a foot on the bottom rung of the metal staircase. A man hurried down, waving his arms around as though he was juggling pins.

"Now, my dear, this is much too dangerous for those of the fairer sex to navigate."

She lowered her lashes demurely but the thing that ran through her veins wanted to tear him apart.

"Could you do something for me, sir?" she asked.

"Of course, my sweet. What is it?"

She could smell the sweat on his body despite his fine clothes.

"Could you give this to Mr. Dawson? It's for his eyes only." Hikari slipped a note into the man's podgy fingers.

"Ah, a fan of the great man, I see. Totally understandable." He was all pomp and fluster and Hikari had to grind her teeth together to stop the words she wanted to say erupting.

She watched as he clambered back up the steps, his grunts of exertion falling into the humid air.

Now she retreated from the staircase, wandering to a spot by a glossy-leaved Chinese dogwood. She watched as the man handed the note over and saw Mr. Dawson open it, his eyes quickly scanning the words.

He folded it again quickly and stuffed it into his pocket but his gaze found hers as he did so. A sly smile broke upon his face. She continued the act by brushing a stray lock of hair behind her ear. Coquettishness did not come easily but this was a means to an end.

She had laid her bait. Now it was up to him.

Priscilla appeared holding a glass of water and Hikari took it eagerly. Her throat was sandpaper dry. All her muscles throbbed in time with her heartbeat. They were preparing themselves, layers of sinew undulating within her flesh.

"It's terribly warm in here," she said, "may I go outside? Arabella is there with her guardian and it would be so lovely to stroll around the grounds."

Hikari knew that Priscilla would have her eye on the sumptuous spread of cake and tea the organizers had laid on.

"I should really check, to make sure it's not inconvenient…"

Priscilla glanced down at Hikari's pleading eyes.

"Oh, be off with you before I change my mind. And stay with Arabella at all times."

Hikari was out of the door in a very unladylike rush before Priscilla's words had faded.

Some part of her felt incredibly guilty about the lie. But this could be her only chance and she intended to take it whatever the consequences.

Quickly, she hurried along the path, watching for people and taking a different route if they came too close. She knew where she was headed, had studied the plan of this jewel of the Victorian age until she felt as though she knew it by heart.

A breeze took up, scattering dried leaves across her path.

Sweat dotted her brow as she fought against the pull of instinct. *Not now. Not just yet.*

She ran down a line of narrow stone steps, their edges green with moss. A wooden door barred her way.

If it was locked, what would she do?

But fate was on her side, as one pull of the latch and the door opened inwards, the smell of cold stone assaulting her senses. Further and further she trod, until the dim light from the door was swallowed by the darkness.

Her heartbeat raced in her ears, the enormity of what she was about to do crushing the air from her lungs.

And then she remembered what had happened on that terrible day. How the intruders had burst into their place of sanctuary, had murdered her sisters and brothers without mercy as they raced to escape.

Her lips tightened into a thin line. She spread her fingers, felt the throb in the tips as she stopped fighting against the pull of something that wanted to be.

***

Time passed and Hikari sat in the dark. She had removed her gown and undergarments, letting them puddle around her waist as she sat on the floor. Had let her hair fall down her back. Ebony against ivory. Dark against the light.

The senses now in her body felt different. She was aware of every tremor on the ground and from the walls. She could feel them through her legs. Her sense of smell was acute.

And now she could hear someone tramping down the stone steps. Ah, yes, it was him.

She clicked her jaw, moved it from side to side. Her skin tightened as something coiled beneath it.

"My dear, Hikari. Where are you?" His voice escaped into the gloom. The sound of a struck match.

She heard the exhalation of his breath as his eyes found her form, hidden behind a curtain of old spider web.

"Come closer, Nathan," she whispered, unapologetically familiar. 'I've waited so long for this moment.'

His clumsy footfall echoed behind her. His muttered curse as the match burned down to his fingers. He struck another.

The harsh rip of cobweb as he forced his way towards her.

He didn't see the smile on her face vanish, to be replaced by something else. He didn't see the busy movement of her hands across her abdomen.

"I understand the need to be secret, my dear, but this place isn't suitable."

She wanted to say that it was perfect.

Here in the dark, close to all of the treasures he had stolen.

"Damn it." The sound of a match book hitting the stone floor.

She could hear him coming closer, irritated curses falling from his lips as he pushed deeper and deeper into the strands of cobweb.

Then his voice changed. It adopted a slightly more panicked air.

She quickened her movements, letting the sticky silk thread spin out.

Electricity pulsed through her new form as she stretched and tested each limb. To fully give in to the feeling, that was the question. She rather liked the half-creature she had become.

He was so close now she could hear his exerted breathing.

"This is most unbecoming, but I appear to be stuck. Could you lend me your hand, my sweet?"

Oh, she would lend him more than a hand.

Hikari raised herself up and moved towards him. She could smell the fear in his sweat and she was both repulsed and attracted.

Hunger gnawed in her distended plump abdomen.

His movements became erratic, terror-driven, though he had not seen her yet.

Even the hunter knows when he is hunted.

He jumped as she reached out towards him. She felt the thick strands of web he was encased in, his struggles only succeeding in tangling him further.

She tore the coils from one of his arms so he had access to his pockets.

"Thank you." His breathless gratitude as he fumbled for another match book.

She drew back, letting the sway of the web play against her senses.

A few moments as he passed the book to his tied hand, fingers clumsy and panic-stricken.

A small flame flickered.

Enough for him to see the pretty human head upon the plump round body of a furred tarantula.

She lifted one of her eight limbs, admired the subtle orange markings, stroked his face with its tip.

His eyes widened, the horror within them a living thing. His lips muttered a prayer.

She busied herself with more web.

As he drew breath to scream, she quickly spun thick strands across his mouth, making him swallow his own terror.

Trussed up like a fly he could do nothing but tremble.

Hikari scuttled across the stone floor towards the closed door, spun a curtain of sticky web across it. Enough to keep out those who may search for a little while.

She returned to him, this pitiable quaking wreck, contemplated simply leaving him here.

But then she would never know the joy of devouring something alive.

Her fangs glistened with venom. She wondered which part of him to inject. Which part of him to liquefy before sucking him into her stomach?

She moved through the old cobweb and into the fresh strands she had spun.

His terrified eyes beseeched her but she paid him no heed.

For one long moment she let her thoughts drift back to her family. How he had destroyed their habitat without a second thought. How she had heard the soft squelch as boots descended on tiny spiderlings.

She had not known then what she was, too young for her mother and father to impart the secret, but she remembered them going into the forest each full moon and returning later with their bellies full.

Hikari gave in to the urgent instinct in her blood. She felt her jaw dislocating, her bones shifting, face melting into its predatory form.

She heard his heartbeat quicken, felt the throb of it beneath his rib cage.

So ripe and tender.

Yes, she would begin there, because the heart of the matter is always what counts.

Garden Landscape

by Cynthia Pelayo

Pluck my wings, haven't you ever done this before?
Painted lady legs pressed tight against the surface
I shed my chrysalides a long time ago, processing
Developed across distances, spread across fringes
Look past my wingspan and I'll tell you about years
Frequenting reaches, nestled between thistles, you
There, it's always been you, cultivated in good years
Dormant in famines, I like to smell fear on your breath
I revel in the trembling of your skin as it sloughs off
Heaps of red soaked flesh, I'll sneak within the fibers
Patrol your arteries and weave a silk tent in the place
Once beating, a shelter, my place, stitched together
We'll huddle in our depressed sunlight, of colorful
Wonders, your decay spreads across winter nights
When I emerge again, shedding silk and blood and rot
From our damaged openings, I'll whisper my names
In the remnant of your ears and feel you vibrate with
Your hate of me, loathe me, detest me, wrap round
The butterfly inside

Fight or Flight
by Elle Turpitt

The itch between her shoulder blades was insect-bite intense, right at the spot where she couldn't reach and scratch it herself. One of the biggest drawbacks of being single – no one else to scratch it for her. Erin groaned, pushing herself against the doorframe, desperate to relieve the itch.

The niggling, uncomfortable sensation remained as she pottered about the kitchen, rummaging through her cupboards to check exactly what she had in. The flat was small, just about big enough for one person, with the kitchenette connected to the living room, no separation between cooking and relaxing.

Her phone vibrated, *Mam* flashing across the screen, and Erin stopped rummaging.

The itch intensified.

She grabbed the phone, swiped to answer, and held it to her ear.

"Hey, Mam."

"Thought you would have called me by now."

"Yeah, well, I haven't been up long." Not true. Erin barely slept at the best of times, and now it seemed she couldn't even have a weekend lay in past seven.

"I'm sure. Well?"

"Well, wh—" The itch burned, extending outwards. "Oh, shit, right. Um, happy Mother's Day, Mam."

"Thank you. Well, it's nice to hear it, even if—"

"What did Pete get you?" She lowered herself next
to the breakfast bar, eyeing the sharp edge.

"Well, he's popping around later, isn't he? He said he's going to take me—"

Her mother rambled on about how amazing Pete was, despite the fact he wouldn't even show, judging by past behavior. She'd looked up to her brother once, but tomorrow she'd have her mother on the phone, explaining something had come up and Pete couldn't possibly drop everything just to see her such a lonely old woman…

It wasn't until the end of the call her mother said, "Oh, thank you for that card. And the perfume. I wonder what your brother's card— "

She pressed her back against the table, wincing as her mother rambled and Erin thought of her brother, how she'd taken his promises to look out for her as real.

Her mother finished and they said their goodbyes and Erin groaned, looking around as she reached over her shoulder, desperately trying to reach the itch.

***

In the bathroom, the bath running nice and hot, she stood before the mirror, peeling off her top. She dropped it to the floor, averted her eyes from her stretch marks, and looked at her shoulder.

The doctor—a lovely if old GP on the verge of retirement, a man who sometimes just didn't understand—had admonished her for jogging at night.

"I didn't realize how dark it was until I was the other side of the woods. I had to get back somehow."

The council had been talking for years about putting lights in on the path, but there'd been pushback. It was nature, after all. Erin was torn. It would be nice to see the path, but she shouldn't have been there. Not after all the…accounts. She knew what happened to the women who passed through. Some men, too, but not as many. The police claimed animal attack, but what kind of animal so ruthlessly shredded victims, left them uneaten?

She really hadn't realized how dark it was until she came out on the other side, above the river, a path winding down towards it and the city on the other side.

"You were lucky," the GP said the next day. "Just a bird. Nothing worse."

Just a bird. The same words she'd told herself when she heard a screeching kind of scream, making her way back through the woods. She sped up, and something tore out of the trees. Pain erupted in her shoulder, claws digging in and ripping flesh as she whacked it with her hand.

It flew back, not even allowing her to get a good look at it before it was gone, the leaves rustling above her.

For her, just a bird. And yes, Doctor Anderson was right. It could have been worse. Her face on the news, using some old photo they dug up from social media because she hated photos and didn't have any recent ones. First missing, but who would report her? Who would notice she was gone? Until her mother called, but would she investigate, or assume she was being ignored?

By the time her mother stopped complaining, she'd be left to rot until it was almost too late to identify her, when some dog walker would stumble across her body like the others, a woman ripped apart.

She put her fingers to the bottom of the scars. And they were scars, already. Paler than pale new skin forming over the wounds. Except for the initial pain, she hadn't felt them the first evening. Getting home, exhaustion drove her straight to bed without even changing, and it wasn't until she woke up to a throbbing, bleeding shoulder she realized she needed to see her doctor.

By the time she dressed the cuts had stopped bleeding, and when Doctor Anderson examined them, he said, "So it's been about a week, correct?"

For some reason, she just nodded. "It's throbbing. And itching."

"It's healing. I'll prescribe some cream for you. Twice a day. Once in the morning, once before bed. Make sure the area is clean and dry."

She lowered herself into the bath, wincing for a moment at the heat, taking it slow to let her body grow used to the temperature. The scars looked like someone tried to take a chunk out of her shoulder, dug in with talons in an attempt to rip her apart.

But if that had been what had happened, the injuries would be worse. Not yet healed. She let the water wash over her, let it soothe the itch on her back. As it lapped over the scars, she winced, prepared for shots of pain. Nothing came, and she exhaled slowly, watching as steam drifted through the room.

***

She called in sick to work. The moment she woke on Monday morning, she knew there was no way she was getting in. Pain forced her to remain in bed, and though she knew the spot it came from, it had stretched over night. Engulfed her. A migraine throbbed in her head, and she yanked the duvet over her to block out the sunlight. Nausea made her stomach a frothing and rolling sea. Yet it was her shoulder blades where it was worst, as if her skin was being torn apart. Parts of her she didn't know existed were in pain, her foot cramping, her muscles stretched. She opened her mouth, keeping herself from screaming for the sake of her flat neighbors. She rolled off the bed and hit the floor, throwing herself onto her back and staring at the ceiling, tears clouding her vision.

She closed her eyes, and when the pain got too much, she passed out.

Waking, she managed to muster enough energy to get out of the bedroom and into the living room. It was already growing dark out. A packet of painkillers waited on the kitchen counter, and she popped out two, dry swallowing them before making her way to the sofa. Agony screamed in her as she fell onto it, flicking on the TV and waiting for the news channel to boot up.

Sometimes she didn't know why she bothered, depressing as it was. A habit, really, picked up from her father; wake up, check the news. Keep updated, knowledgeable, know what was going on.

She focused through the haze of pain. The "highlights" showed protestors running from police, one turning and throwing back a Molotov cocktail. Common enough scenes. Julian Turner, pop star, walking out of court after being cleared of all charges. Her heart sank, as she lifted herself from the sofa, watching the smug git grin as he waltzed out, raising a hand to greet the crowd.

Six women. *Six!* She licked her teeth, tasted blood, as the scene dissolved and the news shifted to regional. The familiar face of Angharad Evans appeared on the screen, looking grave.

"More reports…attacks…Fforest Fach walk…"

Cut to police officers at a press conference the day before, saying these were just animal attacks.

Her head swam. Her jaw throbbed. Toothache? She swallowed, tasted metal, the image of Turner filling her mind, as Angharad Evans explained police were now actively seeking suspects over the killings and assaults in the woodland area, after victims came forward, giving new eyewitness testimony that could be key to solving the crimes.

Erin tilted her head, listening. Two women reported getting to the path entrance, a man emerging from the trees. Dusk, the sun setting but not quite there. Both times. All times. Women out for a jog who thought they could get to one end of the path and back before it got dangerous.

A silhouette appeared on the news.

"It was at the start of the path, where the gate is? Coming up to it I see this…this man, coming out of the trees. And he looked, you know, like…like he needed help, so I asked him. I said, 'are you okay, sir?'. He just looked at me, and…his eyes were yellow. The way the light caught; he just shook his head. 'No, no, I'm fine, thank you. You going in there?' And he tilted his head in this…weird way. I usually jog through the woods, and yes, normally daylight, but I just got distracted and the nights are getting longer, I kind of forgot the time. I couldn't…really see him. Just his eyes and shape. He goes, 'Wouldn't go in there, if I were you. Dangerous animals.' 'I'll be quick.'

"I went into the trees. Like I said it was just…I can do that path in ten minutes, right? It's not long. And halfway down, I felt something push me. Sharp. Not quite…it didn't break skin, but it was sharp, like bird's claws. Talons? I fell, but I got up, and ran. Back, towards the entrance."

"When did this happen?"

"Um, oh, when did—it was the night before Jennifer Fields."

"That's over a month ago."

"Yes."

"Why didn't you come forward then?"

She shifted, and over the microphone came the wet sound of a mouth opening and closing.

Erin put her hands to her head, tumbling off the sofa as the pain made every inch of fabric irritate her skin.

"I…didn't think…it sounds weird. Until…" A pause, more wet sounds, gathering of thoughts.

Erin hugged herself, kneeling on the floor and trying to focus.

"Until?" the interviewer prompted.

"It's going around social media, isn't it? That other girl's account."

The interview cut out. Angharad Evans back on screen, face pale. Her gaze locked on the teleprompt, just beyond the camera, and she nodded. "We—the social media…this account was taken from…"

The sound cut out, replaced by a buzzing in Erin's ears, but she could still read, as a Facebook message appeared. She trembled, narrowing her eyes, the pain in her back exploding.

Don't go to Fforest Fach! Multiple women have come forward…describing the same man…attacked by talons…police are saying bird, but we know better, ladies.

She screamed, letting it all out, letting the noise drown everything.

Something pierced through her noise, and she threw herself towards the wide, tall windows at the front of the flat. Something, someone, struggling, words carried on the wind.

Words she should not have been able to hear.

No, no, please, no…

Angharad, on the TV. "Very unusual, police ask anyone with information…"

Erin inhaled, her eyes widening, vision wavering for a moment before it sharpened. And she could see, the street below, the flats opposite, and there, towards the top, two figures, wrestling.

Heat filled her, and Erin moved back, focusing on the flats. Something else drove her, something primal. She screamed again, ran forward. Glass smashed as she went through and plummeted.

As she shrieked, the sound changed, shifted, as pain erupted in her shoulder blades, something breaking free. Her bones broke, reformed. Erin felt every one, felt the way her body curled, shrank, then settled. Spreading her wings, the hawk oriented herself, shot towards the wrestling couple.

Her beak broke through glass first, jagged edges catching feathers, but she made it into the room. Bigger than an average bird of prey, but still much smaller than a human, she dived at the man, talons raking through skin. He twisted, hands flapping at her. The woman screamed and scrambled back, as Erin's feet found his neck, her talons digging in then yanking back.

The man clasped, hand over wound, eyes wide as Erin spread her wings and hovered, then landed, her body creaking and cracking until she was a woman again, naked and panting and full of fury. The man swayed, collapsed, blood across his neck and chest.

Erin turned, caught sight of herself in a mirror above a mantelpiece. Her eyes shone, pupils ringed in amber. "Are you okay?"

The trembling woman stared at the dead man. "You killed my friend. He…offered to walk me home…and you…you…" Her gaze snapped to Erin. "What are you?"

Erin's arm jittered, and she pressed her nails into her palm, trying to still it. She didn't think "I don't know" was the answer the woman wanted. She could taste the blood in her mouth, feel it drying on her feet. What was she?

What if she changed, and attacked? Could she control it? She pushed off the ground, this time letting the sensation flow over her, fill her. It hurt, pain wrecking her body, but it was easier. Erin flew out the window, focused on getting to one place and one place only.

***

She circled Fforest Fach, wishing she could relish her new form, enjoy this freedom. She spotted rabbits, squirrels, even a mouse, darting across the path, running under foliage. She wheeled around, as day let go completely and night extended its full reach. The rumble of a car drew her attention, and she dove down, slipping under the trees and landing on a branch, watching.

The car turned, following the narrow road leading away from the entrance and towards the car park. Erin waited as the car stopped. Far enough to be hidden. A man appeared at the entrance, cap pulled low, shielding his face.

Yet he was familiar, all the same.

Rage made her tremble. He tilted then turned his head, as if he could hear something. She waited, as still as possible, as his eyes, dark pupils ringed in gold, searched the trees.

Women must have listened to the warnings, stayed away.

She hadn't.

Why had he come back? Why here, why now?

She waited, he waited, pacing around the entrance, stopping occasionally to listen, and listen, and listen…

Her head jerked, hearing the crunch on the woodchips from the nearby playground.

A shape emerged further up the path, and the man turned, unmistakable smile across his face. The woman who came into view was young, pretty, and she slowed as she came towards the fenced off path entrance, as if startled to find herself there.

The man stepped forward, towards her, and raised his hand.

"Hi, sorry to bother you—"

Erin screeched. The woman staggered back, head-phone wires trailing from her ears beneath her thin jacket. Erin launched from the trees, and the woman's eyes widened, the man turning.

"No." The word tumbled, breathless, from his lips, and the woman ran, as Erin wheeled around and came at the man. "How?" He whipped off his cap, baring his teeth. "You shouldn't exist."

Erin landed and changed, allowing the shift to draw her back to form. She stood, naked, shoulders back, looking at him.

"You did this to me, didn't you?"

His eyes drifted to her shoulder, to the not-quite-faint pink scars. "I didn't go deep enough. Shit."

"You didn't kill me, you mean."

"Exactly."

It struck her, why he was familiar. It flashed through her mind, the articles about the assaults, the brief press conferences. The insistence from the police that it was just an animal, they were looking into it, women just had to stay away.

She stretched her fingers out, curled them back, let everything roll into her.

"Officer," she said, feeling the urge to fly, attack, rip into him. "Peter Mackenzie, right?"

He grinned, a feral, unhinged look. "Ain't that sweet. You remembered my name."

She kept her hands at her sides, instinct kicking in. Make yourself small, smile, be polite. Give way to the man; he could kill you.

But he was no longer the only animal.

"I can't wait," she said, keeping her voice steady, "to see it engraved in stone."

"You don't have control. Not yet. You can't."

She lifted her head, and found the smile was no longer forced. "I've had to control myself much longer than you, boy. Didn't want to upset the poor, fragile men, after all."

He opened his mouth to say more, but she was in the air, aware of another advantage she had over him.

Women were, after all, built for the kind of extended pain that came with the transformation.

By the time she flew at him, he'd grown only a little smaller, had time for the feathers to appear but not the wings.

He lifted his still human head, eyes widening as she pressed her wings against her body, panic on his face as she flew at him like a bullet, beak out.

He held out a hand. "Stop! I can help you control—"

Her beak connected with skin—chest—and broke through, and Erin was drenched in warm blood, until she burrowed into something thick and pulsating. Her talons found his chest, and she spread her wings, pushing against him until she pulled out and back. She landed not far from him, watching as blood leaked from his chest, mouth. His body convulsed, the feathers disappearing.

He collapsed, and she flew off. There was more work to be done, and a pop star to visit.

Snowbound, Bloodbound

by Stephanie Ellis

It was their turn. Childbirth, family illness, weather—even sales that just couldn't be missed—had prevented their attendance at Aunt Caroline's previous February Gatherings. This year, Maggie had been unable to come up with any excuse. Her sister, Marian, had usually covered for her, but she was still in mourning for her late husband, said her daughter had taken it particularly badly. February was the first anniversary of his death and so it was down to Maggie to represent the family. She looked back at Brian who remained warm and snug in the car along with their sixteen-year-old daughter, still glued to her phone, unaware they'd arrived. Brian gave her an encouraging smile and she turned, took a deep breath, and knocked on the door.

She felt small, standing there beneath the gaze of her aunt's mansion. A mishmash of styles, the earliest part dated to the seventeenth century, though it was known the family had lived on the same site even earlier than that. In all this time, it had never gone out of the family's ownership.

Apart from a gentle glow peeking through the curtains of one of the ground-floor windows, the rest of the house was in darkness. It felt as if no one was in. Well, if no one answered, they couldn't blame her if she left, booked a room at the Premier Inn ten miles back, returned home—Maggie had almost completed her mental escape when the door opened and all thoughts of reprieve vanished.

"Maggie! Come in, come in, my dear. I've been worrying myself silly with the snow coming down as it is now."

Maggie found herself pulled into the woman's ample body. It was like being smothered by a pillow. Her mother had been the same and she knew her own size was following the family trend. Eventually, she was released and pulled further into the house, allowed only the briefest of moments to beckon her husband in. For now, Maggie appeared to be Caroline's sole focus.

"It is so lovely to have you here at this time, after all these years."

Maggie smiled at her aunt. The woman made it sound as though she never visited. She did. Just not at this time. A habit picked up from her mother who long ago had expressed her aversion to the Gathering.

"Any other time," her mum had said, "is fine." She had never explained why, allowed Maggie one visit during the dreaded month of February when she was small and then steadfastly refused all subsequent invitations. She would do her familial duty, she said—at other times of the year.

Maggie, herself, could remember little of that early visit, only that something had upset her—in the dark. The dark. She looked around her and shivered. Her aunt was guiding her to the lit drawing room, whilst everything else was buried in shadow.

"Hurry up and close that door!" Caroline looked back at the stragglers. "Don't want to let all the heat out. Charlie! Wonderful to see you!"

Heat? The place felt like a freezer.

"Bills," said Caroline. "This place is a real drain on the purse. Costs a fortune in upkeep."

"Have you thought about selling?" asked Maggie, sighing with relief at the sight of a fire blazing in the hearth. Her body relaxed and she realized how tense she had been. The drive, in almost blizzard conditions, had not done her nerves any good. Caroline ignored her question.

"Take off your coats. Brian, you can hang them up in the hall. Come here, Charlie. Let me take a look at you."

Charlie rolled her eyes at Maggie but obediently suffered her aunt's enveloping hug.

Unlike Caroline's all-embracing welcome of Maggie and her daughter, the woman barely gave her husband a second glance. Unusual as it was normally the other way round on those visits later on in the year. The number of times Caroline insisted Brian needed fattening up had become a running joke between the three of them.

"Sit down, sit down. I've just the thing for you after a journey like that."

Caroline moved to the sideboard where she poured four tumblers of brandy and brought them over. The three sat side-by-side on the sofa opposite Caroline's wing-backed chair. Like children in front of the headmistress. Charlie grinned as she took her glass. Maggie was about to stop her when Caroline gave her a look.

"She's old enough," she said. "No harm in this one. Call it a rite of passage."

Maggie held her tongue. Everybody did what they were told in Caroline's house.

She sipped her own drink, felt herself relax even further. "Where's everyone else?"

The house still felt empty.

"You're the first to arrive, my dear," said Caroline, looking towards the window. A gap in the curtains revealed the ongoing blizzard. "I've had two calls to cancel already. Your cousins Jenny and Helen and their families. The roads are impassable. Even the river's frozen. I've not heard from Elise or Victoria."

"I hope they're alright," said Maggie. "We barely got through. I'd hate to be stuck out in that."

"Oh, I think they'll manage. Those two have never missed yet." Caroline gave her a pointed look and then her face broke into a smile. "But you're here now, and that's all that matters."

Maggie silently hoped this would be currency enough for them to miss the February Gathering for the next, oh, thirty years. By that time, Caroline would surely have passed on. She stopped herself. Wishing someone dead was not who she was. A week, that was all they were required to spend here. Yet the snow was continuing its onslaught and the forecast wasn't good. Something told her they would be staying longer than planned.

She looked at the rug in front of the fire. It always unnerved her, having the head still attached, the eyes watching, ears pricked up. Caroline caught her stare and reached down to stroke the pelt. It could almost be the family pet, except this was no animal anyone could tame and merely the remains of what once had been a beautiful creature.

"Magnificent specimen, isn't she," said Caroline.

"She would've been more magnificent left whole—and alive," said Maggie.

"Oh, she is," said Caroline. "She is."

"You mean was," said Charlie.

"No," said Caroline. "I know what I meant. Now, you've had a long drive and you must be worn out. I suggest you turn in. You're in your usual rooms." She was already at the door, holding it open for them. They had no choice but to obey this abrupt dismissal.

Despite her exhaustion, Maggie slept badly. Her old childhood nightmares resurfaced in waves. She had kept them at bay for so long, why would they return now? Brian held her, reassured her nothing would get her. But that hadn't been the scary part of her dream. What terrified her had been what *she'd* done in her sleep world. She could almost taste the blood in her mouth.

At breakfast, she felt the full force of Caroline's appraisal. An almost hypnotic gaze against which she could not keep her eyes open.

"Go back to bed," said Caroline.

"You could do with a few extra hours," said Brian. "We'll be fine. It's stopped snowing and a walk'll do me and Charlie good."

She didn't argue, almost sleepwalked her way back to her room. Barely heard her husband and daughter laughing beneath her window as they pelted each other with snowballs. Only faintly registered the weight of an extra cover being laid over her by her aunt. Warm and soft, it sent her spinning into the darkness, burying the sound of her husband's screams, allowing her to sleep on.

When she woke it was well past noon. She sat up and stretched, felt more relaxed, more—sated—than she had done in a long time. Sated? A strange choice of word which she quickly dismissed. Then she noticed her clothes. They were no longer the jeans and jumper she had thrown on first thing but her pajamas. And there was no extra blanket.

Confused, she grabbed her dressing gown and made her way downstairs.

"Ah, good," said Caroline, positively beaming at her. "You look much better. Amazing what a few hours' sleep will do. I've just made a pot of tea—join me."

"My clothes," said Maggie, taking the same seat opposite as the night before.

"Oh, yes. Caught you sleepwalking. You'd made it outside. Obviously, I had to get you changed."

"Sleepwalking? But I—"

"Now, now dear. Don't fret yourself. It's not the first time."

No, it wasn't. But that last time had been when she had made her first and only February visit. She didn't want to think about it.

"Where's Brian and Charlie?"

"Oh, they went out again," said Caroline. "Fathers and daughters, eh?"

Maggie laughed. Then her eye fell on the bear rug. The fur looked more luxuriant, fuller, the eyes brighter.

As if by habit, Caroline reached down and stroked the fur and for a moment, it was almost as if Maggie herself was being petted. She got up and went to look out at the wintry landscape. The season always had its last cruel blast at this time. She could see no sign of her family, everything blanketed with snow and silence. A nagging unease blossomed in her mind.

"Don't worry," said Caroline. "They're off having fun. Make the most of the peace and quiet."

Maggie returned to her chair, picked up a battered old book from a nearby coffee table and began to flick through.

"Good choice," said Caroline. "Time you learned something of our family history."

She had a vague idea of her heritage, the Bersseck name. Her mother had told her of their Norman ancestors and, via them, their Viking forebears. She had laughed it off. Now she found herself tracing back century after century of detailed trees, potted histories, land records and wills.

"Whoever lives here, adds their generation's details," said Caroline.

Maggie glanced at the other volumes. One had her aunt's name on the front and her date of birth. Each volume had a name—a woman's name—and the image of a bear stamped in gold.

"The women always look after our history," said Caroline. "You could say we are the guardians of both land and name."

It was fascinating. Maggie wondered why she had never seen the books before.

Again, Caroline seemed to read her thoughts. "We only bring these books out at the Gathering. As you can see, many are very old. I was sharing them with Charlie before you came down."

Maggie's eyes flicked to the rug, noticed her daughter's phone nestled in the fur, the flattened hair showing where it seemed she had been lying. Her thoughts turned back to the Gathering.

"Anyone else arrived yet?"

The stillness of the house gave her the answer.

"Elise and Victoria rang. They'll be here later. Just waiting for the roads to clear."

Maggie returned to the book, found herself smiling as she read through a will dated 1600. In amongst the looping, almost unintelligible, script, she discerned a mother bequeathing a bear pelt to her oldest daughter, '*to be looked after as family*'.

"It can't be the same, surely?" she asked her aunt, holding up the page and tapping it with her finger.

"No? If you take care of something, what's to say it won't last forever?"

The pages continued to pull her in. Another volume, further and further back. Then she had to stop. The dense Latin prevented any further examination.

She flipped back to the more recent pages. Her mother's name next to Caroline's caused a sudden pang. Her death, more than two years ago, continued to hit hard. She felt as if a layer of protection had vanished with her passing.

"She never really got over the death of your father," said Caroline. "It kept you from us all this time. You did so well on your first hunt of the Gathering. A good kill. A pity your mother didn't see it that way."

Maggie felt the squeeze of her aunt's hand as her nightmare threatened to return. She pushed it back as her mother had taught her and busied herself once more in the stories of others.

When she looked up again, night had fallen. She frowned. She had lost track of time so easily.

"Brian and Charlie—"

"Oh, I meant to tell you, dear. They rang to say they walked further than intended. They made it to the village, might stop at the local B&B for the night. Brian said he'd decide after they've had a drink."

It irked they'd been able to escape Caroline's clutches so soon.

"Couldn't they get a taxi?"

Caroline shook her head. "The roads are still bad. Ploughs will be out tomorrow. They called me because your phone is apparently always turned off."

Maggie laughed and pulled out her mobile. Rarely used, it was dead. She'd forgotten to charge it. "They know me so well."

She tried to suppress a yawn.

"Why don't you turn in? Another good night's rest will set you right."

Maggie rose, gave her aunt a peck on the cheek and made her way back to bed. Only as sleep claimed her did she remember she'd eaten nothing, didn't feel hungry. She stirred slightly, as the weight of an extra blanket was placed over her. *Her aunt fussing*, she thought, a slight smile on her lips as she heard Caroline calling Charlie and her daughter replying. They'd made it home after all! Maggie relaxed and allowed herself to slide into unconsciousness.

This time, she dreamed. Across snow-covered fields she ran, warm beneath her fur, enjoying the clear air, the stars, the thrill of the chase. She could smell prey, meat to fill her belly, feed her cub. On she ran until she caught them. Two-legged creatures into which she tore, burying her muzzle in their warm blood, drinking it in.

She came too with a start. Shaken by the vision. Maggie glanced down. What on earth was she wearing? And where was she? Not in her bed but out in the hallway, wrapped in that hideous bearskin. Part of her wanted to throw it off immediately, the other part noted how warm it was, and so she kept it on. It was still the middle of the night, dream and reality blurring. Her mouth felt dry and the need for water roused her from her stupor. A drink would clear her head. Making her way downstairs, she noticed how her muscles ached, as if she'd been running.

A lamp had been left on in the drawing room, but her aunt was not there. A sound from the corridor leading to the kitchen and cellars caught her attention.

Slowly, she made her way along, noting the sound of claws tapping on wood, paws padding. Strangely unafraid, she ambled on, the chill receding as fur regrew. Down the stairs.

She smelt family. Her aunt. Her cousins. Their cubs. Her cub. They all turned to her as she entered their circle. Blood slicked their muzzles, coated their fur. Her stomach rumbled. There was enough left for her. She tore into the meat.

Maggie awoke, disoriented. What she recalled had seemed too real to be a dream and yet the bear pelt was back, covering her on the bed. The scene in the cellar—that couldn't have been real. *No?* the bear's eyes seemed to ask her. Maggie clambered out of bed and picked up the bearskin. It was heavy, so much easier to carry if you just wore it. She put aside her revulsion and wrapped the fur around her. Improbably, a feeling of *rightness* enveloped her, the disgust vanishing. Caroline appeared at the door.

"Such a beautiful transformation," she said. "You were born to this role."

Maggie felt her perspective change, found herself on all fours, sensed the strength within her grow as muscle formed.

"Brian—,"

"Don't worry about him, dear. Husbands have always provided for the family."

"Charlie—" her voice mutated, became a growl.

"Did well," said her aunt, "She's resting up. The first time can be overwhelming."

A mercifully brief vision of teeth tearing flesh, a recognized scent, vanished. There was no fear, only release.

***

Caroline led the bear downstairs and opened the door. Outside, two more waited, young cubs behind them. Elise and Victoria had arrived the previous evening with their children. It was time Maggie got to know them better. Learn the ways of the Bersseck clan, or rather, as it had once been spelt—Bersirkir. She'd already proved a good hunter and her daughter showed so much promise.

"Off you go, dear. Time to have a bit of fun with the girls. You've earned it."

Caroline watched the group gambol in the snow. The family had fed well at their Gathering. The bear would sleep for another year. Pity about Brian. She'd rung the emergency services, set his story in motion to prevent any questions. They'd been most sympathetic. Trying to cross the ice on the river was always dangerous. Sadly, bodies were often never recovered. She smiled and pulled on her own fur coat. Time to play.

Shift Left for Love

by Theresa Derwin

Tabitha toddled over to the play area, nervous, but wanting to at least try to be with the regular kids on her first day of primary school. Her mom, tears in her bright, blue eyes, had whispered, "Try, Tabby, try to be *normal*. For Mommy, please?"

Then she left in her expensive car, not once looking back at her four-year-old daughter with trembling lips…

Tabby walked across the massive playground to the sandbox. Shortly after, a shadow passed across her. She looked up to see a four-year-old boy with bright, furiously red hair, looming over the area. He leaned over her, sniffed, then pushed her forward onto the gritty sand.

She fell face-first into the sandpit, spluttering, tiny, pale legs kicking up in the air as she bawled, before flopping over onto her back, pink knickers showing.

The boy stuck his tongue out at her. "Poo-face!" Then, for no reason her young mind could fathom, he said, "Me Joseph. You smell funny."

Anger soared through Tabby's veins. Her chubby hands making little fists, she climbed awkwardly to the edge of the sandpit, stumbled forward, screaming, "Big pooer-face," and pushed him back.

A little blonde doll—Alisa—ran over to Tabby as she curled into a ball, crying, not understanding why the Joseph seemed to hate her. Mrs. Yo-Yo, the primary teacher, ran over to the cluster of children.

"What happened?" she asked, voice firm as she leaned over to check the grazes they both sported.

"Miss Yo-Yo! Him! Him," Tabby wailed, sitting up to point at the boy, who shook his head from side-to-side.

Alisa nodded, pointed, and Miss Yo-Yo shook her head in dismay.

"Joseph O'Rourke, tell me what happened please?"

Oh oh, thought Tabby, she using the voice.

Alisa and Tabby became instant BFFs.

Joseph never pushed Tabby again, though he did have a terrible habit of teasing her from then on.

***

Adult Tabitha snickered, then sighed, a deep pang of emptiness and loss as she remembered the last time Joseph tried to tease her. Her little plan for revenge. Then him moving away, with no warning, after his last attack, the one she thought at first she had caused.

Tall, rangy and freckled, fourteen-year-old Joseph was still cute as far as Tabitha was concerned. It annoyed her that she kind of liked him, despite his proverbially pulling her pigtails. No, she'd never been a pigtail kind of girl.

In fact, like some of the other girls, she would watch the boys playing football. Every now and again the ball would fly their way and they'd duck to avoid broken noses, she'd catch it easily, then throw it back. But for some inane reason Joseph found it funny to run straight back to her with it, like he was bestowing on her the ultimate gift.

He'd grin and drop it at her feet, wink and stand there watching until she threw it back onto the pitch.

Yeah, he'd been a weird one, but she still liked him even when he was annoying her.

Their school hi-jinks were infamous, Alisa watching eagerly to find out who would throw the next punch.

Tabitha's finest, and worst hour, was the day of the sandwich battle.

It was lunch hour and, as usual, she had found a bench outside and Joseph had followed her, like a lost puppy.

"Hey, how's life at the morgue? *Life*!" he yelled, grabbing a seat on a bench and opening his packed lunch.

"I don't know, where's ya pot 'o' gold, ya eejit?" she snapped back at him.

Yeah, two could play at that game, she thought.

Tabitha watched covertly, smirking as he unwrapped his sandwich and bit into it.

Instantly he started gagging, choking on the sandwich, then he spit out the remains of mulched bread and something grey and slimy, glaring at Tabitha.

"YA COW!!!"

He jumped up, his face ruddy, teeth bared at her as he pulled a wriggly, muddy worm out of his lunch box.

Tabitha blew him a kiss and snorted, looking forward to the next battle, but Joseph started coughing again, sweat pouring from his flushed skin.

"Oh shit," she breathed, dashing over to him and smacking his back loudly.

"I'm sorry, Joe, Joe, please don't die on me!"

"Not. Dying. Yet. Morticia" he growled between chugging in great gasps of air, then, "Phone. Mom!"

Mom? Mom, he wants his mom?

Head hung over, his eyes flashing from green to gold, rolling back, Tabitha gasped, panic nearly overwhelming her. What if he was allergic to worms? Oh crap.

Grabbing his rucksack, she opened it, emptying everything onto the wooden table, finally spotting his silver flip phone.

"Ambulance?" she yelled, watching Joseph's already flushed skin turn redder.

"MOM!"

"Okay. Hang on, it'll be okay."

She was crying now, blindly hitting the contacts and calling Marie, his mom.

"Joe honey, what—"

"No, it's Joseph he's…, I think it's a seizure, please."

"It's okay hon, we're coming."

Tabitha dropped the phone and started to run towards the teacher on duty, until a firm hand grasped hers.

"I'm okay," Joseph hissed, holding onto her hand like a lifeline.

She waited with him, watched as his breathing finally calmed down and his mom, a glamorous woman in heels with a mass of curly hair, arrived and shooed her away.

The next day in class, Miss Guinan announced he wasn't coming back to school.

His family had moved away.

***

"Shift Left for Love. How may I help you?" a husky, female voice asked.

Tabitha's heavy breathing echoed down the phone line.

"Hello?" the woman asked.

Maybe she thinks I'm a stalker?

"Um... I, er. That is," Tabitha mumbled.

Her palms were getting sweaty, and she'd only just dialed the damn number on the advice of Alisa, her BFF who had acquired her latest boyfriend through the dating company.

"Don't worry, petal," the voice on the phone said, "I'm Natalia, It's difficult for everyone the first time."

Having first assumed a grouchy older woman, Tabitha revised her estimate back to mid-thirties. She now sounded more empathetic, perhaps. And had a beautiful, exotic accent she couldn't place.

"You'll be fine," she continued. "What's your name?"

Tabitha humphed, let out a deep sigh and told her the unfortunate name she'd been given—*Tabitha* (her mom was basically a weird hippie and was doused in patchouli).

She then confessed to the kind of help she was looking for.

At the end of the long, embarrassing call, she felt like she'd been interrogated by MI5, not a specialty dating agency.

But instead of using a flashlight and a fist, Natalia had used kind words.

She'd turned into her agony aunt. The kind of aunt who knows your most intimate details, whether you're allergic to dogs and even what color of knickers you wear on a Tuesday.

That was black, by the way. She always wore black. Until they invented a shade darker, she'd live in it. She snorted as she remembered the nickname she'd been given by Joseph: Morticia. He'd called her Morticia.

And that was why she couldn't get a date.

At least according to her bestie.

Tabitha's goth image, her brain, her very generous curves, and her refusal to wear pink.

Apparently, those things made grown men run screaming into the night.

Yeah, she didn't get why she and Alisa were friends either.

It was like Elle Woods from *Legally Blonde* hanging out with Morticia Addams from *The Addams Family*. Complicated, contradictory—yet somehow it worked.

They'd met at school and been close ever since Alisa had comforted her after being pushed into the sandbox.

After finishing the call with, "Oh, just call me Nat,"—her new Agony Aunt from Hell—Tabitha sighed, changed into her Jack Skellington PJs, and called Alisa.

Unfortunately, her BFF had just met "Mr. Right"—or possibly "Mr. Right Now"—a few weeks ago and she was in *luuurve*. Tabitha hadn't met him yet, but Alisa reckoned Grant was "worlds away" from any other man.

She answered the phone mid yell.

"—off. No!!! I'm not going anywhere with you!"

Oh oh.

Trouble in Paradise?

"Hey, soz Tab, I was just *discussing* our plans for the weekend."

Tabitha snorted. "Discussing? Really? And you're giving me romantic advice?"

Alisa laughed, then whispered, "He wants me to go *camping*?"

Tabitha burst out laughing, sounding a little like a constipated donkey as her snorts and chuckles became chortles. "No way!" she said, when she'd calmed down enough to speak without having an asthma attack.

"I know!!"

"Disaster! I bet Roberto Cavali doesn't even do tents!"

"Oh, you're so funny. Anyway, how did it go?"

They chatted for a good half hour or so, Tabby with her dragon slippers on, Alisa most likely draped in chiffon or silk.

In the midst of their chat, Tabitha's phone pinged and she gasped.

"I have to go! I have a meeting with them! Tomorrow!"

She could still hear Alisa's squeals of delight as she hit "end".

There it was. The notification she'd been waiting for. An advisor was meeting her tomorrow at Marshall's, her local coffee shop by the train station.

Why did she need an advisor anyway? She'd already been questioned so much it felt like she was auditioning for *Love Island*. Hey, maybe they were making a new show; *Geek Island*. She did love her geeks, but her dream guy was something else.

***

Tabitha got to Marshall's Coffee Shop thirty minutes early. She was so nervous her throat was dry and she was babbling vague introductions to herself in preparation—and it wasn't even the date.

Apparently, this was round two of the assessment to find her "kindred spirit". Yep, they used phrases like that. Marshalls was a local place—*for local people*—with a cool hipster vibe, minus the pretentiousness.

She could smell the rich, roast blend of quality coffee wafting in the air as soon as she entered.

Between the vintage seats, dark varnished tables, scattered rugs and mosaic lamps, Marshall's was perfect for chilling with a cuppa and a good book.

She headed to a wingback leather chair by a low coffee table ensconced in the corner next to a bookshelf brimming with horror, SF, Fantasy and about ten copies of *Fifty Shades of Something or Other*. Quality reading. Well, most of it.

Two brothers, Matt and Dave, had opened it up a couple of months ago, decorating the walls with old hessian coffee sacks, packing crates, and vintage artwork.

Matt, the older, bearded, tattooed brother in a Megadeth muscle top and leather bracelets, waved as he spotted her.

He was busy whipping up some fancy, marshmallow-topped concoction for a mum and her young daughter, whilst Dave, the quieter one with dark hair and light stubble, restocked the cake display.

145

Yep, they'd been expecting her alright.

There was her favorite Belgian chocolate slice, already plated on one of the random pieces of crockery they owned.

Tabitha waved at him, then grabbed the empty armchair in the reading nook.

Dave hooked her up with a load of coke—not the white stuff but the stuff that fizzes—and she sighed as she took her first bubbly sip.

***

Tabitha was drumming her fingers on the table when she suddenly felt uneasy, like she was being watched, and her hackles rose.

She cleared her throat and put her Kindle down, looking up to see what had nudged her invisible "leave-me-alone" wall.

Then gasped a little as a massive man stepped up to her table.

At least six-four, he was muscled, yet his movements were fluid as he nodded, grabbed a spare chair and sat across from her, firm legs on display.

"I'm waiting for someone," she said, giving him the stare-of-death.

He grinned, dropped an iPad she hadn't seen him holding onto the table and held out his hand.

"Yeah, me," he said, voice deep, a hint of Irish brogue to it. "Rourke. You must be Tabitha. I'd remember that grimace anywhere…"

What?? She was flustered. For the first time in her life, she was absolutely flustered.

He was delicious, and smelled of sunshine and sage, triggering memories from a long, long time ago, that she couldn't quite grasp.

With his dark, auburn hair that reached to his shoulders, short beard and twinkling green eyes, this was not her idea of a matchmaker.

Matchmakers were cute old women with scarves around their heads who sang random songs with Barbara Streisand.

This guy had no business in a dating agency. He was better suited to modelling naked on motorbikes.

All this went through her head in about two seconds flat.

She stopped drumming and wiped her hand on her leggings then shook his hand, jumping at the jolt of static that hit her.

"Sorry, I expected … Well, not you. And don't for the love of God call me Tabitha. It's Tabby."

"And here I was," he said with a grin, "thinking it was Morticia."

Ever delicate, she started coughing and pounding her chest, and the gorgeous man stood up, instantly behind her and rubbing her back.

The alluring scent of male musk and something like a sun-dew morning in a forest hit her senses.

Her breathing finally calmed down and she collapsed back into her seat.

"Joseph?" she asked.

"Yep," he answered, looking happy with himself.

"Where the fuck did you go?" she whispered, her voice cracking.

"Well now, it's a long story, luv, but I'll have to make it shorter."

David approached, quietly, and handed Joseph a mug of coffee with a nod, then slipped away.

"So?" Tabitha asked.

***

Rourke, aka Joseph O'Rourke, had messed up straight away and called Tabby "luv".

147

What a monumental fuck up from start to finish.

How in the hell was he supposed to convince her of the truth about what he was? What she was to him, even?

Jesus.

Rourke cleared his throat with a big gulp of coffee. He nodded his thanks at David, who continued to clear tables whilst guarding the front door, as Rourke had ordered.

After all, he was the local alpha – and this coffee shop owed him.

He'd helped finance it from pack funds, mostly so he could keep tabs on Tabs.

He snorted at that and returned his gaze to her. The girl he'd teased, taunted and tortured at school all in the hope she'd pay him attention.

As a four-year-old she'd smelt 'funny' to him.

Ten years later the Irish Wolfhound in him perked up its nose, smelling violets and cherry blossom, and something that was… *his*.

***

"So?" Tabitha asked.

She still smelled of spring flowers beneath the perfume she wore. He could feel his pulse racing, his skin hot, the large wolfhound throbbing underneath, wanting out.

They were both running out of time.

"Okay, the long and the short of it is this," he said. "Bollocks to it. This is easier."

He signaled the lads and David locked the door, pulling down the shutters. The last customer except him and Tabby had already left.

Rourke stood, pushing away from the chair. "There's not much time."

Muscles rippling, his once-pale skin now tanned, he pulled off his t-shirt and threw it on the floor. "And the thing is, when I hit

148

fourteen, something in me changed. You triggered my change. And me and me Ma had to run and hide 'til I was strong enough."

Tabitha's mouth watered as Joseph ripped off his t-shirt, then his strong hands popped the buttons on his Levi's, swiftly pulling them down and stepping out of them.

She shook her head to try and focus. She finally heard him say "had to run and hide," then made herself pay attention.

She gulped.

"What are you—holy shit!"

Tabitha jumped up from her seat, knocking it to the floor and scooted back a few steps, then burst out laughing, a kind of hysterical keening sound, surprising the coffee shop owners and the massive, five-foot high, shaggy red wolfhound that stood panting, tongue lolling, where Joseph had just stood.

"You okay?" Matt asked, addressing the large alpha and inching towards Tabby in case she fled, or screamed the place down.

Mouth gaping, she stared at the humungous hound, then started whispering something rapidly, then slower and slower until her breathing steadied.

She looked into those flashing gold eyes and remembered where she'd seen them before.

Joseph's *not-seizure* just before he'd left the school for good.

Her heart was still racing, but surprisingly not with fear.

No, excitement danced along her nerves as the dog made a chugging sound, loped towards her and slathered his tongue over her outstretched hand, licking her to death as those gold eyes stared into hers.

No wonder he'd had to run, but…

"Why are you back now, Joe? What's going on?"

She continued to pet him, unable to stop herself as she met those beautiful eyes of his. He was a dog, after all, and who doesn't love a dog?

He started herding her backwards until her bum fell into the chair that Matt must've righted for her.

His giant head landed in her lap, doggie eyes and doggie grin entrancing her.

She looked up at Matt, then David.

"You too?"

They nodded.

"Husky," said David.

"Proper wolf, not like this mangy git," Matt said, and David growled at him.

"Well, he can't talk, why is he here now? Why am I here?"

Matt took the seat Rourke had vacated and David passed him an open beer. He sighed in relief as he took a long swig, then put the bottle down.

"Right, you read all that horror and *Twilight* stuff, right?"

He nodded at the full bookcase behind her, and she snorted. "Not *Twilight*. But yes. What's that got to do with me though?"

"Well." Matt rubbed his eyes, cleared his throat then let out a big huff of breath. "That wolfhound there is your mate. And if he doesn't confirm the mating soon, and I mean very soon, he'll be given to the Wild Hunt for a hundred years."

"You're shitting me!" Tabitha squeaked, staring down with annoyance, then anger, at the dog she'd been absently petting. He whined at her, feeling her distress, and she felt that anger melt away as she looked at him.

The dating agency, Alisa forcing fliers and a phone number on her, it had all been a set up. And how the hell was Alisa involved?

These were all questions for later

She should've been furious, but that tiny ember inside her heart that had wanted to meet someone, that had also felt something for the big pile of fur in front of her since childhood, turned that ember into a spark, then heat soared through her heart, and spread outwards, touching every single part of her.

Mine, she suddenly thought, and the flame erupted inside her.

Just as the shutters blew inward under a gale force wind and she screamed.

Joseph swung round growling and Tabitha ran behind the wingback chair. It wasn't much of a defense but it was something.

"The Hunt!" Matt half-growled and before she could blink, she was guarded by fur and muscle; Matt an impressive, chestnut brown wolf, David a majestic husky with arctic blue eyes and her own bright-red wolfhound that nearly towered over her on four legs.

Green mist swirled into the café followed by the smell of dirt, forest and ozone.

Then in they came.

She'd read a bit about the Wild Hunt in the urban fantasy books she'd read, about sexy guys and wolves and horses and magical creatures.

None of that reading prepared her for the seven-foot-tall armored skeleton with twisting antlers that strode into the room, pieces of rotten, stinky flesh dripping from its bones.

"Joseph O'Rourke!" the thing called, the wind howling through its voice. "You must join our Hunt."

Two scabby, skinny hounds with dirty absinthe pelts followed him in, hunched low on either side of their master.

No! Hell no, Tabby thought, the scream rattling around inside her head. *You don't get to take him from me. I just found him.*

The other shifters surrounded her, in defense positions, spreading out, encircling her, claws clicking on the hardwood floor, ready to fight.

One of the sickly hounds lunged, then another, fangs bared and already bloody, those sharp teeth tore the skin of her protectors, drool spilling into the torn flesh left behind from their bites.

Matt howled as the drool hit and sizzled on his fur like acid.

But still the trio of shifters fought, Joseph in his powerful wolfhound form, his fur a bright auburn, attacking the leader of the Hunt, but there was no flesh to grab onto, just withered bones.

It was a losing battle, the barista-shifters being forced back, so Tabitha grabbed the nearest bottle, smashed the end on the table and brandished it, swiping it across the vile dead hounds, letting her rage soar.

A flash of light blinded them and suddenly the animals whimpered as a very naked Joseph stood in front of his pack.

He dodged the fist powering towards him like a freight train; his movements fluid, effortless, his joints moving as if oiled. Tabitha watched, entranced, remembering all the times they'd played at fighting in the school yard or the park. He'd been skinny then, but strapping. Loose limbs and a dancer's skill. Now he was, well, awesome.

Fierce, and damn fine too. It was like watching *The Matrix* on steroids meets *Sons of Anarchy*.

Yet he was no match for the leader of the hunt.

"Give it up boy, you have no claim here," the leader roared, grabbing Joseph by his throat and lifting him to dangle above.

"I DO!"

Tabitha pushed her way through blood and fur to face the Rider.

"I have a claim," she gasped, the knowledge rushing through her as her eyes met Joseph's golden gaze.

"He's mine, you can't take him!"

The Rider paused and sniffed Joseph's neck, uttering a roar as it threw Joseph to the floor.

Shaking, she froze as the Rider leaned down, its antlers touching her hair as he sniffed her.

Then they were gone.

In the blink of an eye, the scent of putrescence, forest and earth had disappeared along with the murky green mist and the Hunt itself,

Legs like jelly, she crumpled, landing on very hot, very bloody, very *naked* Joseph O'Rourke.

And she wanted to pet him in this form too.

Brief flashes of light and the crunching of bones like tearing into chicken wings, and Matt and David were human again, quickly throwing spare joggers on to preserve their dignity.

One strong arm reached up and pulled her close to him.

"You smell the same," he whispered, throat hoarse.

"Ya mean, funny?" she said, smiling at him.

"No, violets and cherry blossom. Spring."

He sniffed her hair, then bestowed a light kiss on her forehead.

"Thank you for claiming me," he said, "I wasn't sure you would. It was Nat's idea, my cousin."

Ahh, Nat, Agony Aunt from Hell.

"I think I claimed you when you pushed me into the sandpit," she said and he chuckled, fluttering kisses across her collar bone.

"Well, it seems you've adopted a dog," he answered between kisses and she snorted.

Yes, well.

A good thing she wasn't allergic to big annoying hounds, after all.

The Fragility of Birds
by Christina Sng

Too many decades now
I have spent coasting
High in the skies,
My wings outstretched,
Reaching for freedom.
Yet, once every year,
I return to the ground,
Return to human-form
And visit my mother
On her birthday.
"How are your adventures,"
She asks as she always does.
"The same," I reply.
She leans closer this time.
"I mean, the ones in the sky."
I startle and widen my eyes
While she leans back and smiles.
"I once flew as you do,
Until your father got tired of it
And cut off my wings."
She stands and shows me
The two scarred nubs on her back.
I weep for all she has missed
But she embraces me, smiling,
"You were worth it."
I gather her bird-fragile body
Gently into my arms, whispering,

"Hold on tight, Momma,"
As we take to the sky together
Forever.

Wife to the Wild

by Clara Madrigano

My mother told me this story, which she heard from her mother, and now I'm telling you; every part of this story is true, you must remember. Consider it a treasure, the passing down of this story; it concerns a time long-gone, a time when such things were possible. That doesn't happen anymore, not after we burned the forests and poisoned the rivers. But, believe me, there was time when men and nature lived side by side, when the line that divided us was so thin you could barely see it, and then you'd step over it and there you'd be, in the land where men ruled nothing, where you had to bow to nature and its children. It's the truth, all of this.

Back in those days, in the North of Minas Gerais, near where the forest grew thick with green, there was a village for the families of the men employed by the big farms. Men would come with their families, set them in little wooden houses they'd erect with their bare hands and survive and work and survive and work; for when working with soil, the precious things that may grow or may not from it, the things that may sustain or, if they decide not to grow, the very things that may damn you, that's what you did: you survived. You could go for months digging the earth and planting the seeds while the sun scorched your head, made you faint with heat; you'd eat a flour-and-beans mixture day after day, without complaining, and drink water when water was available. And the children, they couldn't be children for long. They had to grow up fast, make themselves useful, earn the right of having their mouths fed.

White men in white linen suits, with their hats and precious shoes, would arrive by train so they could watch with their own eyes

156

progress being made. A white man who owned a farm as such, Mr. Santos, made the point of visiting often; he was the kind of white man who wanted the workers to know how caring and good he was, so as not to lose his men to competition—slavery was gone, if only by a few decades, and now workers had to be paid, had to be, as Mr. Santos would say, pampered. But there's only so much caring and goodness that can be shown by white men with big farms. Mr. Santos wasn't beyond sending away workers as he saw fit, including the family of a man who'd been terribly mauled by a jaguar, on the occasion he found himself by the river, cleaning his plate after a fast and poor lunch.

He'd lost an eye, this man, and the jaguar had scarred him so deeply on one side that his arm, once proclaimed saved, could never be moved again the way it had been before. When the man came screaming out of the woods, holding his bloody arm, the right side of his face almost beyond recognition, nobody believed he'd survive the night. They held a small vigil; as the man lay on the kitchen table of his own house, burning in fever, neighbors came and prayed to the saints and to other entities—those that weren't Christian enough, that couldn't be spoke of aloud, who had accompanied them since their ancestors had been forced to cross the seas. Food was served to the young ones, to the man's children, whose eyes were wide like saucers, black and moist with tears. Mr. Santos came to the vigil. He took off his white hat in respect, had a few words with the man's wife. He held her thin hands and said whatever comforting phrases he had, and the woman wept silently.

It was during the vigil that Mr. Santos first saw her.

Maria.

She came with her family; her little brother, her mother and her father. Her head was covered by a white veil, but the black strands of her hair fell over her simple dress—an old dress that once belonged to her grandmother, or other relative (clothes were just mended and handed down, after all; who could afford new dresses?).

It is said it happened that very night—a night impregnated with the scent of blood and fever. That night, Mr. Santos fell in love, and in lust, with young Maria.

What was she at the time? A girl of sixteen, maybe. And Mr. Santos, a man in his early forties. Now, of course, things were different back then; sixteen was a reasonable age for a girl to contract marriage—yes, contract; just like that, like a disease. Not that Maria had any plans of getting married, and not that she'd ever been proposed to, despite being considered a beauty, with a sheer dark brown skin, with eyes black and big as jabuticabas. And not that Mr. Santos, already married by then, was the type of man who, once besotted by a young woman, was in the business of proposing; men like that, then and now, then and in every age, had always the mind of taking whatever it was that they wanted, without asking for permission.

After the vigil, a night that seemed to have no ending, he survived, the man who had been attacked by the jaguar. But he'd lost an eye, and his arm was useless for the work he did until now. Mr. Santos fired him after a few weeks—people weren't warned of that. One day, they woke up to find the house the man had lived in with his family empty. And, just a few days later, another family moved in; new workers, all of them with two healthy eyes and arms.

Mr. Santos kept coming from his farm to visit: to visit Maria's family, specifically, and you'd never refuse Mr. Santos. So, Maria's mother would always have some watery coffee ready, some bread Mr. Santos could munch on—it was all they could afford, and it was more precious than gold, that little food. Maria herself, however, was usually absent from these visits. But Mr. Santos had time at his disposal; time, money, and he could spend it all in that one pursuit, a cat playing with his meal.

"Is your daughter unengaged as of yet?" he'd ask, and Maria's parents would exchange looks. Everyone knew that, yes, Maria wasn't engaged, probably would never be. The boys from the neighboring families all treated her with some deference—and some distance. No, no boy would be foolish enough to try something with Maria, because they all heard the stories. Maria, as pious as she might look, was wild; Maria wasn't to be tamed. She had once fought a boy who whispered to her things a man shouldn't whisper to a girl, and Maria answered by leaving his face marked with her nails, as if nails were claws. That boy took a beating from his father, for the shame of having been hurt by a girl, and never again spoke a word, whispered or not, to Maria.

"She's a pretty girl—she ought to have a good husband, good children of her own," Mr. Santos said. "I can help you find a decent man." Which was to say: Mr. Santos would get her married to someone of his choosing, once he had his way with Maria. Maria's parents said nothing to this. Only her mother, at one point, while serving Mr. Santos with another cup of coffee, dared to share her feelings: "Maria is very young."

Mr. Santos laughed heartily at this, while Maria's mother stared him with her dark eyes, as dark as her daughter's, no trace of amusement on her face.

By coincidence—a stroke of luck, Mr. Santos would think—Maria was coming back home just as he was leaving. Mr. Santos stood by the house's small door, took his hat in respect as Maria, eyes widened, looked from her parents to their visitor.

"A sight for sore eyes," he said. "I was just having coffee with your dear parents. Now, Maria—would you mind showing me the garden? I heard it's thriving."

Maria did as she was asked, but their garden wasn't exactly thriving, and it was no Eden: it just a patch of land where a few things grew well, and others didn't. As Maria caressed the plants, naming them to satiate the curiosity of Mr. Santos, he couldn't help but notice the dirt beneath her fingernails, the mud on her beautiful little feet; neither could he pretend not to see the red, burning welts on her legs, welts that rose and hid under Maria's old skirt, the place where Mr. Santos wanted to touch her so badly.

A wild child, indeed, he thought to himself. But it didn't make him desire her any less. After Maria said her goodbyes and went inside her home, her brother, back from working by the river, accompanied Mr. Santos to where his horse waited for him, near a bucket filled with water, huge flies bothering the poor animal. Mr. Santos swatted them as he climbed on his horse.

"Sir, Maria is not meant for men…" the boy said, all of a sudden.

"Excuse me?" Mr. Santos asked. The boy looked a lot like his sister. Which was to say they all looked a lot like their mother. Same brown skin, same dark eyes, nothing to amuse them, to curl their lips in a smile.

"She should be left as she is." The boy made no attempt to explain himself any further, but those words buried deep inside Mr. Santos, buried like thorns. That night, he had three of his most trusted men to meet him inside his farmhouse. It was late, and Mr. Santos sat by one corner of his massive dining table, drinking his fine spirits, which he offered to the men. He told them he wanted young Maria to be followed—whatever business she attended to when she wasn't home, helping her mother, should be reported to him; whatever business she had in the forest, where her hands got dirty and her skin welted. The men agreed; they armed themselves and mounted their horses, and promised to be the eyes Mr. Santos needed.

When they came back, a fortnight later, their eyes shone with fear, with shock.

The first man said, "She lays with the devil himself." And Mr. Santos had him sit down and gave him a drink.

The second man said, "She lays with a beast." And Mr. Santos had him sit down and gave him a drink, too.

The third man was wiser than the others—his mother had been an indigenous healer, it was said, and he carried her heritage in his long, black hair, in the silent way he would come and go, drawing no attention if he so wished. The third man, calmly, thumbs resting inside his belt, said, "Not the devil, not a beast. Something in between. But something that is human, too." And Mr. Santos offered him a drink, too, but he refused.

"I'll give you money," Mr. Santos promised. "I'll give everything you want, if you only show me…"

"I want no money. But I'll show you what my eyes have seen, if you wish so. And then you'll understand that some things should be left as they are." That strange echo, almost the very same thing Maria's little brother had said. And, still, Mr. Santos wished so.

About the first two men: don't be bothered by them, they are no longer part of this story. You can imagine they went their ways, and for years, until Death knocked on their doors, told their weird tale to their children, then to their grandchildren. Or they died young: violent deaths, an ambush while they traveled the road by horses. Or else their hearts failed them: after what they witnessed in the forest, fear traveled with them wherever they went, until fear dug a deep hole inside their hearts and—that was it. Either way, let them go; they are none of our concern anymore.

What? Yes, it is like a fairy-tale, child. No, I didn't make this up. Every story of our past is a fairy-tale, and you should know this already. When you're old, and you remember this time we shared, you and I, you'll think of it as a fairy-tale, too. Be quiet. Listen to me, for what I'm about to tell might save your life, someday. If you ever find yourself lost in the forest, there's something you should know about the jaguar.

Here, in our country, the jaguar is king and queen of the forest. You'll know when the jaguar is near when you hear its war-cry. That means whenever it's dark, when you can hardly breathe in the warmth of the forest, if you happen to hear a cry like that of a woman mourning the loss of her love, like that of a child mourning the loss of a mother, then you should run. That's the sad cry of the jaguar, but it's not really sadness it speaks of; it speaks of hunger; it's the sound that precedes death.

It's exactly what that third man told Mr. Santos as they dismounted from their horses and stood before the dark vastness of the forest, that deep and warm green that threatened to engulf one's soul; for Mr. Santos did cross himself at that sight, the moon shining bright and almost red in the sky. "If you hear the cry of a child, as heartbreaking as it may sound" said the man, "you run, senhor, because that's no child."

He used a machete to make his way inside the forest. The third man knew well enough where to put his feet, but Mr. Santos followed him with some difficulty, running out of breath, trying to swat away the mosquitos that hungered for his blood. At the distance, he could hear water running; perhaps a little stream, perhaps something more, water that would definitely lead to the great Rio Doce.

The third man said Mr. Santos should be careful now, for they were entering the domain of things such that men should never come to know. The third man had Mr. Santos half-kneel as they approached the source of the sound of water. The man kept his machete ready, and he was very silent as he parted the bushes so they could look; on to the clearing, over the stream, the water making the sound of the touching of glass against glass. And there was Maria. Laying down on one of the rocks that run side by side with the stream. Naked, beautiful Maria, her wet hair spread over the rock. And, with half of its body resting on her belly—the jaguar.

Mr. Santos didn't scream. The image petrified him, but he made no sound. He never thought of the embrace of a wild beast and a human as anything but the embrace of death and violence. But the scene before his eyes, that was different. The way Maria's hand carefully caressed the fur of the beast, and those guttural purrs of pleasure the jaguar produced, and how its claws traced, almost with sweetness, Maria's skin—the red welts… that was lust.

Lust. Just as Mr. Santos once felt.

Rage boiled his blood and, before the third man could say or do anything at all, Mr. Santos already had his gun pointed at the beast. A single shot exploded through that night, through the forest. And then, the screaming.

Maria's screams, but also the screams of the shot jaguar, now convulsing on the ground.

Yes, the beast was screaming. Mr. Santos went pale, trembling at what he was seeing: the jaguar, trashing while his skin was being ripped by something that existed inside. The jaguar's mighty claws fell, bloody as everything else; human hands rose from under that discarded skin, human feet—and soon enough, what lay by the bed of the stream, with his head cradled on Maria's lap, was a man. A man of copperish skin, hair as dark as the night. A man with lines of red that ran through his body like veins; ink, red ink, tattooed deep in his skin.

Maria was crying, begging in whispers, something meant to be heard only by her lover—because, yes, he was her lover, this man, this jaguar. A man who now held one side of his torso where the bullet had opened his flesh and spilled his innards in the same way of a smashed ripe fruit, its color a dark crimson, a spoiled prune.

"What have you done…" the third man muttered. But Mr. Santos, sweaty, face reddened, had recovered from his shock—and now crossed the stream, puffing all the way; rage itself, was that man. He grabbed Maria by her arm and she screamed—not at the pain, but at being separated from her lover.

"How can you… how could you…" Mr. Santos shook young Maria by her arm and she clawed at him, she fought him, wild

Maria, even though she was small and bony next to sturdy Mr. Santos. Mr. Santos was panting, his face still red, but now a little bloated. Without saying much else, he let go of Maria's arm and grabbed his own; his hand traveled up that arm, and then to his chest, as if he was trying to get hold of a snake running under his own skin. He fell to his knees, gasping. His lips moved, and he said something—perhaps his mother's name, or perhaps something else. It doesn't matter. Nobody heard his words, so they are not part of this story. What is part of this story is that Mr. Santos toppled over on the bank of the stream, and there he died.

What? Yes, he did die.

What do you mean?

Oh, I see—you expected some sort of justice exacted by Maria, or maybe by her jaguar. But it didn't happen like that. Mr. Santos died because of the shock of what he had experienced. It happens; to people of any age, at any time. What do you care? Nobody mourned him. Not his wife, not even his children, in fact. We won't mourn him either. He died, and that was it.

Now, the third man—who had witnessed all—approached Maria and the jaguar-man, paying little to no attention to the body of the now gone Mr. Santos. He put a hand on Maria's shoulders, and she, again cradling the body of her dying lover, answered with a snarl. But the third man meant them no harm, and Maria saw that inside his black eyes. He looked at the jaguar-man, who was now coughing up blood. A beautiful creature, eyes like amber, teeth so sharp, but now painted red; a ferocious smile, struggling with the pain. The third man showed him his pistol. After a few seconds, the jaguar-man nodded. Maria cried, and the third man asked her to close her eyes.

Maria didn't see it, so you won't, either. But you can imagine her pain, there, in the dark. The sound of the firing of the gun, the way her heart jumped, and how she stopped listening to her lover's painful breath. A relief, in a sense. But what a loss.

And that little sound? The sound of glass shattering little by little? That's the sound of Maria's heart.

The third man took her back home. Maria, now dressed, surrendered into his arms, blood smeared on her skirt. She kept saying his name, over and over, the name of her lover. No, I don't know his name. She never told anyone else, and the third man kept her secret.

Maria was pregnant. They didn't know at the time, but it became obvious in the weeks that came. Maria's father fell in a deep despair, and Maria's mother said prayer after prayer to the little statues of the saints closer to her heart. It made no difference, because Maria wouldn't name her lover. She barely spoke, barely ate. The third man ended up marrying her; of course he did. Maria needed a man to protect her reputation, and, in the eyes of her family, the third man was as good as any. The secret they both shared, however—the third man and Maria—that was between them.

Nine months later, Maria had her labor pains. It took a whole day and a whole night, and poor Maria was pale, covered in a cold sweat when she finally managed to expel the baby from her belly. Her mother screamed: for the baby she held in her arms was no human baby. It was a grotesque thing, a cat of golden fur, but eyes of a human, nose and mouth of a human. When the baby let out its first cry, it was the cry of the jaguar, the sound that instills a fear in every man's heart. Maria's mother was so horrified, she dropped the baby. And just like a cat, the baby landed with his paws on the floor, let out another cry and then ran for the open door of the little house. Maria's father wanted to shoot the creature, his own grandchild, but the third man stopped him. And Maria's brother, who was waiting outside, feeding the chickens, was the last one to see the jaguar-boy—his nephew—running away, still covered with blood and mucus, towards the forest, where he disappeared forever.

Of course it's true. Yes, everything I told you.

Mr. Santos? No, they never found his body. Nor that of the jaguar-man. You see, the forest is hungry, and it will eat whatever it is offered, since we offer it so little, and take so much. Maybe their bones are still there, somewhere; maybe the stream polished them into beautiful rocks. Who knows?

Maria lived a good life, in a sense. She and her husband had more children, but she could never let go of her firstborn, of course. During the nights, Maria would sit by the window, sewing under the lamp—electric light! Who could have imagined such a thing?—listening to the distant sounds of the forest. Whenever she heard the cry of a jaguar—and those were rarer and rarer as Maria got older—she would lift her head, a pang felt inside her heart, and wonder if that was her boy, crying for her.

My grandmother knew Maria. She remembers Maria buying her vegetables in the market square, gently pressing every potato, every squash, before putting them in her bag. My grandmother was the one who told my mother that, when Maria was eighty, long after her husband, her good third man, had died, she stripped off her clothes, entered the forest and was never seen again. It's true. After nobody had seen her for a whole day, her neighbors went to her house and found the discarded pile of clothes by the door. Maria's brother told them not to waste their time. Maria belonged somewhere else— always had.

Perhaps Maria had something of a jaguar inside herself, too. Perhaps she knew it was time to change skins, once her human life was done, her children raised, her husband buried.

Oh, mock me if you want. But you know it's true; in your bones and in your blood, you know it's true. Here, I'll leave the window open. Close your eyes. Listen to the forest—listen to what the winds carries with it. They say it's hard to find a jaguar, nowadays. But I still believe it is the king and the queen of the forest. So, listen carefully; perhaps you will hear its cry. And it will speak to you, and you'll know my words are true.

Good night, my darling.

Of Foxbites & Sorrow
by Villimey Mist

From across the lake,
Past the singing cicadas,
Faints sounds of footsteps.

A topknot bounces,
Heavy breathing in the air,
Butterflies flutter.

Cheeks painted in white,
Fireflies stick to cotton,
Crimson lips smiling.

Secluded kisses,
Out of bounds fast emotions,
Man and woman embrace.

"I want this for life,"
"Let's run away from our home,"
Heated decisions.

Passion dominant,
Responsibilities haze,
His hand slides down.

Moans flee the abyss,
Excitement ever bubbling,
A fox tail emerges.

Hand touches soft fur,
The forest leaves hold their breaths,
Frightened voice whimpers.

"Are you someone else?"
Frantic shake of the head,
His hand pulls the tail.

A sound like a yip,
Abrupt stomps rebound the lake,
The birds disappear.

"Wretched thing, you're finished!"
Sharp metal glints in the moonlight,
"Accept your tranquil death."

Skin stretches like bow,
Bristled fur encases muscles,
Jagged teeth snarling.

The man advances,
The fox howls and pounces,
Blood spatters the ground.

Sinews and nerves,
Suck in the air, blood spurting,
Ribbons of torn skin.

Knees crumple the grass,
Heart pumps feebly in its sleep,
Eyes reflect the moon.

Salty taste in flesh,
Tears corrupt the youthful face,
Wails fill the forest.

Forbidden amour,
Tricks the naïve hearts,
Cycle of nature.

Absinthe Dreams
by H.R. Boldwood

Stiffs had a way of piling up at The Green Mill Lounge. I tried to keep a low profile, but that ain't easy for a mook like me. I sat at the bar, slouched behind a copy of *The Times*, eyeballing the door like it was a pastrami on rye. Popping peanuts, tipping bootleg Tanqueray. And waiting. Waiting for *her*—Capone's girl.

I was dizzy for the dame.

Every night at seven, she'd strut in, a long, tall drink of water, black hair blazing beneath the spotlights.

What a looker. And what a set of pipes.

She'd sidle up to the stage and croon a couple of sets, sounding sexier than Dietrich. Then she'd saunter back to the last booth on the Lawrence Street side of the bar—*his* booth.

The saddest, loneliest looking skirt I ever saw, waiting on a schmuck like him.

Plenty of saps put the moves on her, but they beat feet once Manny, the barkeep, put 'em wise. Nobody poached Capone's girl.

Come ten p.m., King Alphonse and his goons owned the joint. He'd slide into the booth beside her, darting his eyes from door to door, watching for trouble. Then he'd order a Southside Fizz, and pal it up with his *goombahs*, barely noticing the high-class tootsie by his side.

Stupid rat bastard.

Well, that skirt ain't sad any more. And she sure as hell ain't lonely. I should know. I'm the one been putting a smile on her face for the last few weeks. She might have been Capone's Estelle. But she was my Stella. And I made her brown eyes dance like the fucking Rockettes.

The door opened and rain swept into the bar. Stella hovered at the threshold, standing in the mist, a streetlight burning through the fog behind her. Made her look like an angel. She sashayed inside, hips swaying like coconut palms in the breeze, then sallied up to the bar and tossed Manny a wink. "Hey fella. Word is a gal can wet her whistle in this dive."

The barkeep frowned as her fuck-me-red fingertips stroked the back of my hand. "The usual, ma'am?" He cleared his throat to get my attention. Manny don't like no dustups in his place. Especially ones involving Public Enemy Number One.

"That'd be swell," Stella said, slipping out of her coat. She fixed me in a smokey stare. "Pauly." She called me Pauly. "Butt me, would ya, baby?"

I fired up one of my Luckies. She wrapped her pouty red lips around it and blew, working it soft and slow. Sweet Mother Machree, my Johnson liked to explode.

Screw Scarface. He could only kill me once. I needed that doll more than air.

Manny turned his back to reach for a glass. Stella stood on the brass foot rail, and leaned way over the bar. She rummaged through the understock and fished out a swanky metal flask. I'd seen it before. Some fancy-schmancy giggle juice she liked.

Manny's got eyes in the back of his head. He swiveled around and shot her the stink eye for messing with his bar. But nobody could stay sore at Stella for long. He gave her a crooked smile and set a snifter in front of her. She filled it halfway, then brought it to her lips and gazed into my eyes.

"To us, baby," she whispered, tossing it back.

The piano guy gave her the high sign. She handed me her flask and strutted toward the stage on gams that put Garbo's to shame. I settled back, sucked down another Tanqueray and refilled her snifter. Thick red goo oozed into the glass. I wrinkled my nose.

"What is this shit, Manny?"

He lowered his eyes and scrubbed an invisible speck of dirt on the bar. "Miss Estelle's private label, sir. Pardon me, won't you?" He took off to wait on some other Joe before I could get the real skinny.

Stella ended her set with, "Someone to Watch Over Me." *Our* song. Her dark eyes drifted across the bar and zeroed in on mine. When the last note faded, she took a bow and gave me the nod. I picked up our drinks and moved us over to *his* booth.

So much for keeping a low profile.

Manny darted his eyes to the clock, real regular-like, making sure I took his meaning. But he kept our elbows bent. Stella got pie-eyed. Strong juice, this hooch of hers. I picked up her snifter and swirled it beneath the light of a wall sconce.

"What is this, dollface?"

"Absinthe." She giggled and dabbed a drop of it off the table with her fingertip. Then she licked her lips, stuck her finger in her mouth and sucked it like a Hoover.

"No way," I murmured, imagining that was me in her mouth. "Absinthe is green." Between her, me, and my woody, the booth was getting tight. I took a breath and shifted sideways.

Her finger slipped from her mouth and brushed down her lip real slow. "It's my *special* blend, baby." She waved Manny over. "Pauly would like to try some of my private stock. Be a dear and bring him a snifter."

The barkeep pursed his lips. "That's your *personal* stock, ma'am. It wouldn't be to his… taste. Why don't I serve him the drink of his choice—at his *original* seat?"

"Don't test me, Manny. Bring him a glass. *Now*."

I'd never seen her so riled up. Those pretty brown peepers of hers had gone to soot. Manny plopped the closest snifter in front of me and shook his head at Estelle. "Your friend won't tolerate this well.

Neither will Mr. Capone."

"Snorky? Ha!" Stella threw back her head and cackled. "He doesn't even know I'm alive." Voices went still. Heads turned. Fuck me for an idiot. Manny was right. Time was ticking. If I didn't get the hell out of Dodge, come ten o'clock I'd be pushing up daises in the town dump. Don't get me wrong; I'd take a bullet for the dame. I just didn't wanna do it here, tonight.

I grabbed the flask from Stella and poured a splash into the snifters. "Okay, Toots. One drink. Then I gotta amscray."

"But Pauly—"

Manny growled.

"No buts."

Stella raised her drink and blew me a kiss.

"To us," I said, clinking my glass against hers.

"Down the hatch." *Shit.* That special blend of hers tasted like skunk juice and kicked like a mule. My head began to swim.

She snatched the flask from my hand and poured us another round.

"Love me, Pauly?"

"To the moon and back."

Her lips curved into a smile. "Trust me?"

"Sure. Why not?" Trust? Did she say trust? What the—

"Come with me," she said, snagging the hooch with one hand and my arm with the other. She dragged me from the booth, through the kitchen, and out the back door into the alley. We were finally alone. She guzzled that swill straight from the flask, then swiped her mouth with the back of her hand.

"How'd you like to fly away from here, Pauly? Just you and me. We could live forever."

Between Big Al and that high-test horse piss of hers, I wouldn't have made book on the next ten minutes.

She tipped another dose down my gullet.

"Let's leave, now. Tonight. Fly away, free as the birds."

I couldn't have crawled away. Did I still have legs? Hell, I didn't know.

"Don't you see, Pauly?" she whispered." I coulda left that fat cat Capone anytime I wanted. But I woulda been alone. Then you came along, and everything changed. We can do this, baby. Just you and me."

My knees buckled.

"Maybe tomorrow, dollface." I stumbled into the trash can, slid to the ground, and closed by eyes. "I don't feel so hot."

"Just one more swig. For us."

Stella dumped the rest of that dreck into my mouth. I choked it back but doubted it would stay put. She plopped down beside me, wrapped me in her arms, and nuzzled my neck.

"We did it, baby. You and me. Forever."

I opened a bleary eye and squinted into the night. The sky looked different. The rain had stopped. A full moon hung high over Stella's shoulder. She looked different, too. Her amber eyes blazed in the dark. Little feathers poked through her skin and covered her entire body. Her bones started snapping and popping and cracking and breaking. She turned her face to the sky and stretched out her arms. They turned into giant fricking wings! One by one, her pretty red nails gnarled into three-inch talons.

Stella had turned into a big-ass bird!

It all made sense in a romantic, creepy kind of way. The swill I'd been drinking had been changing me, too. How else could we fly off together? I should be sprouting my wings any time.

But Stella stomped and shrieked and bobbed her fluffy head. Fear flashed in her beady eyes. Her new coat of feathers shot from her body like tiny porcupine quills. Patches of long black fur burst through her skin in their place. She shrank to the size of a showbox, then popped out a snout and a fuzzy, striped tail.

The world spun. I rolled onto my stomach and spewed a river of Stella's special blend across the pavement. As the lights went out, she chittered in my ear.

"I'm so sorry, baby. I'll fix this. I swear."

***

Next thing I knew, the sun was up. I was sprawled spread-eagle, face-down in the alley, naked and covered with dew, my gut twisted like a pretzel, and my mouth drier than an old hooker's cooch.

I'd have given my left nut for a Bromo-Selzer.

I hauled my ass off the ground and twenty-three-skidooed before the coppers showed up. What the fuck had happened? A picture popped into my noggin: Stella.

Bits of the night looped through my brain like a bad B-movie. Stella getting me zozzled on that Jake-juice, and me sick as a dog. Flashes of glowing eyes, tails, and talons. The sound of snapping bones—and strike me dead if I'm lying—talking shoeboxes.

I was lucky I hadn't woken up dead. I swore I'd never touch her home-brewed absinthe again. Turns out, I never got the chance.

Stella disappeared like a puff of smoke.

I went back to the Green Mill and looked for her, but no dice. Big Al squatted in his booth, eyeing the doors like always, and making time with some new tootsie. I was safe. The clueless goon didn't even know I was alive.

A month or so later, I wasn't feeling myself, so I called it a night and settled up early with Manny. "There's a gorgeous moon tonight, sir," he said. "Why not step out back and get some air? You'll feel better."

Out back? In *that* alley? Not a fucking chance. "Thanks anyway, Manny. Here's a ten-spot. Keep the change."

He drummed his fingers on the bar.

"Sir, I've been meaning to apologize for the, ah, …mix-up. Quite the gaff, really."

I yanked him up by his collar, bringing us nose-to-nose.

"What mix-up?"

"All water under the bridge now," he said, cocking his head toward the door. "Follow me, please."

He pulled me through the kitchen, shoved me out the back door, and slammed it closed behind me.

At the end of the alley stood Stella. I'd have known her anywhere. Same jet-black hair, but with a single white streak down the middle. And she was shorter, lots shorter with four legs and a tail. Behind her was the fullest, brightest moon I'd ever seen. She trotted to me, wagged her furry striped tail, and sniffed my hand.

One by one, my bones broke and splintered. I doubled over and howled as they smashed back together, leaving me the size of a chihuahua, with four legs instead of two and the same striped tail as Stella.

Stella slurped my face like it was made of egg cream.

"Sorry about the screw-up, baby."

"Enough with the tongue," I growled, batting her away with my paw.

"You was supposed to turn into a Were-raptor, like me, so we could fly away. But I grabbed Benny the bouncer's flask by mistake. He's a Were…rodent. And well, now we're—"

"Skunks, Stella. We're freaking skunks."

"Aw, don't be sore, Pauly," she chittered. "Let's blow this popsicle stand. We're free. And we're going to live forever."

Stella and me. Were-skunks. Together. Forever.

Fuck me for an idiot.

Darkness Peering

by Ben Monroe

Bertram Thomassen rattled the shop's security gate open, sliding it up overhead, then glanced at the chipped and worn watch on his wrist. It was 11:25 in the morning and while Bertram felt a bit guilty about opening the shop half an hour past the posted opening time, he also knew there was little chance he'd missed any potential customers. Business at his shop, Bits & Pieces, had never been what anyone would consider brisk.

The store sold bric-a-brac, collectibles, and antiques. Seemingly random items he'd purchased or collected over the years. Mostly things that Bertram found on his travels and wanderings, and the occasional heirloom or gewgaw brought in by someone in need of quick cash. Still, he had an expert eye and the store turned a modest profit.

Rainwater drizzled from his scalp and got in his eyes as he unlocked the shop. Bertram ran a hand through his unkempt, rain-soaked jet-black hair to get it out of his face. Blinking water from his eyes, he unlocked the shop's front door and walked inside.

He flipped on the lights as he entered the shop. A quick glance around showed him that nothing had moved, or been removed. Bits & Pieces wasn't the sort of place that got robbed for its stock. Assorted taxidermied animal heads hung on the walls overhead: deer, boar, and alligator. The north wall held a large variety of unorganized paperback books of multiple genres and topics. Snow globes, lace doilies, porcelain miniatures, and an astounding array of random ephemera filled the center of the store. He kept the only items of any real worth in the back, where a nonsensical array of jewelry, watches, collectible coins and stamps, and other semiprecious small items, lurked under a glass counter where he could monitor them.

He took a deep breath, inhaled the heady scent of dust, polish, and disappointment. He breathed out a long sigh and entered the store, grudgingly ready to start the day.

Shortly past noon, while Bertram was dusting a shelf of clocks, two young women entered the shop. One blonde, one brunette, both dressed casually and sprinkled with a smattering of glittering raindrops. He turned toward them and said, "Please let me know if there's anything I can help you with." He recognized one of them, the blonde. Kelly, he remembered. She worked at the cafe a few blocks down from his shop. He'd eaten there a few times, and she'd always been pleasant to him.

As the women perused the wares, he heard them whispering. "It's like an episode of *Hoarders* threw up all over this place," the brunette said, then skirted around a stack of *National Geographics* to skim the wall of paperbacks.

Bertram smiled to himself. He couldn't say she was wrong. He finished up the dusting and took up his position behind the shop's counter.

"Excuse me," the blonde said as she approached.

"Yes, how may I help you?" he said, forcing a smile and tenting his fingers as he leaned forward.

She paused.

"Don't I know you?" she said.

He nodded. "You work at the Spring Chicken Café, don't you?" he asked. "I've eaten there before. Kelly, right?"

"Oh, sure," she said. "That must be it. How do you know my name?"

"You've waited on me a few times, I think. And you usually wear a name badge. I have a good memory."

"Of course."

"So, how may I help you?" He couldn't help noticing that up close, she was altogether lovely.

"I have a few items I was hoping to sell." She reached into her purse and removed a small wooden jewelry box. Opening it, she turned it toward him. Inside were a few rings, necklaces, earrings. Gold, silver, and a few small diamonds glittered in the shop's gloom.

"I see," Bertram said. He took the box between his long-fingered hands, sliding it closer toward him. He leaned over and peered at the contents.

"Do you mind if I ask why you want to sell these?" he asked.

"They were my grandmother's," she said. "She passed away a couple of years ago and left them to me. They're lovely, but they're really not my style. And, well…" she trailed off.

"You find yourself in need of quick cash?" Bertram said, looking up at her. He noticed a quick flash of distress cross her face.

"Yes," she said. "I suppose that's it."

"I understand," he replied. "And you're looking to sell, not pawn?"

"Right," she said. "I just need the cash."

"Well. Let's take a closer look, shall we?" He slid on a pair of cotton gloves, took a jeweler's loupe from a small soft cloth bag and examined each piece. He held each one up to a bright light and viewed it through the loupe, noticing the generally excellent condition of each item.

"Your grandmother took good care of these pieces," he said. "And you're certain you want to sell them?"

She shrugged and nodded.

"Yes," she said. "I'm certain."

He mulled them over in his head.

"I can offer you $750 cash."

It was a fair price, he thought, but noticed an obvious disappointment cross her face. She was closer to him now, and in the lamp's light he saw a fading bruise around the right side of her face. She'd covered it with makeup, but he could still make out the pale blue and yellow corona around her eye.

"Can I think about it for a minute?" Kelly asked.

"Of course," he said. "Take all the time you need."

She turned and walked across the store to meet her friend. They chatted for a minute, their voices low and quiet. Bertram turned to the shop's computer, while watching the women out of the corner of his eye. After a moment, Kelly returned, forcing a smile.

"Okay, I'll take it," she said.

"Marvelous," Bertram replied. Under the counter he kept a few thousand dollars in cash for purchases such as this. He counted out $750 and slid it across toward her. "Would you like to keep the box?"

"No," she replied. "You keep it."

She placed the cash into her purse and turned to go.

"I'm sorry, one last thing," he said, as he opened a receipt book. "I need your name and address for my records. It's a formality, but if I get audited…" He trailed off and shrugged.

"Of course," she said, and handed him her driver's license.

Bertram noted her name, address, and the details of the transaction on a receipt. He tore off the customer copy and handed it to her, staring into pale blue eyes. She took the receipt and shoved it into her purse.

"Thanks," she said and turned to leave.

"You're quite welcome," he replied. He watched her and her companion leave the shop. As the door closed behind them, his eyes dropped to the receipt book and her address. It wasn't far from the shop. Only a few blocks north.

For the next half hour, he wrote prices on little white stickers for each of the items she'd sold. It would take a while to move them, but he stood to make a decent profit in time. She wasn't the first young person who'd come into his shop looking to sell something for quick cash. But he couldn't help wondering what it was she needed the money for.

***

Kelly Felix sat at the small desk in her apartment, looking out onto a sparse yard. The open window faced east, and with the sun setting in the west, the yard before her was bathed in shadow. A warm breeze fluttered the curtains pulled open on either side of the window, carrying a faint scent of jasmine with it.

She spread the bills she'd received at the pawn shop out in front of her, counting them again to make sure they were all there. She hadn't bothered counting them at the store, as the guy behind the counter had given her the creeps and she'd wanted to leave before the creep asked her out on a date. And he knew where she worked, too, which added a whole extra layer of creepy to the guy.

Still, she wouldn't be working there much longer. And she could thank the creep for that. The money he'd paid her for her grandmother's jewelry would get her a bus ticket out of town and settled somewhere else. She was disheartened about having sold the jewelry, but her grandmother would have understood.

She glanced out the window, staring at the large Japanese maple tree in the yard in front of her building. The crimson leaves were returning with the start of spring. The tree's branches had grown up around the power lines, and she saw a large raven perched on the line. It was larger than any bird she'd ever seen outside of a zoo. Almost hidden behind a tangle of branches, it was staring back at her. As if it had been observing her when she glanced up.

182

A knock at her bedroom door shook her out of her thoughts.

"Kelly?" her roommate, Tabitha, asked from beyond the door. "You okay in there?"

Kelly turned to the door.

"Yeah, Tabs, come on in," she said.

The door opened as Tabitha entered.

"Think you've got enough?" she said, pointing at the stack of bills.

"I think so," Kelly said. "Enough to get me out of town, anyway. I won't go home in style, but I'll be okay. I can stay with my folks while I get back on my feet."

"I'll be sorry to see you go," Tabitha said. "But I understand, of course."

"Thanks," Kelly said. "I hate to leave you in a pinch. You're sure you won't have trouble finding a new roommate?"

Tabitha shook her head.

"No, not at all. Don't worry about it. When are you leaving?"

"A couple of days, I think. Joe's out of town for another few days. I want to be long gone before he gets back."

Tabitha nodded.

"Too bad you can't just call the cops on him."

Kelly turned back to her desk, scooped up the cash and stuffed it into a drawer.

"Fat lot of good that would do. Blue brotherhood and all that bullshit."

"You don't think he'll be able to track you down?"

"I don't know. Maybe," Kelly said. "I guess I'm just hoping that he won't bother when I'm on the other side of the continent."

Tabitha leaned forward and gave Kelly a long hug. "You'll be fine," she said. "Just get California behind you. Everything will work out. You'll see."

Kelly hugged her back, then pulled away.

"Sure," she said.

"One day at a time."

She looked out the window again. The raven remained in the tree just a few yards away.

"Guess I should get ready for work," Kelly said. "You want me to bring you anything?"

"I wouldn't say no to a slice of Gene's famous cherry pie," Tabitha said.

"You got it."

***

The day's rain had ended by mid-afternoon, and washed the coastal city of Alcosta, California clean. The warm scent of petrichor still hung in the air as Bertram walked along the darkening streets. The sun had just set, and full dark was still at least an hour away. He snugged into his dark overcoat, keeping the evening's growing chill at bay.

The Spring Chicken was only a short walk from Bits & Pieces, and it didn't take him long to get there. He walked past a large window facing the street and was pleased to see the little cafe wasn't very busy that evening. He saw the girl who'd stopped by the shop earlier within, waiting on a table. She was wearing light blue jeans, her hair pulled back in a tight ponytail. He paused for a moment, then opened the oak-framed glass door and entered the small cafe. The smells of coffee, fresh bread and pastries saturated him.

Kelly recognized him when he came in and gave him a half-hearted smile. She wiped her hands on her apron and approached him.

"Hello again," she said.

Bertram could tell she was sizing him up.

Probably thinks I'm stalking her, he thought. He smiled back at her.

"Indeed," he said. "Just stopped by on my way home for a cup of coffee."

"Well, we have plenty of that," she said, and gestured toward the menu board hanging over the counter where a dizzying array of coffees and drink styles were scrawled in multicolored chalk. A tall, thin man stood behind the counter, reading the day's paper, and keeping an eye on their conversation.

Bertram nodded as he looked at the menu, then leaned in closer, lowering his voice to a conspiratorial whisper.

"I was also hoping to speak with you briefly," he said.

Kelly's face went stoic, stone-like.

"Look, you seem like a nice guy, but I'm not really interested. I have a boyfriend."

Bertram smiled, a razor-thin smirk.

"Of course you do. A pretty woman such as yourself? That's to be expected."

"Right," she said, and walked toward the counter. "So what can I get you?"

"Oh, an espresso, and one of those biscotti," he said, pointing at a glass jar full of the hard cookies. "But I didn't stroll over here to inquire about a date. Rather, I feel I owe you something of an apology."

Her left eye arched up. In surprise or cynicism, he couldn't be sure. She turned to the barista, "Gene, can you pour an espresso?" The barista gave her a thumb's up. "How's that?" she said, turning back to Bertram.

"Well, I spent some time looking over the items you brought in earlier, and I fear they're worth a bit more than I'd estimated."

"Is that so?" she said, crossing her arms and leaning back against the countertop.

"Indeed it is," he said. "I feel like I owe you a bit more than I'd paid you." He fished in the pocket of his dark overcoat, pulled out a thick letter-sized envelope, and presented it to her.

She looked at it suspiciously.

"You could have just kept it and I'd have been none the wiser."

"I suppose I could have done that," Bertram replied. "But the guilt would peck at me. Please take it."

He handed the envelope to her again. Kelly took it, opened it up and stared in disbelief at the sheaf of bills inside.

"No strings, no tricks," he said.

The barista slid the espresso and biscotti across the counter. Bertram handed him a bill in return and then deposited the change in the tip jar.

"Besides," Bertram said. "You look like you needed it."

"Why do you say that?" Kelly asked.

A thin smile creased his lips.

"Just say a little bird told me."

Kelly was about to reply when the door chimed as someone entered the cafe. She glanced at the door and her eyes went wide.

"Shit," she muttered.

Bertram turned around to see who had caught her eye. Standing in front of the door stood a mountain of a man, disheveled and looking like he was getting over a three-day binge.

"Someone you know?" he said to Kelly.

She walked past him, dismissive.

"Who's that?" Bertram said to the barista.

"Joe Mesling. Her boyfriend," Gene replied. "Dude's an asshole. I don't know what she sees in him."

Bertram watched as Kelly approached the man and gave him a quick hug.

"I thought you weren't coming back for a few days," she said. She could smell the beer on his breath. Never a good sign.

"Got bored," he said. "Hunting was no good, and I got tired of fishing. Besides, Cliff's an asshole and I got sick of him running his mouth."

Bertram took his order and sat at a small table. He placed himself so he could monitor the exchange.

"What time you get off tonight?" Joe said. His eyes crawled over her curves like some loathsome clinging insect.

"Late," she said.

"I'll wait around," Joe replied. Then he noticed the envelope tucked into the pocket of her apron.

"What's that?"

She looked down. Bertram could tell she was becoming anxious. He saw her hands trembling and a flush rise in her cheeks.

"Nothing," she said.

Joe's hand shot out and pinched the envelope between two sausage-like fingers, sliding it out of her apron in one smooth motion.

"Doesn't look like nothing," he said. He ripped the envelope open and saw the stack of bills inside.

"What's this?" he growled.

"It's none of your business, Joe," she replied and took a step back. Joe's other hand shot out and grabbed her by the wrist.

"Stop it," she said, squirming and pulling her arm. "Joe, you're hurting me."

She looked to Gene for help, but the barista just lowered his eyes to the floor.

He held the bills up in front of her face.

"I'm going to ask you again, where'd you get these?"

Bertram stood and approached the pair.

"With all due respect," he said. "I think she asked you to let her go."

Joe turned his head and looked at Bertram with cold, dark eyes.

Bertram thought they looked like wolf's eyes. Feral and mean. Joe stood at least a foot taller than Bertram and glared down at him.

"And who the hell are you, pal?" Joe said.

"Nobody that concerns you. But you seem to be hurting the young lady, and I can't stand for that."

"Do you know who I am?" Joe said.

"Joe, stop it," Kelly said, tugging her hand again. Joe let her go, and she stumbled back when unexpectedly released.

"I do," Bertram said. "You're Kelly's boyfriend, and a police officer. And I think you should leave."

Joe looked around the cafe. There were only two other patrons within, who'd forgotten their coffees and were staring at the confrontation.

"You gonna make me, tough guy?" Joe said, taking a step toward Bertram.

"If necessary," Bertram replied. "I'm not fond of bullies."

Joe turned as if to leave, then snapped back, delivering a hammer blow with his fist to the side of Bertram's head. Bertram dropped to the floor, then tried to rise onto his hands and knees. Distantly, as if through water, Bertram heard Kelly yelling at Joe, telling him to stop. Pain exploded through his side as Joe's foot collided with his ribs. He felt himself dragged up off the ground. Joe had him by the collar and lifted a foot above the floor.

Then he was sailing through the air. He flew through the glass of the front window into the night outside. Bertram hit the concrete sidewalk in front of the cafe in a glittering spray of broken glass.

But when Kelly sprinted through the door, searching the street for any sign of him, he was gone. She looked up and down the street but he'd disappeared.

Joe lumbered through after her.

"Chicken-shit asshole took off," Joe said.

"Damn you," Kelly said, turning to him, her eyes full of hate. "You could have really hurt him."

"Big fucking deal," Joe said. "Now, you going to tell me where you got that money, or not? You steal it?"

"Get out of here," she said. "I never want to see you—" Her sentence was cut off as Joe's meaty hand collided across the side of her face with a sharp, cracking slap. Kelly fell to the sidewalk and pain shot through her leg as her knee collided with the hard concrete.

Joe took a step forward.

"Why do you always push me like that?" he said.

He leaned forward, grabbed her by the wrist and dragged her up. She pulled away, slapping at his arm with her free hand.

"Let me go, you bastard!" she yelled.

He raised his hand overhead. Just as it began its descent, something black flashed between them and Joe shrieked. A line of scarlet formed across his left cheek and up to his forehead, and suddenly blood flowed.

"What the hell?" he said, letting go of Kelly and slapping his hand to his face. Blood ran out between his fingers, down his wrist.

The black shape fell out of the night sky again. A raven, huge and menacing. Large like the one Kelly had seen peeking in her window earlier that afternoon. It buffeted Joe with its wings while tearing at his face and scalp with its talons. Joe flailed at it with his free hand as blood flooded down his torn face.

Joe stumbled backward. His heel caught on a crack in the sidewalk, and he fell onto his back. In an instant, the massive raven was on him, pecking and tearing. Joe shrieked as the bird stabbed out his eyes one after the other. Again and again, it pecked at the sockets, deeper each time.

Joe grabbed at the bird, catching it by one wing and squeezing. Kelly heard something snap, and the raven reared its head back, opening its beak wide and croaking in a strangely human cry of pain.

Then a thrust of its beak, stabbing deep into Joe's left eye socket. A last spasm, and Joe lay still on the ground. Blood trickled from his torn face, mixing with thick, jellied vitreous which oozed from the ruin of his eyes.

The raven hopped off Joe's chest and walked toward Kelly, dragging its broken wing beside it. It looked at her, stared right at her, then to her amazement it lowered its head as if bowing. A final *kaw* and it hopped away, down past the café, disappearing into an alley. She watched after it for a moment before turning back to Joe.

A single thought—*I'm free*—was drowned out by the sound of distant sirens approaching.

***

Golden morning sunlight gleamed through the front window of Bits & Pieces as Bertram tidied the displays of knick-knacks with his off-hand. He was alphabetizing a box of vintage LPs when the front door opened with a faint tinkle from the bell overhead. He looked up to see Kelly enter, carrying a pink box in one hand.

"Hello again," he said as she stepped into the shop.

"Hi," she replied. "I wanted to check in. Make sure you were okay."

Bertram shrugged and raised his arm. It was bound in a plaster cast and supported in a sling wrapped around his shoulder.

"A bit worse for wear, but I'll survive," he said.

"That's good," she said. "I brought you this."

She placed the pink box on the counter.

"Cherry pie, specialty of the house. Just to say thanks, and that I'm sorry."

He nodded toward her. For a moment, Kelly thought of the raven the night before. The way it had seemed to bow to her.

"I'm sorry to hear about your friend," he said. "I assume the police will be giving him a hero's send off."

She shrugged.

"Probably. It was the damnedest thing," Kelly said. "I've never seen anything like it. That bird just came out of nowhere and attacked him."

Bertram nodded. "Ravens are curious creatures," he said. "Very territorial, and can be quite protective. In any case, I dare say you're better off without him in your life. You're free of him now."

"I am," she said. She seemed to stand a little taller when she spoke. As if a burden had been lifted off her shoulders.

"I'll never have to worry about him hurting me ever again."

"No, you certainly won't," Bertram said. "Nevermore."

The Crow's Nest
by Stephanie Wytovich

I am a murder, blood-soaked and
ravenous, the black cloud perched
outside your house, my belly
swollen, the bones of mice lodged
in my throat.
I break my nose into beaks, spread
my arms into wings. I am a reaper,
a war cry, a voyeur to the study
of carnage, my eyes a violence
piercing through a hangman's tree.
When the moon sleeps, I hold a
funeral, my body a switch blade,
a spell falling from the sky: naked,
anointed. I am feathers and darkness,
an exhalation of flight, of shadow—
      my nest a church, a convent,
      an ever-expanding grave.

The Travelers

by Laurel Hightower

The witch hunters had come for her. Jill wanted to believe differently, but she didn't have the luxury. The rising hum of voices from her lawn was too familiar, the atmosphere charged with the tang of threatened violence.

She kept her head in the sand long enough to finish her thought, then closed the leather-bound journal Daron had found for her two houses ago, when she first realized she needed to make a record. She kept her hands on its soft front cover, taking comfort from the words inside. At least if things went bad this time, there would be a part of herself left for her girls. She pushed away from the little writing desk in the corner of the sky-blue living room and went to the window, her stomach churning. Parting the soft white curtains, she saw what she knew she would. A mob. Only ten or so strong, but it would get bigger. They always did.

She sighed, exhaustion settling in her chest and shoulders. Three and a half weeks. That was a new record – it usually didn't take this long for the inquisition to come. Her mouth twisted and she wished she could lay down on the scuffed maple floors and never move again.

"Daron," she called up the stairs.

"I see them," he replied, a grim note in his voice. He was already transitioning from happy-suburban-dad to survival-man, and a rush of gratitude lifted her heart before guilt brought it crashing back down.

The sound of opening drawers and backpack zippers floated down to her. The girls would be packing, too, better at it than they should have to be. It was a shit world they lived in now, but it shouldn't be this shit. Other survivors had made lives for themselves, created a new normal. That was all she wanted for her family, but it never seemed to stick.

She looked around the cheerful living room, to the brick fireplace they'd been looking forward to using when the nights got colder. To the little white desk she wrote at every day, and those curtains like puffy clouds against the blue walls. Tears started in her eyes and regret dropped her stomach. She shouldn't have gotten attached. But she was so tired, they all were, and things had seemed perfect at The Enclave. She thought they'd put enough distance between themselves and the last place that they might have a chance, but the Puritan spirit of blaming your fellows for acts of God was still alive and well in New England.

She went to the window again, saw the crowd had doubled. At least twenty of her neighbors stood outside on her lawn, faces drawn and closed against her, sunglasses shading any chance she had of looking into their hearts. Most of the women stood with their arms crossed, hugging themselves in the heat, and Jill wanted to believe it was because they weren't okay with what was about to happen. It was too much to hope for anyone to stand up for them – that was a rare occurrence, and one she never pinned her chances on. But believing at least some of these women wished her well, that would ease the sting.

Daron called something unintelligible to the girls before coming down the stairs to stand at Jill's back, a hand on her shoulder.

"How bad?" he asked.

Jill shrugged.

"They haven't thrown anything yet, and I don't see any weapons, but it's only a matter of time. I think they're waiting on someone."

"That Tybee asshole?" he asked, his tone hardening.

"I'd assume so."

"I hate that fucker," Daron said, teeth grinding.

She patted his hand, drew in a shaky breath.

"If it wasn't him, it'd be someone else. You know how this goes. How are the girls?"

He sighed and put his free hand on her other shoulder.

"About like you'd expect. Layla's crying—she likes that Thorne boy. She doesn't want to leave him behind."

Jill felt a stab of pain for her youngest daughter. Thirteen was hard, and budding romance was one of the few joys of life at that age.

"What about Hailey?" she asked, knowing the answer already.

Daron's grip on her shoulders tightened. "She's pissed."

"How pissed?"

He shrugged, gazing out at the people working themselves into a lather a few feet away.

"She's not talking, but I know that look." He kissed her jaw. "Seen it often enough on her mom."

Jill nodded, a low throb of worry making her queasy. They had time, but not much.

"Is it worth it, do you think?" She gestured to the crowd outside. "To try to talk them out of it? Maybe all they need is to see that we're like them. An answer to whatever Tybee's accused us of."

Daron snorted.

"Lawrence Tybee is one of the dumbest sons a bitches I've come across, so in a straightforward battle of intellect, you'd win, no problem."

"But," she prodded him.

"But you can't argue with zealotry. They've decided to pin something on us, and they won't let it go."

"On me, you mean," she said, giving him a faint smile so he wouldn't feel the need to refute it. "I wonder what it is, this time. Think somebody ended up with a two-headed calf?"

"You don't know of anything?" he asked, refusing to be drawn into her lame joke.

"Not that I've heard." She chewed her lip, trying not to get lost in the tide of *it's not fair* threatening to sweep her away. She caught sight of Clint Channing, standing far back by the road, his craggy face stoic, his jaw set. He was one of the good ones, a social worker in his prior life. Often treated as a de facto leader in the settlement, but that didn't mean he could stop what was about to happen. Still, seeing him gave her enough hope to make an effort.

"Jillie, please don't," said Daron when he felt her shoulders go back, her spine straighten. "It won't do any good. We need to just finish getting what we can and get out of here. If we go now, they might let us out without trouble." Fear cracked his voice on the last word, and she almost let it sway her.

Her gaze caught on the cutting board stretched across the sink, all the cans of food and jars of spices Daron experimented with on a nightly basis. Relearning to cook with limited supplies, finding his place in the world again. She took a breath, turned and stood on tiptoe to kiss him. "Make sure the girls are done. Do you mind to pack my bag?"

His mouth twisted on one side.

"Already done."

He gripped her shoulders for long seconds before he let her go, resignation deflating him.

"Be safe, okay? You only *think* you're invincible. One of these days you're going to get hurt."

She squeezed his hand.

"If it gets bad, I'll give it up. *Before* anything bad happens. Promise."

He followed her to the door, kissed her again, and closed it behind her after she'd stepped out into the waning afternoon sun. She tucked her trembling hands into her pockets, breathed slow to steady her thumping heart. She went to the edge of the wooden, wraparound porch, and peered into the crowd. They got quiet. Maybe they hadn't expected to have to face her before they drove her family out of town. She studied them; the way they'd moved closer together as soon as they saw her. The hard lines of their mouths, the way no one would meet her eye, even behind sunglasses.

"Clint?" she called. "What's going on here?"

He met her eyes and his mouth went sour, then he ambled a few steps closer, favoring his left knee.

"Wish I knew, Jill," he replied in a voice that cut easily through the ambient noise. "I'm hoping these folks are gonna come to their senses and leave you nice people alone."

"Nice people?" came an exaggerated drawl from the yard of a vacant house further down the street. "Now I don't think you can really say that in all honesty, can you, Clint?"

Jill bit her lips. Lawrence Tybee was from New Jersey, but he loved recasting himself as a good ole' country boy, just for moments like this. As a native southerner it pissed her off. Have the courage to be a bigot in your own accent, she thought.

He came into sight, moving in a theatrical manner, hands at his belt. He was nothing special, a middle-aged man the same flavor you used to be able to find all over the country. Her trepidation made him appear sinister, larger than he was. His denim jacket, too hot for the temperature, was open just enough to show a cross-body gun holster. Whether he actually had a firearm and the ammunition to back it up, she didn't know, but she felt her window of time slamming closed.

"We *believed* they were nice folks—that's why we let them in. Why we opened our arms and hearts, offered the protection of our borders. Hell, I brought 'em a six pack by way of welcome."

He shook his head.

"We thought they were survivors, like any of us."

Jill remembered Tybee's visit, on their first full day at The Enclave. The way he lingered, eyes on everything, his smile anything but sincere. She hadn't liked him, got an off vibe from him, the kind she never used to give herself permission to pay attention to. But Jill's days of repressing her own instincts were long gone. She'd rather turn away a hundred good people than let her guard down with a single predator in the midst of her family. And anyway, the six pack he brought had been IPA. No points for that one.

"We *are* just like any of you," she said, the strength of her voice carrying over the length of the street. "We're just people, trying to put ourselves back together. We're grateful for the community here. We need it as much as any of you. My girls—"

"Your *girls* are why we're here, Jill," he interrupted.

A spike of adrenaline ran through her like lightning. She tamped down on the immediate desire to jump the guy and kick his teeth in. It helped that she could feel the crowd pulling away from Tybee, a wave of unease rippling through a crowd that had grown to thirty or more.

"What about my girls?" Jill asked in a low, calm voice.

He stopped a few yards away from the porch, and the crowd made room for him.

"Look around you. At the devastation these good people have suffered. Since two Novembers ago, every person in this community has lost loved ones. Ever since the red sky, when those sickos showed up, there ain't a one of us that hasn't had family ripped from us. Some of us came back to empty houses, some had to watch while our children or wives or husbands were dragged away screaming, but either way, we all knew where they'd end up. Nothing but scattered teeth in a pile of shit."

He stepped closer, pulled his sunglasses off to meet Jill's eye.

"You ever tried to identify someone you loved by their dentals like that? *Know* they'd been eaten by their own kind?"

There was a muffled sob from somewhere in the back, and Jill hoped it meant Tybee had gone too far. People were still healing, many never would. No one wanted to hear their suffering drilled down to something like that. She might have a chance.

She looked out into the sea of faces, many of them pointed at the ground now.

"I haven't had to do that, no. I thank God for it every day, and my heart aches for those of you who have."

"But *why* haven't you, Jill? Why is it that out of every blessed person in this whole world, you're the only one whose family is intact?"

He gestured to the home behind her, and her heart rate kicked up. She took a breath, counted the release. She couldn't afford to lose her temper.

"I don't know why. There's nothing special about us—just blind luck. We've been all over since it happened, and I've seen the same suffering everywhere. I wish I could help, that no one had to deal with it, but I won't apologize for my family's safety."

Tybee turned, hands on his hips, and paced a few steps to his right before looking at her again.

"That's another interesting thing about y'all."

The "y'all" was stiff on his lips, not a colloquialism he was comfortable using, and it grated on her.

"You *have* been all over, haven't you? Traveled halfway across the country, even as unsafe as it is. Roving bands moving into the cities, and as soon as the sun goes down…" He made a whistling sound through his teeth and clapped his hands together.

Jill assumed he meant to convey the idea of cannibals creeping out from the darkness. Ones that no one had seen or known about until the day the sky went red all over the world. Not a good red, like before a storm, or a particularly striking sunset. A dark, unhealthy red, stilling the breeze, suffocating the sky. She'd expected heat, like maybe the sun had finally gotten tired of their shit and was going to wipe them out, but instead everything was just still. Waiting.

Until they came slinking from the shadows that night. The sun had gone down like always, but it hadn't had an effect on the eerie red light. No one was sleeping, or going to work, or doing anything much but staring at the sky, so people were watching when the first ones appeared. Hulking, ragged forms with dead eyes and filed teeth, hair matted and filthy, a stench like body odor smeared with feces. What clothing they wore was stiff with blood and other fluids, and Jill had been close enough to see what looked like a bit of fallen flesh smeared into the cloth.

She'd been standing on her porch, the first one, back at their real home in South Carolina. Watched as things that could almost be human pulled themselves across silent streets, moving low to the ground, oozing across lawns and up porch steps. Their familiarity almost tricked her—she stayed still too long, heart pounding, wondering if they could be what she'd looked for all her life. Had they come here for her?

Then one slithered to the ground floor window of her neighbor's ranch house across the street, stretched to its full height, and hope came crashing down. These were people, yet not—dirty husks full of nothing but hunger. And they were dining on her neighbors.

Jill wanted to warn them, had already stepped onto her walkway to holler though she didn't know what name to call. People on their street knew the names of dogs and kids, but never adults, and until right that second, she'd loved the arrangement. But before she could decide whether screaming the dog's name would elicit the right attention, the creature punched its way through the glass and climbed inside, moving too fast to give the people inside a chance.

Screaming from deeper in the house started after that, and

barking, but Jill caught movement in her right peripheral. She turned, almost too late to stop the man, monster, whatever the fuck it was from grabbing her by the hair. She dodged its swiping hands, her eyes watering at the stench of it, then she made it to the front door and into the house, gathering her family to make a run for it.

They'd been running ever since. It was incredible how fast things had fallen apart. It didn't seem possible that subhuman cannibals could have consumed so much of the world's population in such a short time, and there were theories that the red sky had caused other catastrophes, killed in other ways. Contaminated food, water, air. It had stayed crimson for a full week before fading; anything could have happened. Jill never stopped running long enough to investigate.

Sometimes they lived in settlements like The Enclave, more often they were on their own. That was the dangerous time. The maneaters had learned early on that a well-prepared group of humans could inflict a hell of a lot of damage, now they knew what to expect. That wariness accounted for some of the safety in numbers, but it made her uneasy, wondering what the things were up to when they weren't hunting. Whether they were leaving pockets of humanity intact for some nefarious purpose. Whatever the reason, they preferred to pick off the lonely and the weak. Jill Lanscombe was anything but weak, and she'd done what she needed to keep her family alive. It pissed her off to hear Tybee dismiss that effort, like she hadn't earned her family's lives.

"You're right. Being on the road like that is dangerous as hell, which is why we're here now. Why we want to *stay* here."

Tybee shook his head.

"Amazing that even after all that time, all that traveling, you still didn't lose anybody. That's more than good luck – it's damn near unbelievable."

She held his smug gaze, her molars grinding.

"It wasn't easy."

He hitched his pants up and smiled.

"I'd imagine not. Maybe you can fill us all in on how you managed it, seeing as how even here, with all the protections we have in place, we've still lost people. If you know the secret to keeping safe from these things, we'd love to hear it."

She knew they wouldn't. No one ever did, but telling them so only made things worse, so she kept her silence.

Tybee raised his eyebrows, threw his hands up when she didn't answer.

"If that one's too hard, maybe you could tell us why you had to do all that travelin'. Why you waited this long to settle somewhere, seek out your fellow man."

Jill's skin erupted in goose bumps, her face alternately hot and cold while her panicked mind sought an answer. He couldn't know about those other places. People didn't travel the way they used to, and there were no methods of long-distance communication left. No phones, no internet, no mail service. If news needed to travel, it went by foot, and with the dangers that presented, news usually stayed put.

Looking at Tybee, that shit-eating grin plastered across his face, she knew it didn't matter how he knew, or if he even did. Maybe he'd just guessed, was throwing everything at the wall to see what would stick. If so, he'd gotten lucky—Jill knew from experience there was no right answer she could give.

The mood of the crowd got dark again, faces hardening, angry words muttered. She was an idiot to have attempted this, and she knew Daron was going crazy inside the house. She hoped he would get the girls out the back and trust her to take care of herself.

"We're waiting," said Tybee.

Jill looked over at Clint, reading regret in his hound dog expression, but no salvation. She lifted her shoulders. Nothing to lose now by telling the truth.

"We've tried it before," she said, her voice low. "Joined places like this. But people don't like newcomers, past a certain point. Once they've gotten over the worry, they'll never see another person again, once they've made themselves comfortable, anyone after that becomes an outsider."

She gave a tired smile.

"Outsiders are easy to blame for things that go wrong."

He nodded.

"Uh huh, uh huh. I can see that. So just a big misunderstanding, huh?"

Jill's lips thinned.

"You could call it that."

"Mm hmm. A big ole misunderstanding, nine different times." He whistled. "That's quite the record."

Fuck. He *had* known, had talked to someone, but who? She would have recognized anyone who came from those places. Her eyes scanned the crowd as another ripple ran through it, voices getting louder, eyes running up and down her with blatant distrust. She saw Julia Thorne, the mother of Layla's boyfriend, step back from Tybee, her mouth twisting, refusing to look at Jill. Damn. They'd taught the girls to be so careful, but Layla was thirteen. She needed kids her own age, and confidantes that didn't include her family. Jill bit her lip and hoped her daughter never learned who'd betrayed them. She didn't need to carry that kind of guilt on top of everything else.

Jill lifted her chin.

"It doesn't matter what I say. Your minds are made up. Whatever inconvenience, oddity, bad luck you're blaming on us, you're going to keep doing it. We'll go."

He almost let her. She was close enough to brush the door handle when his voice cut through all the others, quivering with righteous indignation.

"Bad luck? *Inconvenience*? That's what you call it when a man is murdered?"

She froze, stomach in free fall.

"Murdered?" she said, turning. "How?"

"Eaten," he said, the single word clenching the gut of everyone in hearing.

"By *them*."

She stared past him, mind working, presenting possibilities that were all discarded.

"That's not possible," she said.

Tybee crowed; it was the moment he'd been waiting for but she didn't understand why. The maneaters might be nominally human, but they were easily distinguishable from everyone else. He couldn't believe anyone in her family had done this.

He took several steps closer, set one boot on the lowest step of the porch.

"Maybe you can tell me why it's impossible that Mike Angel was pulled from the path where he was walking patrol last night, dragged half a mile from town, and chewed on like a dog toy. World's full of maneaters now, isn't it? Why'd you find it hard to believe one of them breached our perimeter, took one of our people? It's happened before."

She couldn't answer him, couldn't tell these people she would have known if one of the cannibals had gotten through. She shook her head, squinted against a nascent headache.

"I still don't understand what you're accusing us of."

Tybee climbed to the next step; his gaze locked with hers.

"I know exactly what you are, Jill Lanscombe, and your chickens have come home to roost."

Fear flared her nostrils and stiffened her back. For the length of three heartbeats, she believed him. Believed he could look into her soul and see the secrets hidden there. Part of her was glad. The relief of it, of being able to give up, stop running, stop hiding. She almost gave into it, into him.

Then she thought of Daron, and the girls. Of the leather-bound journal with so many pages left unfilled, and she drew back from him. She let anger rise and burn through her, lifting a derisive lip.

"And what am I?"

There was a long silence while she waited for the truth to come, for these people to see her for who she was.

"You're a damned turncoat is what you are," snarled the man, triumph in his voice.

It took her seconds to process his words.

"A what?" she asked finally.

"A betraying bitch—you led those bastards straight to us, let them in, showed them how to get to the meat inside. You've probably been doing it since the beginning—selling out your neighbors to save your own skin. *That's* why nine other settlements have chased you off."

Jill laughed. It was the wrong reaction—the crowd would call her callous, take it to mean she didn't care about Mike Angel or any of the rest of them. But she couldn't help herself—she'd been ready to give everything up, put her fate in this faux redneck's hands, actually believing he'd somehow seen through her. Instead, he thought she was sneaking through the shadows, making deals with creatures that had no capacity for empathy or reason. That she somehow had the power to not only barter with the maneaters, but hold them to their promises. The first laugh was joined by a second, and she put a hand across her mouth to stifle more.

If she'd reacted any other way, they might have let her go—at the core, these were tired, frightened people who only wanted life to go back to the way it had been. They had little capacity for violence, and no energy to waste on chasing her down and enacting a vengeance only half of them believed in. But laughter flips a switch in some people, and Lawrence Tybee was one of them.

He lunged the rest of the way up the steps, grabbed her arm in a painful grip.

"Funny, is it? Think it'll still be funny when we string you up? Leave you dangling until night time, when your friends will come out of the shadows and finish our work?"

"What?" she asked, trying to pull away as he yanked her off balance, dragged her down the steps. She fell hard on her knees before smashing her chin into the concrete walkway. The impact was jarring, the pain immediate, but Tybee didn't hesitate to twist her arm back, bringing her to her feet again. Blood pooled in her mouth and she spat it out, raising a trembling hand to her aching jaw.

More hands grabbed for her, pulling at her clothing, pinching the skin of her arms, someone grabbing her hair. It happened in the space of seconds, and she had no time to react, no time to think through what happened next.

Rage flooded her system, her vision changing, narrowing, tunneling into a bloody haze. Her breathing grew ragged, skin bubbling under the hands of her attackers. Most of them let go at the rough feel of thick fur bursting through her follicles, standing away from her but not far enough. Tybee held on, even as others began to scream.

Her joints separated and reformed with wet, gristly pops. Her jaw relocated and extended, making room for bigger, sharper teeth. Long claws burst from her fingertips and her eyes went round and black. The pain receded and she straightened to her full height, panting.

Silence reigned for several seconds while her neighbors took in what she was. Did they see, now, what they'd cost themselves? The safety she had offered?

Tybee let go of her arm and backed away, squeezing between neighbors, turning them into human shields. Jill dropped heavily to all fours and stalked after him, her enormous body swaying, ears back. People moved aside, slowly at first, until someone tried to stop her. A baseball bat made contact with her shoulder, enough to hurt, but one swipe of her three-inch claws hurt her attacker a lot more. The man screamed, his shirt and gut in ribbons. She stood once more and roared, and after that her path to Tybee cleared quickly.

He tried to run. They always did. She increased her speed, loping after him, then swiped again, claws cutting through his back like hot butter. He crashed to the ground screaming, belatedly doing the smart thing and staying down, making himself as small as possible.

She leaned in close, snuffling at his nape, his ears. The smell of shit wrinkled her sensitive nose. Lawrence Tybee was offensive, right to the very end. She lunged, locking his head in her great jaws, and felt his screams echo down her own throat. They cut off when she bit down, crushing the man's skull like a pinata. Blood and brain matter spilled from his ears down her gullet, warming her belly.

She dragged Tybee's body up to her covered porch, the one that had felt like home. His foot spasmed as it thumped up the steps, but that didn't last long. She dug her snout into his back, where she'd already cut him open, clawing his spine out of the way of the juicy innards, the tender bits.

There was no one left on the cul-de-sac to disturb her meal, not even the man she'd disemboweled. Too bad—winter was coming, and she and Hailey needed to build up their fat stores. The girl needed guidance—killing Angel had been sloppy, but that's what parents were for, after all. To teach, and to protect. They'd do better at the next place—she wouldn't let this happen again.

Nobody fucked with Mama Bear.

Trouble's Braids

A Sam Hunter Story
by Jonathan Maberry

-1-

I was sitting at my desk trying not to feel like my life was a sinking ship when the kid walked in.

Didn't know the kid. Just a kid. I knew it was a kid from the smell. Yeah, I can smell that kind of thing. Really good sense of smell. Great eyesight and hearing, too. Business sense? Not so much.

There was a little tiny knock first. Three soft raps.

"Yeah," I called.

She paused outside for a moment. Clients do that sometimes. They've gotten all the way to a private investigator's office, laden with purpose and need, but they pause at the act of commission as if my threshold is some kind of line in the sand. It usually is.

I waited.

When she opened my door, it was a tentative thing, like she was sorry for touching it, for bothering me, for a lot of stuff. Little Black girl. Big eyes and braids.

Maybe twelve, but there was something in her eyes that made her look older. Not in a good way. Not like she wanted to grow up fast; more like something had a hook in her, pulling her up out of childhood. Too fast, too far. In this part of town, you see a lot of that. Saw a lot of it back in Minneapolis when I lived there before moving to Philly. Black neighborhoods, white neighborhoods, any kind of neighborhoods where growing up poor is like being stranded on a desert island full of snakes and tigers. There's a lot of kids

208

growing up wrong because the adults in their lives never matured past their own needs into being parents. Am I bitter about that sort of shit? Yeah. No apologies.

The little girl looked at me across the nothing that was my office. I had a threadbare couch, a couple filing cabinets, a card table that was stacked with magazines and mail I didn't want to read, my desk and two visitor chairs. You could buy everything in the room for the price of a good pair of jeans. I could see her measuring the room and me against her expectations.

"You Mr. Hunter?" she asked. My name was on the door and the mailbox downstairs, but I don't toss off any of my patented smartass comments to kids.

"Sure," I said. "You need something?"

She stood in the doorway, still holding onto the knob. Still unsure.

"Google says you're a cop. Private cop. That true?"

"Sure," I said again. "Used to be a real cop but now I'm a licensed investigator."

"Google says you help people," she said.

"Depends on the kind of help. You lose something?"

"No," she said, but her eyes shifted away for a moment. There was something about my question that triggered a defensive reaction, but I'm no good at reading kids' faces. I could smell her fear, though.

"Someone go missing?" I suggested. "Your mom or dad skip out?"

She shook her head. "In the ad on the computer it says you do stuff for people."

Ah. My online ad listed my services, but I rattled off to see which one rang a bell.

"I do a bunch of things," I said. "Discrete investigations, surveillance, infidelity investigations, missing persons, skip tracing, child custody and recovery, pre-employment screenings, loss prevention, attorney services, tenant screening, service of process, deadbeat dads and moms, assets investigation, and personal protection services."

"Yeah," she said. "That one."

"Which one?"

"That last one."

"Protection services?" I asked.

She nodded. "Can I hire you for that?"

I smiled. "You want to hire me to protect you?"

"No."

"Then—?"

"It's my little brother," she said.

My smile felt like a plastic mask. "What about him?"

The girl took a small step into the room, but didn't let go of the handle. "I need you to protect him."

"Is someone hurting him?" I asked, trying not to lean too hard on the word 'hurting,' because it has all kinds of meanings and it's a fragile damn word.

Her answer surprised me, though. "No," she said. "No one's hurt him."

"Okay, so what—?"

"But they're gonna."

There was so much raw emotion in her eyes that it was painful to look at. And her small brown hand clutched the doorknob with aching force.

I said, "Then maybe you better come in and tell me about it."

-2-

The little girl's name was Kenya.

"Like the country?" I asked, smiling again.

She blinked. "Like my grandma."

"Right," I said.

Kenya perched on the edge of one of my wooden chairs. She wore a pair of overalls that were two sizes too big and twenty-five years out of fashion. Red and white long-sleeve Where's Waldo-looking pullover shirt under it. Bunch of plastic clips in her braids. Butterflies and My Little Pony. Stuff that was a few years too young for her. But the clothes were clean and the small places here and there where they'd been mended were done with neat, careful stitch work. Would have bet a hundred bucks she did her own sewing. She looked the type. Self-sufficient, smart, and diligent. The kind of girl that would grow into a strong woman if the world let her. And maybe she'd do it even if the world was a dick about it. I liked her.

"Anyone know you're here?" I asked.

"No."

"No one?"

"Who would I tell?" she asked.

"Your mom, maybe."

A shadow passed across the kid's face and for a moment her eyes were forty years older and filled with disappointment.

"Mama don't care much where I am or who I'm with or what I'm doing."

"Sorry," I said.

"For what? You don't make her go out all the time. You don't make her smoke that stuff."

"Rock?" I asked.

Kenya sighed and nodded, and the jaded look slipped away. The little girl was there, hurt and strong and alone and brave.

"You have any other family? Dad?"

She paused and gave an icy and cynical raise of one eyebrow. "Don't know who that is."

"Aunts, uncles…?"

"Just me and Marcus."

"How old is Marcus?" I asked.

"He's six."

I sat back and folded my hands on my lap. "Okay," I said, "so who wants to hurt your brother?"

"Mr. Sassy-Bones Sam."

I smiled.

"It ain't funny," she snapped.

"The name is. Sassy-Bones Sam? That's a little funny."

Her stare was as hard and cold as ice. "That all you going to do? Make fun and laugh?"

I wiped the smile off my face. "Sorry. It's just that the name *sounds* funny. Sassy-Bones Sam. It's not even a cool street name. It's old-fashioned. Like some a zoot-suiter would think was cool back in the day. Like someone headlining a Cab Calloway show."

"I don't know what any of that stuff means."

"Doesn't matter. Sorry. Is that his street name?"

"It's what Marcus said his name was." She paused. "The mailman said his name is Jacob Bonsu, but Marcus said Sassy-Bones Sam was his real name."

"Marcus is six," I said.

She shrugged. "Maybe he is, but that don't change what he knows."

"What do you mean by that?" I asked.

"My brother…*knows* stuff. Secrets. Stuff no one told him. Stuff he knows when he wakes up."

"You're saying he dreamed that Sassy-Bones Sam is this man's real name?"

"It sounds stupid when you say it like that," said Kenya, "but that's how it is. Marcus always knows stuff. He…gets it from our grandma. She was like that all the way up 'til when she died from the cancer. Everyone round the way knew she knew things, and they

212

know that Marcus is just like that."

"You mean he's psychic? That he has gifts?"

She nodded. "He knows stuff, but Grandma used to say that it was never no gift. Knowing stuff about people is scary. And it makes people mad sometimes. They don't like you knowing their business' less they ask you to read tea leaves or look at their hands." She touched her palm. "Marcus, though…he don't do that stuff. He just knows stuff when he wakes up. Like when someone on the block is going to get sick, or someone's dog is gonna die. Never fun stuff. He never had no lottery numbers. Now, people up and down the street know that Mr. Sassy-Bone Sam is the right name to call him by. But they don't say the name loud. Anyone says that name whispers like they're afraid he's gonna hear. I seen Mrs. Wilson slap her grown son for saying it once. Slapped him in front of all his friends, and none of them stood up for him. They all looked down like they got yelled at in church, and these are boys who talk back to the police. They don't make jokes about Mr. Sassy-Bones Sam. No one does. Not if they're smart."

At twelve this little girl was more articulate than nine-tenths of the people I hang out with. Okay, so that's a low bar, but my point is the kid was sharp.

"Why is Mr. Sassy-Bones Sam after Marcus?" I asked. "Is it because he found out his real name?"

She nodded. "People started using that name at first. And when Mr. Sassy-Bone Sam found out he was so mad. Last week, when I was walking Marcus home from kindergarten, he spoke to us from an alley. I jumped near out of my skin. There he was, standing in this smelly little alley, smiling with all those nasty metal teeth."

"Metal? Like gold teeth?"

"I guess. Metal, anyway. And he points a finger at Marcus and says, 'You know my name, boy. Now everyone knows it and I'm going to make you sorry.'"

"Were those his exact words?" I asked.

"Near as I can remember."

"Did he try to hurt Marcus? Did he touch him at all?"

Kenya looked away, then past me out my window, then down at her hands. Anywhere but at me. She started to speak a few times, stopped, shook her head, and then sat with her little fingers knotting and twisting together.

"He…" she said in a small voice, then shook her head again. She seemed to be suddenly alarmed by what she was saying and what it might mean.

"Kenya," I urged gently, "it's okay. You can tell me."

"Maybe I shouldn't have come here," she said in a small voice. "He'll know. God, he'll know…"

"Kenya," I said.

She shook her head and I could see the panic rising in her eyes. It hurt me that after being brave enough to look me up and come over here, the kid's courage was failing. Or maybe it was that this Bones guy was enough of a scary son-of-a-bitch that saying more might cross some line. At least in her mind.

"Kenya," I said again, "*he's* not here. He doesn't know *you're* here. He can't know what we're talking about."

"He'll *know*."

"It doesn't matter," I insisted. "You came here for my help."

"Maybe I shouldn't have come here at all," she said.

"You came here to protect your little brother. If you think this guy is going to hurt Marcus, then there's no going back."

Now her eyes clicked up to meet mine and I saw equal parts fear and anger. A whole lot of each. "Yeah, but what if he finds out before you can do something? Maybe he'll do something worse 'cause I…'cause I…"

Two large tears swelled on her lower lids, broke, and fell down her smooth cheeks. She didn't sob, didn't tremble. Those tears were enough, though. It was proof that behind the iron control there was a terrified little girl.

What to do next was a tough call for me. On one hand, I ought to get her the hell out of my office and back to whoever filled the role of parent or legal guardian. But I already knew that was a cowardly choice lacking in both empathy and compassion. So…no. On the other hand, I could sit and wait her out and let Kenya find her own way back to courage. On the, um, *third* hand, I could push a little and hope it didn't drive her away.

The second choice felt more mature. I went with the third choice, though, because it's what my gut was telling me.

"Kenya," I said, "you came here because of what you read in my online ad. All those services I offer; all the things I do. They're not just for window dressing."

"For what?"

"It's not me bragging," I said. "It's not me saying I can do anything that I can't. I'm good at all that stuff. It's my job. I told you that I used to be a real police detective, and I was very good at that job, too. My office may look like crap, but I'm a good investigator. Maybe a really good one. I can usually find who I want to find. I can figure people out and figure what they want, and if they're bad guys I can usually stop them."

She looked at me. "*Usually*." She repeated the word, not as a question, but as a frank and hollow echo.

"Sure. No one is perfect, and I'll tell you that straight up, but there's one thing I'm really, really good at." I leaned forward and put my elbows on the desk. "When it comes to protecting people, I'm better than anyone you'll ever meet. Better than any gangbanger, better than any cop, better than anyone."

She sat and studied me with those young, wise eyes. The fear wanted her to disbelieve, that was obvious in the way she sat—half twisted like she was ready to bolt and run.

But…

Whatever else this little girl was, she was smart. She had insight.

"What if he has a gun?" she asked. "Do you got a gun?"

"Sure," I said, grinning to show a lot of teeth. "But I don't need one."

We sat there. Staring at each other. Letting the moment figure out the next move for us.

"Okay," she said at last.

"Okay," I said.

She wiped the tears from her face. "Okay," she said again.

"Now, Miss Kenya," I said, "tell me absolutely everything about Mr. Sassy-Bones Sam and your brother Marcus. Everything."

-3-

Kenya told me the story. It was long and she rambled a bit, but here are the bones of it. Yeah, pun intended.

She lived a couple of streets over from my office, so location was as important to her as my claim of protection. Her block was rough; it wasn't the worst in Philadelphia, but it was a contender. A lot of the homes were boarded up, though it didn't mean they were empty. Some were occupied by squatters—the endless flow of the disenfranchised who were on the run from something. Abusive families, bad decisions, their own memories, their lack of expectations. Take your pick. Some of the abandoned places were crack houses or needle palaces, and I guess if you're getting that high you don't give much of a shit about where. Her neighborhood was mostly Black, but the template works for whites, Latinos, or any other group. Race doesn't much matter. Lack of money, an indifferent upper class, and crushed hope deal those cards.

There are gangs all over Philly, just like in any big city. The gang that ran Kenya's neighborhood didn't have a cool nickname. No

'Crips' or 'Bloods' like in L.A. There was more of a dog pack mentality, with the gang gradually taking on the name of whoever was top dog, meaning whoever kicked the most ass. That kind of celebrity was usually short-lived. For the last few years, it had been Baby Hulk's block. Baby Hulk was one Nicholas Powell, a twenty-eight-year-old thug who was only five foot six inches tall but nearly as wide. He'd gone into prison at twenty and when he made parole at twenty-four it was clear he'd spent every minute inside clanking weights. Massive muscles and clinical anger management issues. Hence the name. He took the gang over from his big brother, Donnie, when said sibling went down for a murder-two fall and was sent off to prison for fifteen-to-twenty. Kenya didn't know exactly what Baby Hulk's gang did, but she said, "Probably drugs. I mean…what else is there?"

This is a twelve-year-old girl. The sadness of that kind of worldly wisdom came close to breaking my heart.

Baby Hulk was known to knock teeth out—apparently one of his favorite hobbies. He did it to anyone who gave him shit, and apparently a lot of people fell into that category. Even some of his crew sported gold replacements for teeth he'd forcibly removed. Both of his lieutenants, Grayman and Topper. When I later looked them up, I was surprised to learn that these were not nicknames but actual surnames. Weird.

After Baby Hulk took over the family business, things more or less settled down on the block. There had been some pushback from neighboring gangs, but Baby Hulk and his crew kicked enough ass to reinforce the accepted boundaries, just not so much that the other gangs felt a need to go to war. After all, war would interfere with business, and each of these smaller groups worked part of a bigger drug distribution system run by more dangerous predators higher up on the food chain.

Then, eight months ago, Jacob Bonsu moved into the neighborhood. He was an immigrant from Ghana. He bought a row home sandwiched between a crack house and one filled with transients. He moved in at night, Kenya told me. Her brother Marcus watched from his bedroom window and saw the whole thing –Jacob Bonsu arriving a little past midnight in a U-Haul truck. He said that Bonsu did not carry anything himself, but 'black men' did.

And here's where the story gets a little weird. Kenya asked him 'which' black men, thinking it was maybe delivery guys or someone from the neighborhood. Marcus told her that they weren't real people. They were shadows. Kenya grilled him on it because Marcus seemed genuinely terrified. Marcus kept saying they were black men with no faces. A few weeks later she found some of his drawings and they showed lamps and chairs and boxes being carried into the house by completely featureless shapes that were vaguely humanoid. He colored them in all black and insisted that's how they really looked.

From then on Marcus was both terrified of Mr. Bonsu and strangely fascinated. He walked past the man's house a dozen times each day and often sat on the stoop of an empty house across the street, watching and waiting.

"Waiting for what?" I asked.

Kenya shook her head. "He wanted to see the shadow people again."

"Shadow people," I echoed.

"That's what he calls them," she said. "Now, anyway. He called them black men the first night, but ever since it's shadow people. Crazy, huh?"

I said nothing for a moment.

Shadow people.

That struck a chord with me. Over the last few years there has been a growing number of reports in the conspiracy-theory and paranormal news feeds about shadow people. No one seemed able to agree on what they were. Some of the wilder claims held that they were aliens who were infiltrating the government, and given what was happening in Washington I could see their point. But I don't think that's really it. Among the folks who lean more toward a supernatural or preternatural explanation, there were various theories that they were pernicious ghosts, or demons, or even a kind of vampire. It was the latter theories that seemed to circulate most among the fringe crowd whose opinions I don't easily dismiss.

I've met vampires. One of my first big cases here in Philly involved vampires. A woman hired me to protect her against her ex-husband. He'd been making threats and showing up in her house, despite changed locks, to abuse her. I confronted the guy, thinking maybe he was just some kind of asshole wiseguy wannabe, but damn if he didn't pop some fangs. Him and his boys. They tried real damn hard to turn me into an open bar.

I dissuaded them.

Well, not the 'me' Kenya was talking to on a sunny afternoon. No, when those guys went for me with fangs, I reciprocated in kind. Fangs and, for me, claws. No, I'm not part of the fang gang. Me and my whole family run on all fours. We have the whole package—fur, claws, full set of chompers, enhanced senses, and a healing ability like Wolverine in the movies. They call us *benandanti*. Werewolves of a kind. No full moon bullshit, and silver doesn't mean dick to us. Sure, we can die, but someone has to work real damn hard at it and we are less than cooperative, if you can dig that.

If the shadow people were real and if they were vampires, then maybe this really *was* my kind of thing.

"Did you ask him what he meant by 'shadow people'?"

She paused, then nodded. "He said something stupid. Or…I thought it was stupid at first."

"What did he say?"

"He said that he saw Mr. Sassy-Bones Sam come out of his house one night and he didn't have no shadow. But then Marcus saw his shadow kind of leak out of him."

She described a bizarre scene, where Bonsu stood on the curb of a deserted street, directly under a streetlamp with no shadow at all on the ground. Then he spread his arms and a pool seemed to form around his feet. It spread out until it was about the size of a hula hoop. Then Bonsu turned and walked away, but the pool of darkness was still there.

Marcus saw all this from his bedroom window. As he watched, too terrified to move, the pool shifted and changed and finally broke apart, splashing upward as if a rock had been dropped in it. The splashes did not fall back down, but instead thickened and changed until there were five shapes standing in a circle and no trace of darkness left on the pavement. The shapes were utterly black, but Marcus told his sister that they were like people, with heads and arms and legs.

"Only he said they were all wrong," said Kenya, her voice quiet.

"Wrong how?"

"They were all hunched over and they had really long fingers," she said. "Thin and crooked, like tree branches. Marcus was so scared he wet himself."

"I'm sorry," I said. "I remember being that scared when I was a kid."

And a few times since, I thought, but felt it was best not to say it and ruin what little confidence Kenya had in me.

"Did anyone else see this?"

"No. Only my brother, and before you ask, Marcus don't lie. If he said he saw it, he saw it, and you can take that to church."

"Okay," I said.

"After that is when it got bad," said Kenya. "That night, I mean. 'Cause the shadow people must have seen Marcus in the window."

She described a horrific moment in which the creatures suddenly jerked and turned like startled birds, raising their featureless faces to look across the street and up to the window where little Marcus stood watching. Marcus started to cry and as soon as he did the shadow people *changed.*

"What do you mean?" I asked. "Changed how?"

She licked her lips and her small hands gripped the armrests of the chair so hard her knuckles went pale and the old leather creaked.

"They turned into birds," she said. "Big black ones. Like crows."

The birds flew toward Marcus' window, but he screamed and pulled the shade down and ran for his sister's room. When Kenya calmed him down and went to look at the 'monsters' he claimed were outside, she saw a sight that chilled her to the bone. Mr. Sassy-Bones Sam stood in the middle of the street, looking up at the window. There were crows on his shoulders and standing on the hood of an old stripped-down Chevy. The crows were looking up, too. And Mr. Bones was smiling.

"Ever since then," she said in a quavering voice, "Mr. Sassy-Bones Sam been telling people that he was gonna eat him a little nosy boy. People thought he was joking at first, but after Willie Thomas died, they didn't laugh."

"Who's Willie Thomas?"

"Kid from my grade. They found him in his bed all dried up like an old orange. Lady down the street from me said there wasn't a drop of blood in him, and there wasn't any on his sheets."

I sat back and nodded. I'd heard something about that on the news. A minor story that didn't get a lot of play. A kid abandoned by his junkie father who starved to death and was mummified by the brutal summer heat. I said as much to Kenya, but she started shaking her head.

"I know what they said on the TV, but it ain't true. I saw Willie around the block. Everybody did. I saw him no more than a day before he died. His daddy's a junkie, sure, but he didn't leave Willie alone for that long. No, sir, it was Mr. Sassy-Bones Sam done that."

"How do you know?"

"I know 'cause Willie threw a bottle of water at his house the night before. I saw him do it."

"Why'd Willie do that?"

She looked at me in surprise. "It's what you do when you want to chase away the devil."

I tilted my head. "Is Willie's family Catholic?"

"Yeah."

"Was it holy water?"

"I guess," she said. "He said that his grandma got some from church last time she was there. People been doing that since Mr. Sassy-Bones Sam moved in. Not all of everyone's Catholic, but people who are been getting it for everyone."

She told me why. Since Bonsu moved in there had been a whole bunch of problems. Family dogs died off. Nearly all of them. Some kind of skin disease, though when their bodies were found, the eyes of each and every dog had been pecked out by birds. No one saw anything, though. The cats went next and now there was not one cat left on the block. That opened the door for rats and mice to get much bolder. Then people started getting sick. Kenya said it was like they get old overnight. Even some of the gangbangers appeared to wither into infirmity in the space of a single night. Those that went to the E.R. were given shots but no real answers. A couple of older folks died, too; passing away in the middle of the night and found the next morning with looks of abject horror on their faces. The police and EMTs called it "death spasms" from strokes or heart attacks. Or whatever. No real answers.

Then there were two big incidents and that's what made her come to see me.

First, Baby Hulk decided to do something about the monster on his block. Maybe it was actually acting on civic pride—though I'm not inclined to think so. Or maybe he was losing face because everyone in the neighborhood believed Bonsu was somehow causing all of the sickness and death, and Baby Hulk was supposed to be the local muscle. Whatever it was, the bruiser and a couple of his boys decided to confront Bonsu at his house. They were not nice about it. They didn't knock. Instead, Baby Hulk kicked the door in and five of them stormed inside while everyone in the neighborhood stood across the street and watched. It was the inner-city Philly version of villagers with pitchforks and torches.

In old monster movies there are two distinct scenarios that play out. Either the villagers kill Doctor Frankenstein or stake Dracula…or they get their asses handed to them by a threat much bigger than they expected to encounter. Guess which one this was?

Kenya and little Marcus stood with the others waiting for Bonsu to come flying through an upstairs window, maybe with a dozen bullets in him and his throat cut.

There was nothing as dramatic as that.

Not at first.

The crowd grew restive as minutes passed without a sound from inside the house. Two more of Baby Hulk's crew went in.

Nothing.

A whole hour passed. Not a gunshot, not a scream, not a word.

It was twilight and the sun was falling fast when a figure finally appeared in the doorway. It was Baby Hulk.

Or had been.

He looked twenty years older and much thinner. His brown skin, which had been stretched tight over bulging muscles, was flaccid and wrinkled and blotched. There were patches of gray in the man's hair and dark smudges under his eyes. He stood swaying in the doorway, looking dazed and confused and sickly. He stood there for a long time and it took nearly all of that time for the crowd to realize this was, in fact, Baby Hulk.

The crowd watched him stand there and they saw his shoulders begin to tremble as the man started to cry. Big, deep, broken sobs.

Baby Hulk stumbled down the steps and walked away from Bonsu's house. One by one the members of his gang followed. They, too, looked wasted and old and sick.

The crowd broke apart and fled.

For a while only Kenya and Marcus remained, staring at the now empty doorway. Marcus pulled on Kenya's hand and she followed him across the street. They were both scared, but for some reason her brother wanted to see inside the house. Not *go* in, but look in. Kenya could not explain to me why she let herself be pulled along. They stopped in the street and Marcus put a single foot on the curb, but even he wouldn't go any farther. They stood and looked for just a minute.

That was one minute too long, though. And that's how bad stories become nightmares. As the sun dipped behind the row of houses on the other side of the street from where the kids stood, a wave of shadows seemed to roll outward toward them. Not just the shadows of the houses thrown by the setting sun, but a denser, darker, colder blackness that vomited out of the open doorway. At first it was just a shapeless nothing, but as the darkness reached the street it exploded into a flock of black birds. Crows, maybe, or starlings. Kenya wasn't sure. Her brother called them 'nightbirds,' and that was a term I'd heard before. Never in good places, never under good circumstances. I heard that word used in places like Pine Deep where there is never comfort in the coming of night. My grandmother talked about nightbirds, too. She said that they were lost souls who fed on the light of the living. It was a scary bedtime story when I was a kid. Before I knew who and what she was, and what I was.

The children screamed and ran, but the nightbirds followed.

Once, when Kenya dared look over her shoulder as they raced for home, she saw Mr. Sassy-Bones Sam himself walking down the steps of his house. He was dressed all in black but she could see his eyes. They glowed a red as bright and hellish as the setting sun. He pointed a long and crooked finger and she heard him say one word.

"Mine."

He was pointing at Marcus.

That was a week ago, and her brother had had truly dreadful nightmares ever since. In his dreams he was disappearing a little at a time. In those dreams he imagined that Mr. Sassy-Bones Sam was crouched over him, pressing down on his chest, sucking the life out of him. When he woke up each morning, he was weaker, sicker, paler. They did not have health coverage. Their mother hadn't ever held a job and had let her welfare lapse. The kids were completely on their own.

"Did you check Marcus for bites?" I asked.

Kenya took a long, long time with that, and from the look in her eyes I knew that she knew what I was asking. She never did give me a straight answer. Instead, she caved forward, put her face in her hands, and began to cry.

I sat there like a big, lumpy, stupid fool.

I let a lot of seconds burn off the clock and fall like cinders to the floor.

"I'm going to help you," I said.

-4-

She used my bathroom to clean up but I could hear her crying in there for a while, too. When she came out her face was washed and her clothes straightened, but her eyes were wet and bright.

"I got to pay you," she said, "don't I?"

"No—," I began, but Kenya gave a sharp shake of her head.

"I got to pay you or it's not right. That's how it works. I asked people and they said that's how it works."

"Really, you—"

She dug in her pocket and laid a fortune on the desk.

Six dollar-bills, one dollar and thirty-six cents in change, and five free meal coupons for McDonalds. It constituted everything she owned. She spread it out in a neat row so I could see how much was there.

"It's all I got," she said.

I didn't want to take it. Not a penny of it. But all of her pride, all of her self-worth was calculated in with that amount, and I would have to be the world's biggest asshole to say no.

I reached out and took the McDonalds coupons. "This is my rate for an evening's work. I have never in my life said no to working for food."

She watched me fold the coupons and put them in my wallet.

"Now," I said, "give me his address. I'll be over in a couple of hours. First, I want to do a background check on him. That's how guys like me work. We find out everything we can and then we move."

"Find out stuff like what?" asked Kenya.

"Who knows? Maybe he has something in his past. A crime he's running from, or some debt he owes. You said he's here from Ghana, right? Well maybe his visa is expired. There could be all sorts of things, even some overdue parking tickets. The point is, I don't like to go in cold. I have access to databases that will give me his whole history, and maybe there's something I can hand over to the cops."

"Cops can't stop no monster."

"Depends on what kind of monster he is," I said.

She eyed me with doubt. "And what if he's the kind of monster they can't stop?"

"That," I said, "is why you hired me."

5

I sent her home. It was bright and sunny outside and I promised to be on her block before sunset. She gave me a dubious smile that had barbed wire wrapped around her hope and her fear, binding them together. I returned the smile with a bland one. A safe one.

When she was gone, I could feel my smile change, though. The wolf behind my eyes sometimes smiled, but it wasn't something I would ever show an innocent kid. I'm nasty but I'm not cruel.

6

I searched the net.

Not surprisingly, there was no listing for anyone named Sassy-Bones Sam. However, Jacob Bonsu was in there. He was a legal immigrant and was waiting to take his citizenship test in a few weeks. That was almost funny. A monster—if he was a monster—taking a test like that. No doubt he would play his role well and not smirk too much as he filled in the right answers.

His passport picture showed a very gaunt man with intense eyes and a thin slash of a mouth. He wasn't smiling, so I couldn't see if he had any gold-plated or platinum-plated teeth. Bonsu looked creepy but that was about that. Some of my best friends look creepy. In the right light, or after a hard night of bourbon and bad choices, I looked creepy, too.

Bonsu had no police record at all in the States. Nothing. Not even a parking ticket. No beefs with the cops, not late on any bills, up to date with his forms and taxes and all that. He owned the house, having bought it with a certified check. I noodled around and got his financials, but they were clean to the point of being boring. He'd transferred money here from Ghana and it had cleared all of the appropriate checks and safeguards.

He was, according to all official agencies, clean as a Girl Scout.

Except that he wasn't. Not if Kenya was telling me the truth, and my gut and my judgment were both telling me she was. Besides, let's face it, you don't have to be a supernatural monster to be smart enough to keep all of your public records whitewashed. It was hardly proof of innocence.

Doing deep background in the Republic of Ghana was a little trickier, and I had to call in a few markers with old contacts in the FBI and Interpol. Folks I knew from my old days as a cop in the Twin Cities. It's the internet age, though, and just about everything about everybody was somewhere on the Net.

What I found wasn't much. Beautiful country, beautiful people, and Bonsu was damn near as common a name as Smith is here. And biblical names like Jacob were pretty damn common, too. The country was over seventy percent Christian. I found close to eight hundred people named Jacob Bonsu. Swell. It would take too much of the rest of my life to run each one down. So, I closed my laptop and thought about it for a few minutes.

There was something about the name. Not Jacob

Bonsu, but the name Marcus said was his real one. Sassy-Bones Sam. Why did that ring a bell? It was the kind of mental tickle you get when you're trying to remember something you've read in passing, like when you're reading an article on one subject and your mind half-ass records info on a few tangential details.

Sassy-Bones Sam.

Yeah, there was something there.

I placed a call to a folklorist friend of mine, Dr. Jonatha Corbiel-Newton at the University of Pennsylvania. She wrote stacks of books on weird stuff, with a bias toward supernatural predators. She'd been my Van Helsing four or five times now. But…her voicemail said that she would be away until Monday. Balls. I tried her cell and got the same message.

"Who the fuck goes on vacation and doesn't take their cell

phone?" I asked the empty air of my office.

The answer was in my head already. Smart people. People with their priorities straight.

"Fuck," I said.

The sunlight was slanting through the window and leaving yellow-gold slashes on my cheap area rug. Time to go.

I opened my bottom desk drawer and removed a nylon shoulder holster, then checked the action of my beat-up old Glock 26, slapped in a magazine of hollow-points. On impulse, I slipped a second magazine into my front pants pocket. I put on a sports coat over my white shirt but didn't bother with a tie. I wore clothes I didn't much care about. Just in case.

Then I locked up the office and walked over to Kenya's neighborhood.

-7-

There's always been racial tension in Philadelphia. Back in the 60s and 70s you had neighborhoods like Kensington, where the entrenched whites would firebomb any house a person of color tried to move into. And there was an area around 33rd and Columbia where even the toughest meathead of a white supremacist wouldn't venture. In between those poles you have a lot of neighborhoods where you had poor white, poor Black, and poor Latino smashed in together, with everyone hating just about everyone else. More recently some of those trouble spots —like Fishtown, for example— have become gentrified and people of all kinds mixed and mingled in artsy harmony. That was nice and hopeful, but there was still a lot of intolerance of all kinds elsewhere in the city. I mention this because liberal as I am, I could feel eyes on me as I came walking down the street where Kenya lived. I was a white guy wearing a sports coat on a warm day. I used to be a cop and even though I'm a P.I. now, I still have the cop look. That look, by the way, covers a lot of job descriptions beyond local P.D. I could be vice, ICE, a U.S. marshal, housing authority, DEA, a skip tracer, a process server, a repo man, or any one of a dozen other professions that offer some kind of threat.

No amount of reasonable conversation or explanation was going to wipe away four hundred years of racial intolerance, oppression, mass slaughter, enforced poverty and general inhumane treatment by whites to anyone who was not white. Call me a snowflake—and fuck you if you do—but that's part of the American legacy. We have to own that shit along the way to fixing it. Maybe we will individually and as a culture evolve to the point where no one on either side of the race line cares anymore. I will be dusty bones in a box long before that happens, I expect.

So, sure, I was aware of being looked at with suspicion, fear, anger and hostility. The wolf in me felt defensive and wanted to snarl, but that was a fear reaction. My kind have been oppressed too. We're the bad guys in a lot of books and movies, and thousands of my kind have been tortured and executed by religious groups since Etruscan times. Maybe all the way back to caveman days.

Human beings, man. We have potential but we have a long fucking way to go.

I did not go to Kenya's house. That would have been a bad move and the last thing I wanted to do was put her and little Marcus more squarely in the sites of anyone who might want to do them harm. Like Bonsu or what was left of Baby Hulk's gang.

As I passed their house though, I felt a twinge. It was sharp and struck deep. I have a kind of goofy policy with certain clients. When I accept a case as special as this one, it's like I take the client into my pack. My 'protection' services are a little more personal and a lot more extensive when it comes to standing between innocents and the big bad. There is not much I wouldn't do to protect my pack. I learned that from my grandmother and my aunts. Let me put it this way…there is no one left sucking air who took a serious run at someone under the protection of the Hunter family.

So, I strolled past the little row home and didn't turn to check for faces at the window, but I could *feel* them. And I had Kenya's scent filed away. I picked up Marcus's as well. A bit from when Kenya was in my office and more as I passed their stoop. Little boy scent. Soap and dirty sneakers and baby powder and Cheerios and fear. It all got filed away in a mental slot I labeled 'Marcus.' I caught a whiff of their mom, too. So much pain, so little hope. I could smell the sickness in her. Cancer. She was going to check out soon, which meant the kids would go into the child services system, maybe get separated and probably go to foster homes. The thought stabbed me.

The universe sucks dick sometimes. Artlessly but with enthusiasm.

There were some people sitting on their stoops or on beach chairs by the curb. Watching me. Saying nothing. Giving nothing away in their expressions. I didn't try to start conversations with any of them. Not even when I saw a short, broad, young man with withered muscles and haunted eyes. Baby Hulk and his crew sat on the steps in front of an abandoned row home. They looked at me, but there was no aggression left in them. Mr. Sassy-Bones Sam had stolen it away.

Even though they were criminals, I actually felt bad for them. They were lost, broken. There was so much despair in Baby Hulk's eyes that it made me really sad.

I kept walking.

When I was directly across the street from Bonsu's house, I slowed and stopped. In an ordinary surveillance, I'd have driven past or walked by without a pause, but I wasn't trying to be sneaky. If he was looking, then I wanted him to see me. I turned and faced his front door. There was a telephone pole there, so I leaned my shoulder against it and waited.

The sun was ready to roll off the edge and shadows were already long and dark. There were a few clouds up there and it would be a new moon. I glanced up at the street light and saw jagged glass under the metal hood. Once the sun was down it would be dark as the pit on the street. Mr. Bonsu would probably think that gave him an edge. Time would tell.

Out of the corner of my eye I saw some people standing on their steps watching me. Wondering what I was doing. It was obvious whose house I was looking at since the homes on either side were abandoned. As far as my sense of smell could detect, there weren't even any junkies in those houses, or the places adjoining them. Bonsu had that part of the block all to himself.

The shadows lengthened and thickened and the sky seemed to catch fire over in the west. Gaudy slashes of crimson and orange were torn into the skin of twilight. Murder colors. Very appropriate. The universe doesn't usually stage-dress things for me, so I appreciated the effort.

I caught movement to my right and turned to see Baby Hulk come limping toward me. He stopped thirty feet away when he saw me looking at him.

"Hey, man," he said weakly. "The fuck you doing here?"

He was trying to sound tough, but there was no fire left in him.

"Came to see someone."

We both looked across the street at the closed front door and then back again.

"You the police?"

"No."

"You any kind of police?"

"No," I said.

He began to say something else, stopped, had to swallow and reset himself. He blinked to chase away the wetness in his eyes.

"Don't go in there, man."

His voice was pale, weak, nearly empty.

But not entirely empty.

We studied each other. Baby Hulk was a gangbanger and a criminal and no doubt at all he was someone who had done a lot of harm to a lot of people. Maybe even innocent people. That, as they say, was then. Now he was something else. Whatever had happened to him in Bonsu's house had not merely broken him and stolen his power, it had cracked something open, too. It had broken the locks people like him put on their deepest emotions, the shackles they clamped around their humanity. In that moment, he was no longer a tough Black gangster and I wasn't a tough white private eye. We were two human beings standing on the edge of an abyss. Baby Hulk had looked over the edge and stared too long into the darkness below. He'd stared long enough to see what was inside that darkness.

"Don't go in there," he said again. His voice was a shadow, a whisper. Ashes.

I said, "I have to."

He licked his lips, which were cracked and dry. He wanted to say more, but it would have cost him too much. He shook his head and turned away. I watched him creep like an old man back to his friends. No one else came over.

I couldn't blame them.

Twilight was in full fury now, burning the last of the day away. The shadows near the tops of the east-facing houses were purple infused with the color of dried blood. At street level those shadows were black as the pit.

I was about to step off the curb when my cell phone vibrated in my pocket. When I looked at the screen, I felt an odd flush of relief. I pushed the button.

"Hey, Jonatha," I said.

Dr. Jonatha Corbiel-Newton still had a soft southern accent even though she'd moved to Pennsylvania almost twenty years ago.

"Tell me that voicemail was a joke," she said.

"Why would I make a joke?"

"Mr. Sassy-Bones Sam? Are you kidding me?"

The sun was almost gone. All that was left was a fiery sliver above the rooftops.

"Not really all that much in a kidding mood, Doc. Why? Does that name mean something to you?"

She said something in Cajun that might have been an obscene comment about my sexual habits. Definitely something in that neighborhood.

"Come *on*," she barked. "You call and leave a message about a man from Ghana with the nickname of Sassy-Bones Sam? Either you're making a stupid joke or you are in deep, deep shit."

The sun vanished and immediately the quality of the shadows changed. They went from blocks of empty darkness to something else. Something with more density, more substance. I recoiled a step by reflex and my heart jumped into a different gear.

"How much shit, exactly?" I asked.

The front door of Bonsu's house began creaking open. Yup, just like in a fucking horror movie. Slow, noisy, ominous as a motherfucker.

"First off," said Jonatha, "the name is wrong. In your message you said that a kid dreamed it? Are we talking a vision?"

I quickly explained about Marcus and his gifts, then about the very bad things that had happened in the neighborhood. Missing pets, people getting sick, and what happened to Baby Hulk's crew. And the attacks on Marcus.

"Shit, shit, shit," said Jonatha. "What is it with you and kids? You never learn, do you? You always have to put your ass on a line whenever there's a kid."

"Is now the time for a lecture, Doc?" I asked. Something was moving inside the darkness of that house. Even with my senses I couldn't tell what it was from across the street. The hairs on my head were standing up, though.

I took a steadying breath and stepped off the curb. The shadows on the asphalt seemed to ripple around my feet like a pool of tar. I heard sounds within it, too, like the plaintive lost-child cries of crows. But they weren't crows, I knew. Somewhere inside those shadows were nightbirds.

"Talk to me," I said.

"Sam," said Jonatha, "there's a legend among the Ashanti people of Ghana and Togo about a kind of predatory monster. It looks like a frail and wizened old man, but that's only a glamour, a disguise. It's really very powerful and very, very hard to kill."

"How hard?" I asked as I reached the far side of the street.

"Almost impossible."

"Fuck," I said under my breath. "What is it? Some kind of vampire?"

"The word doesn't really apply, not in the European way it's been used. This isn't a charming gentleman in evening attire. This monster is savage, brutal, and relentless. It has gigantic wings like a bat, but it isn't a bat. It has twisted legs with three-toed feet and it hangs from the branches of trees. It drinks blood but also feeds on life energy, so it's both a hematophagous and essential vampire. But it's more than that. It's incredibly strong and it can make people sick just by looking at them. And, Sam, it has *iron teeth*."

"Well…shit."

"But the name," she said, "the kid was almost right.

It's not Sassy-Bones though…this monster is a *sasabonsam*."

And there it was. That thing that had been niggling at the back of my mind. *Sasabonsam*. It had been in one of Jonatha's own books, one I'd read. But it was a footnote in a chapter about another kind of African witch-vampire called an *obayifo.*

I stopped at the foot of Bonsu's porch steps. "How do I kill it?" I asked.

"Sam," she said, "I'm not sure that you can."

"Shit."

"You need to get out of there, Sam," she implored. "Don't fight this thing. Let me do some research, give me a few days or a couple of weeks. Let me see if there's some kind of protective charm or— "

A voice from inside the house said, "If you are going to come in, then come in."

Into the phone I said, "Might be a little late for that."

-8-

I drew my gun and stepped inside.

The house was utterly black. The windows were totally blocked and only grudging light from the dying twilight painted a strip of illumination for me. I walked to the end of that glow, aware that it was fading.

The darkness inside was not empty, and I could tell right off that Bonsu was not the only one —or only *thing*—in there.

"You are a fool."

The voice came from nowhere and everywhere. The accent was thick, and although I'd never heard a Ghanese accent before, I figured that's what it was. Nice accent. The tone was scary as balls, though.

"Jacob Bonsu," I said, trying to make my voice sound confident and not at all scared shitless. "How about you stop hiding in the shadows like a pussy and let's talk man to man."

Suddenly he was right there behind me. I could feel the heat from his skin and the wetness of his breath as he whispered in my ear. "But I am *not* a man."

I whirled and backpedaled and whipped my Glock out of the holster. "So you're just a pussy then, is that it?"

He chuckled. If he ever wanted to play a mad scientist in a cheesy flick, he could kill the audition with that chuckle. It was beyond creepy. Filled with menace and promise and way too much confidence. This was his house, his game, his rules, and he knew it.

I held my gun with my right and slipped my left into my jacket pocket. My fingers curled around the little Maglite. I'm a big fan of the Boy Scout motto of 'Be Prepared.' Of course, if I was smarter, I'd have been even more prepared and brought a gallon of gas and a book of matches and simply burned the damn place down. Oops.

There was a rustling sound as if someone was moving sheets of leather around. That was not a good sound.

"Listen, Bonsu," I said, trying to sound reasonable, "maybe we can talk this out. Maybe we can find some way where we both get to walk away without losing face. Come out and let's have a real conversation. Tell me what you want. I'm okay with cutting a deal."

That laugh again. Sneaky and low and mean.

"I want them," he said.

"Who?"

"All of them. The cattle on this street. The old ones and the young. Especially the young. They are so delicious. I want them all."

"Looks to me like you already had a full lunch with Baby Hulk."

He snarled and I heard a sharp sound, like him spitting something nasty out of his mouth.

"That one is polluted," growled Bonsu. "His blood is like dirty water, full of chemicals."

"Yeah, well, to be fair you did chomp on a drug dealer, brah. What'd you expect?"

"I want the others. I want the child. I want Marcus. First him, and then his sister. And then all of them. Delicious. All of those delicious children. Their purity is so—"

"Delicious, yeah, I got it. Buy a thesaurus." I kept turning toward where I thought the sound was coming from, letting the gun barrel move in sync with my eyes, but it was pitch black in there. "Well," I said, "the whole eating kids thing? Yeah, that's where our negotiations are going to break down. You can have all the gangbangers you want, but you don't get Marcus or his sister or anyone else."

"And who," he said, coming closer, "will stop me?"

I pivoted and fired three shots into the center of where I thought the voice originated. The muzzle flashes strobed the moment and I caught a flash of a horrific face that was in no way human. Here in his personal darkness Bonsu had shed all pretense of humanity and was pure monster. His eyes were sunk into dark pits and glowed cat yellow in the muzzle fire. He had ridges of scales rising up like a V from nose to temples and there was a spike, like a stubby horn on his head. His body was human enough, but he had short arms and twisted goat-like legs that ended in three savage clawed toes each. From his back two enormous wings stretched out. I caught all of that in the space of those three shots. And I saw one more thing. I saw the iron teeth. They gleamed like steel and they snapped the air inches from my face.

He hissed, but in anger rather than pain, even though I knew that I'd hit him.

Then I was in darkness again, but now there was not even a faint glow from outside. I pulled the Maglite from my pocket and turned it on. The beam was intensely bright and I nearly screamed when I saw that the darkness around me was *filled* with creatures. Not only the *Sasabonsam*, but the nightbirds, too—and they were in mid-transformation, losing their bird shapes and becoming almost human. Like ghosts made of smoke rather than vapor. Dozens and dozens of them. I was trapped and surrounded by an army of monsters. The shadow people.

They rushed at me, howling like demons. Clawed hands slashed at me, and the gun went flying off into a corner where it landed with a clatter. I kicked out and punched and wrestled, but they tore the flashlight away from me, too. It spun wildly through the room and passed in front of Bonsu's face, revealing a wicked leer that was filled with dark hunger and amusement. He was hanging upside-down from a broken light fixture and he was enjoying this.

Then the Maglite stuck the floor and the lens shattered. The bulb flickered weakly but did not go out. Seeing death rush toward me was no comfort at all.

I ran backward, smashing at the shadow people, knocking them aside but doing no damage. My back thumped against the wall, but it was the dividing wall between living room and dining room. The door to the street and to freedom was fifteen feet away, but it might as well have been on the far side of the moon for all the good it did me.

Bonsu dropped to the floor, turning as he fell, flapping his wings once to orient himself as he landed. His claws tore splintery lines in the floorboards and his metal teeth clanged together. The shadow people crowded around me, darting in to slice or pummel, but dodging back away as I tried to stop them.

"Fear is a wonderful thing," said Bonsu, and his voice was even less human than it had been before. Soft and slithery and ancient. The damaged flashlight painted the edges of his features with pale white light, and it made him look even more terrifying. "Fear is a feast and I will dine on yours and be delighted."

His eyes were intense and it was as if I could *feel* him stare at me and into me. My stomach knotted and I gagged. My knees buckled and I sank down to the floor. Jonatha's words burned in my brain. *It's incredibly strong and it can make people sick just by looking at them.*

Yeah. His power was obvious, but now I could feel the magic, too. I was getting sick. My joints began to throb then ache as if arthritis was spreading like wildfire. My gums ached and my teeth felt loose. There was warmth on my upper lip and I tasted blood dripping into my mouth. A fever raced through me. I tore off my jacket and ripped open my shirt. There wasn't enough air in the room and I was dripping with sweat.

The sickness was owning me, draining me, taking me.

And Bonsu was feeding on it. Even from ten feet away he was consuming everything that was healthy in me. He was killing me.

"Do not fear, my friend," said Bonsu. "I will not let you die. No, no, no. Arrogance such as yours should be treasured. You came in here so bold and brave because you were outraged that I would want to harm those children. All of that bravado is as delicious as their innocence. Your despair, as you watch me feast on them, will be beautiful."

"I…won't…let you…" I wheezed, but he only laughed.

"How can you hope to stop me? I am a monster and you are nothing. You are a man and I am like unto a god."

"Please…" I gasped.

"Go on, beg. It's delicious."

"Please," I said again as I dropped to hands and knees, "for the love of God…stop using that motherfucking word."

He blinked, though his smile was still broad and hungry.

I said, "Ancient monster…supernatural engine of destruction, blah blah blah. You talk like a bad horror comic. Jeez-us. And, really, there are other words for something yummy besides delicious. Delectable, tasty, scrumptious. That's a good one. Scrumptious."

His smile flickered. Partly because I didn't sound as sick as I should be. Partly because I was mouthing off to him when he clearly held all the cards.

But mostly because my voice had changed.

It was rougher, deeper, harder to understand.

Because my mouth wasn't shaped for human speech anymore.

And a moment later I couldn't speak at all.

I could snarl. And growl.

There in the darkness, by the uncertain glow of a broken flashlight, I rose from the floor. Not to my two feet, but to my four feet. My claws dug into the floorboards every bit as deeply as his had. My eyes could see in the dark now. Every bit as well as his could. I saw him, all of him, standing there with wings spread and teeth dripping and talons flexing. I saw the dozens upon dozens of misshapen shadow people clustered around him.

And they…well, they did not see Sam Hunter anymore. They'd defeated him. What they saw was something belonging to a much older race. They saw the *benandanti*.

Call it a wolf, but that's only partly correct.

Call what they saw a werewolf, but that's really too shallow a word.

Call it a monster. Sure. That'll work real well.

Call it death.

What I saw was doubt flicker in Bonsu's dark eyes. I saw him try—and fail—to understand. I saw him try to recalculate the value of this encounter and come up with answers that were both right and wrong.

Wrong for him.

Wrong for his shadow people.

Kenya and her little brother Marcus were part of my pack now.

And you never, ever fuck with the pack.

No, you do not.

His screams were terrible and high pitched and I made sure they lasted a long, long time.

What the Night Swallows

by Gabino Iglesias

Jorge sat in his car and watched people go in and out of the Pink Monkey. The strip joint's neon marquee was a pink abomination that featured a cartoonish chimpanzee in a blue bikini. The grinning ape was standing up and holding a pole. When the neon changed and a different portion of the marquee was illuminated, the chimp's round booty popped out. Jorge had a hard time imagining anyone who'd feel attracted to the ape's invitation, but he'd learned that there were a lot of strange people out there and that his own situation in life prevented him from passing judgment on most of them.

The parking lot in the back of the Pink Monkey was a cracked rectangle of darkness that pushed up against undeveloped land in a part of Austin most folks wouldn't even consider Austin. There was a fence that closed off most of the lot, but a drunk driver had knocked down the left corner of it years ago and no one had bothered fixing it. The green world behind it had devoured it quickly and now the lot looked like something you'd see in a post-apocalyptic movie.

The car Jorge was staking out sat in front of the wilderness. The white Lumina soaked up some of the pink light the marquee vomited into the back lot, but it wasn't enough to overpower the darkness. Jorge knew that's what the car's owner liked.

At some point, if all went well, a chubby man of about 45 years of age and sporting an awful combover that did little to disguise his incipient baldness would emerge from the strip joint, sit in that car, send out a text, and wait for a woman that would, must surely, emerge from somewhere beyond the tree line. The chubby man worked at an insurance place near North Lamar. Every Friday night he would come into the Pink Monkey, have a few drinks, grab something to eat, and stare lasciviously at the carnival of flesh on display. Then, surely unable to afford a private dance or the company of the few women who offered it, he'd come outside and get something cheaper, and of less quality, on the outside.

Jorge had learned all this because he had been hanging around the tent city that had grown like mold between the woods that ran up against the back of the Pink Monkey and 180. For a while, homeless folks had been his go-to when he needed a person, but the mental gymnastics required to keep the guilt at bay had been too much and he couldn't bring himself to do it. Luckily for him, he'd spent enough time learning about the hustles some of the homeless folks had going, and that brought him into contact with a different kind of person: assholes who had no qualms about hurting homeless people, slapping around homeless sex workers, or beating transients to death because they knew they wouldn't call the cops and no one would give a shit about another dead homeless person. The chubby man Jorge was waiting on liked to get skull from a rotating group of homeless women and, when he blew his load too quickly or the service wasn't to his liking—or within his budget—he liked to kick the women out of his car and peel out of the parking lot without paying. Jorge had seen him do it twice, and that had made him the perfect candidate.

When the man came out, his legs refusing to carry him in a straight line, Jorge realized the booze was going to give him a little help.

The light that came from the man's cell phone illuminated his bloated features and made him look like a corpse that spent a few days in a shallow stream. Not five minutes later, a thing of a woman wearing jeans and a shirt for a someone twice her size came out of the woods and climbed into the chubby man's car without hesitation.

As Jorge sat and waited for the man's little party to be over, he thought about how everything now fell on him. He was now responsible for the things the night swallows, as his mother always put it. The thought was so heavy he felt like it could crush him under its weight if he dwelled on it for too long.

Jorge and his sister Ana had grown up in a normal home and their childhood, which included a lot of moving around, had been good. At least he remembered it that way. Then, three years ago, his father vanished, and that's when everything crumbled. Ana and him woke up to find their mother crying at the kitchen table. She asked them to sit down and dropped a story on them that changed everything they thought they knew about their happy family.

Isabel, their mother, had moved to Florida from Puerto Rico when she was six. She had no idea why until later. It was the first of many moves. Unluckily for Ana and Jorge, their mother had never been a gifted storyteller. The nighttime stories were something their father, Ronaldo, did since they were kids. In his absence, Isabel was forced to cram her life, her bloodline and its curse, into a few minutes. Her delivery was blunt and what she told them was short in both details and explanations, but it was all she had, and the siblings had accepted it.

Isabel's grandmother, Vicenta, had suffered a lot in life, so when her husband was murdered in the early 1940s out in a cane field in the outskirts of Guánica following an argument with a brute who had a short temper and a sharp machete, she was left alone with three kids. The company said Manolo, her husband, was dead and there was no way of knowing who'd started the fight. They wouldn't give her any money except what Manolo was owed at the time of his death by a machete to the side of the neck. A few weeks later, desperate and with spiced rum running through her veins like a wild horse, Vicenta walked into the woods behind her house while her children slept. In her left hand was the bottle she'd been nursing since dusk. In her right was a large knife she usually used to cut chickens. Her plan was simple: she'd walk far enough into the woods to ensure none of her babies would find her body and then slice her own throat with the knife. She'd heard how single parents dying made the government take care of orphaned kids. Her sacrifice would ensure her children had something to eat and a place to live. It was worth it. Then she ran into something and her plans changed.

That was the part of the story in which Isabel stopped offering names, dates, and details. More than a narrative that resembled a realistic painting, her tale became a sketch drawn with vague, wide strokes that seemed unconnected to Jorge. Isabel's grandmother gave birth to one more child about a year after her husband's violent demise; a girl she named Veronica. Veronica wasn't Manolo's baby and everyone knew that. What they didn't know is that she was the daughter of whatever Vicenta had encountered in the woods. Money and food would show up at Vicenta's door regularly and everyone knew she would sneak out into woods in the middle of the night, but no one dared say anything. They had all heard the sounds that came from the woods from time to time in the middle of the night and anyone who lived near there knew that folks who lived too close to the woods would occasionally go missing. Sometimes folks would find bones or shreds of clothing, but often nothing would be found and the families would be left with an aching heart and the ugly presence of a new absence in their lives.

Ana was the smart one at home, but that didn't mean Jorge was stupid. The bits and pieces of story he got from his mother were enough for him to put together a reasonable facsimile of the whole story. The thing in the woods was evil. Despite his mother not saying it clearly, whatever was out there, whatever had fathered his grandmother, ate people. The story helped him realize his father had vanished because he was out there doing something awful in order to keep his family's secret, his mother's secret. And the secret…well, whatever it was, the first daughter of every family carried it in their DNA: Veronica gave it to Isabel, and Isabel gave it to Ana. Ana found out she had the same thing her mother had that morning because she'd never felt anything weird, so she had a lot of questions. Her mother could answer none of them. She didn't know when she would start feeling a change. She didn't know how Ana would react. Most importantly, she didn't know how they were going to get by without their father. Jorge also had questions. His mother, again, had no answers. Jorge started asking more practical questions. For those, his mother was a bit of help.

It had to be human flesh. Isabel had heard it all from her mother, but she had tried other things anyway. They all failed. If it wasn't human flesh, she wouldn't return to normal after feeding. Jorge asked questions as if his future depended on it, and his mother answered in short sentences without much discussion.

No, she didn't think she was a werewolf. In her mind, werewolves were covered in hair and had amazing strength. She wasn't strong enough to break out of the room her husband had built in the basement for what he called her "episodes."

She always knew when it was coming, so she'd tell her husband then lock herself in the room. He'd go out and bring back what she needed. Now Jorge and Ana had to do all that.

Yes, she felt horrible.

No, there was no cure.

Yes, this was the reason they'd moved so much when they were kids.

Yes, that was what was really happening whenever she vanished for a day or two into her room and the kids were told she had a really bad migraine.

Yes, it was all on them now that their father was gone.

Yes, she felt an episode was coming on.

Yes, their father had gone out to get her a body, but he'd never returned or called. Sadly, yes, she was sure he was dead.

By the time their mother had shown them how to open the secret door to her room, which required moving the kitchen table and lifting up a chunk of the floor, Ana and Jorge were panicking about what they had to do next. Then they did it anyway. They did it because it was their mother. They did it because every family has secrets, and some of them have secrets so dark that they bind them together forever. They did it because they knew they had to get good at it before Ana started suffering from her own episodes.

The first year was bizarre, but they made it work. Ana, the smart one, quickly came up with a solution. She knew a place near the University of Texas at Austin where desperate students went to make some extra cash. Ana was a good-looking brunette with huge almond-shaped eyes and full lips. She had no trouble getting men to invite her into their car. Jorge was always behind them. Ana would distract them and he would open the door and knock them out with a chunk of rebar for which he'd made a black-tape handle. It worked because no one wanted a to fuck with a big brown dude carrying a chunk of rebar. It worked because desperate people doing bad things at night tend to stay in their lane and not mess with anyone else's business. It worked because they were fast and Jorge always parked behind the car his sister went into and because he quickly learned how to put a man's lights out with a single swing. It worked because it was something they did out of love for their mother, so they willed it to work.

Then it stopped working.

Isabel knew when an episode was coming, but she had no idea when that feeling would come. The first summer they spent without their father, she didn't have a single episode. The following year, between February and May, she had one every ten days or so. On a night like any other, he saw a lot of movement as he parked behind the car Ana had climbed into. When he reached the door, he heard her screaming from inside. The door was locked, which was rare but not unheard of because Ana made sure they were always open for him. Jorge saw blood. He broke the window and bashed the man's skull in with the piece of rebar before he was done dragging him out of the car. The fucker had pulled out a knife. Ana had lifted her legs and kicked him back, but not before he slashed her left arm. She needed thirty-six stitches to close the wound. That was the last time he allowed Ana to get into a stranger's car. That's when Jorge started hunting homeless folks.

The space underneath the I-35 overpass at Airport Blvd. was a perfect place. No one reported people when they went missing. Sometimes all Jorge had to do was walk around the periphery or behind the Pok-e-Jo's and he'd find someone whose body was on earth but whose mind was floating somewhere in the stratosphere. Sometimes he had to wash them a bit or pluck the syringes they still had in their arms, but it made his job easier. Then the nightmares started and he couldn't take it. Ana, again, came to the rescue.

Ana knew her brother was a good man and the guilt was killing him, so she taught him how to find what she called "human trash": pimps, guys who jerked off by kiddie parks, and fuckers who abused homeless women…like chubby. The nightmares still came, but the guilt was small enough to be swept away under the rug in Jorge's mind.

Jorge had been lost in his thoughts and didn't realize the chubby man's party was over until he saw the woman walking back into the darkness of the woods. The lack of drama meant the man had paid. That, however, didn't make him a good man.

Driving up next to people in a dark parking lot is a great way to scare them, so Jorge had a bunch of different tactics. With this man, he'd tried the phone and money trick. He'd learned that if you approach people with money in your hands, they tend to be distracted by the money. It also makes them think you're not coming to steal from them. Adding the phone allows you to seem like you have something else going and aren't focused on any evil deeds.

This time, it worked perfectly.

Jorge pulled out his phone, help it up to his face with his shoulder, and approached the man, who was doing something inside the car before surely driving away. Jorge walked up to the driver's side window and saw the man cleaning his jeans with some brown napkins. He tapped on the glass. The man jumped. Jorge smiled.

The man rolled down his window.

"Can I help you?"

"All I got is twenties here, man I need…wait—" Jorge reached back and, in one swift motion, brought out the piece of rebar and smashed the man's nose in with it. The weird position made the blow less hard than Jorge liked. The man was moaning and holding his face in his hands, meaning he could snap out of it at any second and try to drive away. Jorge dropped the rebar and reached into the car with both hands. He grabbed the man's head and slammed it against the door twice with all his strength. The man deflated into his seat. Jorge picked up the rebar, opened the door, pulled the man halfway out, and gave him a solid whack to the side of the head to make sure whatever fight was left in him took a long vacation. Then he looked around and, seeing no one, threw the man over his shoulder and walked to his car. He kept the smile on his face and a story about the man being drunk at the tip of his tongue, in case anyone came out to claim any one of the other four cars in the parking lot. Not bad for a Tuesday.

Jorge now knew why his father always used their garage to keep his car. Driving in and shutting the door before doing anything was part of his MO, and it made him feel a bit safer. He'd also removed the lightbulb from the garage door's motor, so he always drove in in total darkness except for the car's headlights.

The chubby man was still out. His breathing was shallow, but that didn't matter. His breathing would soon be no more.

Jorge dragged the man into the kitchen. His mother was there, waiting at the kitchen table with a cup of tea. She stood up and came to her son, placing a warm hand against his right cheek.

"You're a good son, Jorgito," she said. "You're a great son and a great brother." She looked down at the man on the floor. "I'm sorry I gave this to Ana, but I didn't know it was going to happen. Your grandma was never clear on the…rules of this thing."

Jorge had nothing to say and knew that trying to put his feelings into words would make him sound like he had a wounded bird trapped in his throat. Instead of saying anything, he nodded and looked at the table. Isabel helped him move the table and lift the chunk of floor up.

The darkness inside the hole in their kitchen was absolute. From that inky blackness came a wet snarl. Jorge shivered. He grabbed the man's right leg and pulled him into the hole. The body vanished into the darkness. A loud thud announced the man's arrival at the floor below. A long moan floated up to them. As Jorge lowered the chunk of floor back down, he heard a guttural snarl followed by the sound of something wet. The scream that erupted from the man's throat was short and quickly morphed into a wet gargle that died as soon as the floor was back in its place.

Isabel had moved to the living room. Jorge walked into the room and sat on the big sofa. He looked at his mother, who sat in a lounging chair that had been with them since he could remember. The lack of sound was merciful. He sent out a thank you to his father, wherever he was, for paying attention to so many details.

This was Ana's first episode, and Jorge couldn't stop wondering what she looked like. When Ana and him had taken over for their father, when they knew the truth behind their mother's migraines, they had kept the chunk of floor up and shined a couple of flashlights into the hole one night. They'd seen their mother transform. At first it just looked like her head was getting bigger and becoming longer at the top. Something from inside seemed to push her hair out. Then came the loud cracks. Her bones become longer and her spine curved. Her fingernails exploded into talons and monstrous teeth erupted from their mother's mouth. Ana had stopped looking then, but Jorge couldn't bring himself to look away. He watched as his mother went from a small, somewhat frail woman of five-foot-two to a lanky thing that stood well over six feet tall. When her transformation was done, the howls and shrieks subsided and she— the thing that was now his mother—approached the woman they'd brought her that day. She picked her up with ease and brought the unconscious woman up to her face. The thing that had been his mother and would be his mother again opened its maw and Jorge watched as its jaw dislocated to fit the woman's hole head inside it. The crunch that followed was too much and Jorge decided to stop looking, but right before he did, the thing looked at him. The eyes hadn't changed. The eyes that looked at Jorge were his mother's eyes, the same pretty eyes Ana had, and they looked sadder than he'd ever seen them. Those eyes shattered his soul more than anything he'd experienced until then. He knew he couldn't watch Ana transform. It'd be too much.

Isabel cleared her throat. Jorge knew it was a kind gesture, a motherly way of pulling him out of the waking nightmare that had surely knotted his brow and sped up his breathing.

"Honey," said Isabel. "I need you to…I'm sorry, Jorgito, but I feel it. I think you're gonna have to head out again tomorrow night."

Jorge looked at his mother's eyes, the same eyes that had shattered his soul that day he stupidly insisted on watching her transformation. He still had no answers. He had no permanent solutions. All he had was love, and it was a love so big it turned him into a killer.

Jorge nodded. He needed some rest if he was going to do it all over again the next night. He needed to be sharp.

"I'm sorry, honey," said Isabel. "I wish I could control it." Her voice cracked at the end, filling the space between them with unsaid things. Jorge stood up and bent his big body over the lounging chair to hug his mother.

"It's okay, Mom," he said. "I'll go out. Don't worry about a thing. Summer is coming and you know summers are always better."

As he hugged his mother, Jorge started thinking about his next victim. He was a loving son, a loving brother, but he was also in charge of finding people. No, not people, food; he had to find food. He had to find and bring home what the night swallows.

Lagniappe

During a staff meeting one gloriously stormy night, the idea of having a section titled "Lagniappe" near the end of some of the works published by Brigids Gate Press was discussed. The staff unanimously voted in favor of the idea.

Lagniappe (pronounced LAN-yap) is an old New Orleans tradition where merchants give a little something extra along with every purchase. It's a way of expressing thanks and appreciation to customers.

The Lagniappe section might contain a short story, a small handful of poems, or a non-fiction piece. It might also feature a short novella. It may or may not be connected with the theme of the work.

***

"One and Done" by Cindy O'Quinn

The extra offering for this anthology is "One and Done," a non-fiction piece written by Cindy O'Quinn.

One and Done

by Cindy O'Quinn

April 20th 2021 was a beautiful day, and there were no storms in the forecast. But patches of white dotted the homestead in all the usual places—the shaded areas around the barn and along the trails in the woods that crisscross our property—snow tended to linger. Winter's little reminders; she was the boss of seasons in northern Maine.

It was unusual for early Spring to be so warm. The sun was out and reflecting against those white patches scattered about, causing them to have a silvery glow. They reminded me of the spots on an elderly man's hands. I looked at your hands. The hands of someone who worked hard for nearly fifty years; calloused, but your touch remained gentle. We walked hand in hand anytime we stepped away from our home. The strength in those hands made me feel safe, protected against everything.

You placed yourself between danger and your family, without hesitation, on more than one occasion. You jumped into hero mode the day we were on the Greenbrier River. My innertube did a flip in the rapids, when I kicked away from a wrecked canoe which was wrapped around a rock. I came back down headfirst into the water. My head crashed against the rocks and made a horrifying sound. You got our boys to shore before going upstream to float down to rescue me. I made it to my knees, body braced against the rapids. Screams echoed when I took my hands away from my head. Blood covered them and streaked my arms.

"One shot at this. When I tell you to grab my hands, you better do it!"

You shouted the firm but loving command to me. I glanced over at our young sons on the shore. They watched through teary eyes as

Dad tried to save Mom. I remember the power in your hands that day. In a split second, I was yanked from the rapids and up into your arms. I was cut, bruised, and sorely bent but not broken. Your strong, determined hands saved me and continued to keep me safe for nearly three decades.

Our small family. It was the four of us always, since forever.

Back to the warm day in April, out by the garden. I looked up at you sitting in the chair as I sat on the grass. I wondered what you were thinking. You looked out over the big field, which made me think you were planning out my new herb garden. Were you looking towards the future, or was your mind in the past?

Your hazel eyes were a sparkling green in the spring sun. I thought back to the first day of April when we arrived at the hospital to receive our vaccines. I wanted the two-step, but you insisted on the one dose injection.

"One and done, Mom. One and done."

Those words became a haunting anthem in a real-life nightmare. You had no immune response to your vaccine, not so much as a sore arm. Was it a dud injection? Perhaps it was due to diabetes, and the way it played havoc on your body. By April 13th you were showing symptoms. So many things went wrong in such a short amount of time. Was it because of my agoraphobia that you insisted on the one dose? I was good at finding a way to blame myself for anything bad that ever happened.

There by the unplanted vegetable garden you were quiet. I couldn't leave your side. Not in thirty years, and certainly not then. Your quietness became accompanied by complete stillness. It was that stillness which caused my heart and mind to break. Holding my breath, I waited. I repeated it over and over, waiting for your chest to move. Watched and waited.

Watched and waited.

Begged for your next breath to come.

It never came.

I felt the ground shake beneath me, or was it me who shook while the ground was still? The only world I knew was about to crack open. And when it happened, I just knew it was going to chew me to shreds. Spit me out when it was good and done and not a moment sooner.

Our eldest was home and tried so hard to hold it together. Youngest was at work, and I made a call no one wants to ever make. I asked his boss to bring my son home. No other explanation given. I heard it in his voice when he spoke. He knew. Youngest arrived home, stepped out of the vehicle, and took about three steps before hitting the ground. Eldest and paramedics kept the youngest in the ambulance until he was stable enough to go in the house. No pauses along the way. Two siblings provided comfort to one another, while I stayed out by the garden with you.

People came and went as need be. I remained by your side for hours. No one dared to tear me away. Throughout it all, I watched your face, eyes open but not seeing anything. Unless you did. Maybe you hung around long enough to see me through. I liked to think so. I caught myself glancing at your chest. I knew it had been far too long, but stranger things have happened.

The next breath would never come.

Another vehicle pulled in. I looked up to see something straight out of a horror movie. Chrome outlined the edges of a long black hearse. It moved eerily slow, and my breath caught in my throat, not sure if I was breathing in or out. It rolled to a stop, and the driver looked to me for further direction. I motioned where to park, knowing the driver and his partner needed to be as close as possible to you.

Dear God, they were here to take you away from me.

I wasn't ready to let you go. They stared at me as I gave one last kiss and hug, with whispered words from wife to husband, begging you to visit if you were allowed. Pleading for you to let me know when you were okay. Still wasn't ready to let you go.

The two men from that long black hearse, picked you up, chair and all. They lay you down on something. What was it? A blanket maybe. Something used for the no-longer living. They proceeded to pull the chair from beneath you. I cringed at the motion. They straightened your legs. Next came the task of moving you, my soulmate, to what looked to be a long vinyl bag.

Fuck! A body bag. Really?

They couldn't lift your two-hundred-pound body. This is when you lent me your strong hands. It had to be me, didn't it? Without speaking, I shooed the men away from your head and down towards your feet. They lifted their end of the blanket, and I lifted your top half as though I was suddenly a weightlifter. Your eyes staring at mine. My focus was glued to your face, your eyes, the lips which had kissed me from head to toe for nearly thirty years. Thirty good years, but it wasn't near long enough. I needed you.

Oh Tim, please!

My tears dripped on your face as we lay you down onto that body bag.

Dear God, this can't be happening! Surely this isn't real!

It was real, and never more so as the man in the black suit zipped up the body bag, like it was just a clothing bag.

Hold up! Don't zip it all the way! Not over his face!

My head was spinning. I was losing control.

Not yet, Cindy! Not yet!

I had another duty ahead, lifting you, inside that ugly body bag, up and onto a gurney. Once again, my borrowed strength surpassed that of the two funeral men.

My work was done. I stood and watched as they wheeled the gurney to the nearby hearse. Its back opened like a cavernous mouth as it swallowed you whole. I stepped forward, inches from the foul mouth of the death-wagon. I wanted to climb into the cool, dark grotto with you and go wherever you went. I needed to be with you, Tim. I could feel you pushing me back and away from the hearse.

I looked up and towards another door. Our cabin. Behind that one was our sons. Alone. Waiting for at least one parent. That was me, wasn't it?

The strength you lent me left my body as they slammed the hearse's back door closed. Wham! An alligator snapping its powerful jaws shut. The pain tore through my body like a bullet shredding flesh and bone.

The long, black, ghostly hearse eased from the yard, onto the driveway, and down the lane. Sun glistening off its back glass. One final wink from husband to wife.

With no strength of my own, I fell to my knees in the very spot where you had been sitting when you left your body behind. I wept, wailed, and tore at the grass. I was a mad woman.

Our eldest came out and found me still pawing at the ground. I asked about his little brother. The shock took a toll on his body and mind. He drifted to sleep as big brother sat watching over him.

Elijah helped me up off the ground and to the house. In the bedroom was Zack, asleep. We crawled in bed with him. I was between my sons. There, I quietly wept. Our family of four was now a family of three.

It was on night three when you finally came back to me. You sat on the bed and held my hands in yours. The same strong, calloused hands as before, but death made them even gentler. I felt your warmth all over my body, until I opened my eyes. I had no doubt you were there. Your presence in any room was a strong one, and I still felt it.

An emergency call was placed to my physician, and three days' worth of Klonopin were ordered.

The first few days were a blur. They had to be that way or I wouldn't have made it through. The three of us who remained pooled our money together to pay for your cremation. There was no wake, no funeral, just two boxes of ashes for our two sons. What to do with those ashes hasn't been decided, but there's no rush. That was just under eleven weeks ago.

Wasn't it just yesterday?

Elijah and Zack are doing as well as one could expect. They are back to work, seeing friends, and moving forward. You would be so proud of them. Wherever you are, I'm certain you are proud of them. As for me, well, the mourning tears remain close to the surface. The smallest things trigger them. Anger creeps in from time to time and takes over. The back of our bedroom door has taken one helluva beating.

I hide behind a closed door, hoping our sons won't hear my pain, my cries, and the agony your death has caused. The really bad thoughts come and go on a daily basis. Those are the times which scare me most. I hope they will eventually come less frequently.

My pain is obvious. Anyone can see it in the dark circles around my puffy eyes. Sleep eludes me as if it's against the rules to get a full night's rest. The boys break down when reminders of you reach out. They try to remain strong and supportive for me.

Is there a message of learning or teaching among these words? I don't see any. Is there advice to give? Just my opinion. Mask up, and get vaccinated! I don't believe the horrors of Covid 19 or the variants are anywhere near done with us. A happy ending? No. Not yet.

"One and done, Mom! One and done!"

About the Authors

Linda D. Addison is an award-winning author of five collections, including "How to Recognize a Demon Has Become Your Friend", recipient of the HWA Lifetime Achievement Award, HWA Mentor of the Year and SFPA Grand Master. Addison has published over 370 poems, stories and articles. Her site: LindaAddisonWriter.com.

H.R. Boldwood, author of the Corpse Whisperer series, countless short stories, and Imadjinn Award finalist, is a writer of horror and speculative fiction. In another incarnation, Boldwood is a Pushcart Prize nominee and winner of the 2009 Bilbo Award for creative writing by Thomas More College. Boldwood's characters are often disreputable and not to be trusted. They are kicked to the curb at every conceivable opportunity when some poor unsuspecting publisher welcomes them with open arms. No responsibility is taken by this author for the dastardly and sometimes criminal acts committed by this ragtag group of miscreants.

S.H. Cooper is an award-winning horror author based in Florida. Her work has appeared in publications by Cemetery Gates Media, Burial Day Press, and her most recent novella, Inheriting Her Ghosts, is the launching title for the NoSleep Podcast's imprint, Sleepless Sanctuary Publishing. S.H. Cooper can be found online at www.authorshcooper.com or as @MsPippinacious on Twitter.

Theresa Derwin, HWA member, writes Urban Fantasy & Horror and has over sixty anthology acceptances, one in 'Below the Stairs' with Clive Barker and a number of them in Writing advice and Shallow Waters anthologies from Crystal Lake Publishing. When she became too ill to work, she accepted medical 'escape' to pursue a writing career. As well as physical disabilities she has cognitive function issues, and writing gives her an escape from her illnesses. She's had four collections published; has edited over nine anthologies. Her forthcoming books include 'God's Vengeance' from CLP. Her most recent collection is 'Hearts and Bones' from Demain Publishing. She is the 2019 HWA Mary Shelley Scholarship recipient. She also just survived 22 months of a part time MA Creative Writing and is currently drowning in her final project, praying for help to the elder gods. She blogs at her website www.theresaderwin.co.uk and is on Twitter as @BarbarellaFem.

Ruschelle Dillon is a freelance writer whose efforts focus on the dark humor and the horror genre. Musings are on her blog, Puppets Don't Wear Pants, because…puppets don't. She is a contributor to The Horror Tree website, penning drabble and flash and a frequent interviewer of fellow authors. Her short stories have appeared in various anthologies. Arithmophobia, her collection of short stories published by Mystery and Horror LLC and her latest novella, The Stain, published by Black Bed Sheet Books are available across the Internet. She is a musician who attempts to entertain crowds with her husband and good friends in the acoustic band, The Dillon's. Her love of animals has filled her home with a small ark of cats and dogs that refuse to do any housework or help her with editing.

Stephanie Ellis writes dark speculative prose and poetry and has been published in a variety of magazines and anthologies, including Off Limits Press *Far from Home*, Silver Shamrock's *Midnight in the Pentagram* and *Midnight from Beyond the Stars,* and Demain Publishing's *A Silent Dystopia*. Her poetry has been published in the *HWA Poetry Showcase Volumes VI and VII* as well as in the collections, *The Art of Dying* and *Dark is my Playground*; her dark nursery rhymes are to be found in *One, Two, I See You*. Longer work includes the folk horror novel, *The Five Turns of the Wheel* and the gothic novella, *Bottled,* both published by Silver Shamrock. Her new short story collection, *As the Wheel Turns – More Tales from the Weald* features stories set in the world of the Five Turns. She is co-editor of Trembling With Fear, HorrorTree.com's online magazine and also co-editor at the female-centric, Black Angel Press, producing the *Daughters of Darkness* anthologies. She is an active member of the HWA and can be found at www.stephanieellis.org and on twitter as @el_stevie.

Alyson Faye lives in West Yorkshire, UK with her husband, teen son and rescue animals. Her fiction and poetry have been published in a range of anthologies, (*Diabolica Britannica/Daughters of Darkness*) on the Horror Tree, several Siren's Call editions, in Page and Spine, by Demain Press (*The Lost Girl/Night of the Rider*), in *Trickster's Treats 4*, on *Sylvia* e zine and *The World of Myth*. She has stories coming out in 2021 with Kandisha Press, Space and Time's July magazine and *The Casket of Fictional Delights*. Her work has been read out on BBC Radio, local radio, on several podcasts (Ladies of Horror and The Night's End) and placed in several competitions. She works as an editor for a UK indie press and tutors. She co-runs the indie horror press, Black Angel, with Stephanie Ellis. Their aim is to publish and promote women horror writers, from new voices to more established ones. She swims, sings and is often to be found roaming the moor with her Lab cross, Roxy. She can be found on Twitter as @AlysonFaye2.

Michelle Garza and Melissa Lason have been dubbed the Sisters of Slaughter for their work in the horror and dark fantasy genres. Their work has been published by Thunderstorm Books, Sinister Grin Press, Bloodshot Books, and Death's Head Press. Their debut novel, *Mayan Blue*, was nominated for a Bram Stoker award.

Eric J. Guignard is a writer and editor of dark and speculative fiction, operating from the shadowy outskirts of Los Angeles, where he also runs the small press Dark Moon Books. He's twice won the Bram Stoker Award (the highest literary award of horror fiction), been a finalist for the International Thriller Writers Award, and is a multi-nominee of the Pushcart Prize. He has over 100 stories and non-fiction author credits appearing in publications around the world; has edited multiple anthologies (including the current series, The Horror Writers Association's *Haunted Library of Horror Classics* with co-editor Leslie S. Klinger); and has created an ongoing series of author primers championing modern masters of the dark and macabre, *Exploring Dark Short Fiction* through his press. His latest books are *Last Case at a Baggage Auction*; *Doorways to the Deadeye*; and short story collection *That Which Grows Wild: 16 Tales of Dark Fiction* (Cemetery Dance). Outside the glamorous and jet-setting world of indie fiction, Eric's a technical writer and college professor, and he stumbles home each day to a wife, children, dogs, and a terrarium filled with mischievous beetles. Visit Eric online at his blog, www.ericjguignard.com, or on Twitter as @ericjguignard.

Kev Harrison is a British writer of horror and dark fiction, living on the outskirts of Lisbon, Portugal. His latest release, *Below*, a novella of subterranean horror, is out now from Silver Shamrock Publishing, and his debut collection, *Paths Best Left Untrodden* is available now from Northern Republic. When he's not writing dark tales, Kev can be found running, sampling too many craft beers for his own good, singing bizarre songs to his cats and travelling to far flung places with his better half, Ana. You can find him online at www.kevharrisonfiction.com or on Twitter as @LisboetaIngles.

Laurel Hightower grew up in Kentucky, attending college in California and Tennessee before returning home to horse country, where she lives with her husband, son, and a rescue pit bull. She works as a paralegal in a mid-size firm, wrangling litigators by day and writing at night. A bourbon and beer girl, she's a fan of horror movies and true-life ghost stories. She is the author of *Whispers in the Dark* and *Crossroads,* co-edited the charity anthology *We Are Wolves,* and her short fiction has appeared in several anthologies.

Gabino Iglesias is a writer, editor, and literary critic living in Austin, TX. He is the author of ZERO SAINTS and COYOTE SONGS and the editor of BOTH SIDES and HALLDARK HOLIDAYS. His work has been nominated to the Bram Stoker Award, the Locus Award, and won the Wonderland Book Award in 2019. His editing work has been nominated to the Anthony Award and the International Latino Book Awards. He teaches creative writing at SNHU's online MFA program. You can find him on Twitter as @Gabino_Iglesias.

Shane Douglas Keene is a poet, writer, and musician living in Portland, Oregon. He is the co-founder of the Ink Heist Podcast and inkheist.com. He wrote the companion poetry for Josh Malerman's serial novel project, *Carpenter's Farm* in 2020, has short fiction in Cemetery Gates Paranormal Contact, and has multiple other works forthcoming in. He lives with his wife and a small dog who thinks he's royalty because he is.

Ronald Kelly was born and bred in Tennessee and has been an author of Southern-fried horror fiction for nearly 35 years, with fifteen novels, twelve short story collections, and a Grammy-nominated audio collection to his credit. Influenced by such writers as Stephen King, Robert McCammon, Joe R. Lansdale, and Manly

Wade Wellman, Kelly sets his tales of rural darkness in the hills and hollows of his native state and other locales of the American South. His published works include *Fear, Undertaker's Moon, Blood Kin, Hell Hollow, Hindsight, The Buzzard Zone, Midnight Grinding & Other Twilight Terrors, The Essential Sick Stuff, The Halloween Store and Other Tales of All Hallows' Eve, and Irish Gothic: Tales of Celtic Horror*. He lives in a backwoods hollow in Brush Creek, Tennessee with his wife and young'uns.

Beverley Lee is the bestselling author of the Gabriel Davenport series *(The Making of Gabriel Davenport, A Shining in the Shadows* and *The Purity of Crimson) The Ruin of Delicate Things* and *The House of Little Bones* (September 2021). Her shorter fiction has been included in works from Cemetery Gates Media, Kandisha Press and Off Limits Press. In thrall to the written word from an early age, especially the darker side of fiction, she believes that the very best story is the one you have to tell. Supporting fellow authors is also her passion and she is actively involved in social media and writers' groups. You can visit her online at beverleylee.com (where you'll find a free dark and twisted short story download) or on Instagram (@theconstantvoice) and Twitter (@constantvoice).

Baba Jide Low is an experiment in horror fiction. They are curating a stylized archive of the macabre and the fantastic terrible, as rooted in Nigerian experience. They exist on Twitter, for now as @babajidelow.

Jonathan Maberry is a New York Times bestselling author, 5-time Bram Stoker Award-winner, anthology editor, and comic book writer. His vampire apocalypse book series, V-WARS, was a Netflix original series. He writes in multiple genres including suspense, thriller, horror, science fiction, fantasy, and action; and he writes for adults, teens and middle grade. His works include the *Joe Ledger* thrillers, *Ink, Glimpse, the Rot & Ruin* series, *the Dead of Night* series, *The Wolfman, X-Files Origins: Devil's Advocate, Mars One*, and many others. Several of his works are in development for film and TV. He is the editor of high-profile anthologies including *The X-Files, Aliens: Bug Hunt, Out of Tune, New Scary Stories to Tell in the Dark, Baker Street Irregulars, Nights of the Living Dead,* and others. His comics include *Black Panther: DoomWar, The Punisher: Naked Kills* and *Bad Blood.* His *Rot & Ruin* young adult novel was adapted into the #1 comic on Webtoon, and is being developed for film by Alcon Entertainment. He is a board member of the Horror Writers Association, the president of the International Association of Media Tie-in Writers, and the editor of *Weird Tales Magazine*. He lives in San Diego, California. Jonathan Maberry may be found online at www.jonathanmaberry.com.

Clara Madrigano is a Brazilian author of speculative fiction. She publishes both in Portuguese and in English, and you can find her fiction in The Dark and in Clarkesworld. Two of her stories were recently selected for the 2020 Locus Recommended Reading List. For a complete list of all of her stories, go to her website, claramadrigano.com. Clara can be found on Twitter and Instagram as @claramadrigano.

Catherine McCarthy, from deep within the wild Welsh countryside, spins dark yarns that deliver a sting in the tail. She is the author of the collections Door and other twisted tales, Mists and Megaliths, and also the novella, Immortelle (published by Off Limits Press July 2021): a Gothic tale of grief and revenge, set on the West Wales coast. Her short stories and flash fiction have been published in various places online and in anthologies, including The

British Fantasy Society, Flame Tree Press, Kandisha Press and Curiosities. In 2020 she won the Aberystwyth University Prize for creative writing for her magical realism story, The Queen's Attendant. When she is not writing she may be found hiking the Welsh coast path, or huddled among ancient gravestones reading Machen or Poe. Catherine can be found online at her website, www.catherine-mccarthy-author.com, @serialsemantic on Twitter, and as catherine_mccarthy_author on Instagram.

Villimey Mist has always been fascinated by vampires and horror, ever since she watched Bram Stoker's Dracula when she was a little, curious girl. She loves to read and create stories that pop into her head unannounced. She lives in Iceland with her husband and two cats, Skuggi and RoboCop, and is often busy drawing or watching the latest shows on Netflix. Villimey is the author of the Nocturnal series which currently comprises 3 books; *Nocturnal Blood*, *Nocturnal Farm* and *Nocturnal Salvation*. Villimey's work has previously appeared in *Campfire Macabre*, edited by Joe Sullivan and John Brhel, *The One That Got Away: Women of Horror Anthology Vol.3*, edited by Jill Girardi, *Of Cottages and Cauldrons: An Autumn Anthology*, edited by Tiffany Putetis, *Krampus Tales: A Killer Anthology*, edited by Alexandra Rose, *Far from Home: Anthology of Adventure Horror*, edited by Sam Kolesnik.

Ben Monroe has spent most of his life in Northern California, and lives in the East Bay Area with his wife and two children. His most recent published works are *In the Belly of the Beast and Other Tales of Cthulhu Wars*, the graphic novel *Planet Apocalypse* and short stories in several anthologies. His story "Vinegar Syndrome" appears in *Monsters, Movies & Mayhem*, which won the 2020 Colorado Book Award. You can reach him at www.benmonroe.com and on Twitter as @_BenMonroe_.

Cynthia "Cina" Pelayo is a two-time Bram Stoker Awards® nominated poet and author. She is the author of LOTERIA, SANTA MUERTE, THE MISSING, and POEMS OF MY NIGHT, all of which have been nominated for International Latino Book Awards. POEMS OF MY NIGHT was also nominated for an Elgin Award. Her recent collection of poetry, INTO THE FOREST AND ALL THE WAY THROUGH explores true crime, that of the epidemic of missing and murdered women in the United States, and was nominated for a Bram Stoker Award and Elgin Award. Her modern-day horror retelling of the Pied Piper fairy tale, CHILDREN OF CHICAGO, was released by Agora / Polis Books in 2021. She holds a Bachelor of Arts in Journalism from Columbia College, a Master of Science in Marketing from Roosevelt University, a Master of Fine Arts in Writing from The School of the Art Institute of Chicago, and is a Doctoral Candidate in Business Psychology at The Chicago School of Professional Psychology. Cina was raised in inner city Chicago, where she lives with her husband and children.

Cindy O'Quinn is an Appalachian writer who grew up in the mountains of West Virginia. In 2016, Cindy and her family moved to the northern woods of Maine, where she continues to write horror stories and speculative poetry. Her work has been published or is forthcoming in Shotgun Honey Presents Vol 4: RECOIL, The Shirley Jackson Award Winning Anthology: The Twisted Book of Shadows, Shelved: Appalachian Resilience During Covid 19 Anthology, Attack from the 80's Anthology, The Bad Book Anthology, Chiral Mad 5, HWA Poetry Showcase Vol V, Space & Time Magazine, Weirdbook Magazine, Nothing's Sacred Vol 4 & 5, Sanitarium Magazine, & others. Cindy is a two-time Bram Stoker Award Final Nominee. Her poetry has been nominated for both the Rhysling & Dwarf Star Awards. She is a member of HWA, NESW, NEHW, SFPA, Horror Writers of Maine, and Weird Poets Society.

You can follow Cindy for updates on Facebook as @CindyOQuinnWriter, Instagram as cindy.oquinn, and Twitter as @COQuinnWrites.

Christina Sng is the two-time Bram Stoker Award-winning author of A Collection of Dreamscapes and A Collection of Nightmares. Her poetry, fiction, essays, and art appear in numerous venues worldwide. She has garnered many accolades for her work, including multiple nominations for the Rhysling Awards, the Dwarf Stars, the Elgin Award, the Pushcart Prize, and honorable mentions in the Year's Best Fantasy and Horror, and the Best Horror of the Year. Visit her online at christinasng.com and connect on social media @christinasng.

Sara Tantlinger is the author of the Bram Stoker Award-winning *The Devil's Dreamland: Poetry Inspired by H.H. Holmes,* and the Stoker-nominated works *To Be Devoured, Cradleland of Parasites,* and *Not All Monsters.* Along with being a mentor for the HWA Mentorship Program, she is also a co-organizer for the HWA Pittsburgh Chapter. She embraces all things macabre and can be found lurking in graveyards or on Twitter as @SaraTantlinger, at saratantlinger.com and on Instagram as @inkychaotics.

Elle Turpitt is a writer, reviewer and editor living in Cardiff, South Wales. Her short fiction has appeared in anthologies for Seven Deadly Sins: A YA Anthology, and Fantasia Divinity, as well as online. She co-runs Divination Hollow Reviews, and when not writing or editing can often be found with her head in a book or playing video games. Her website is elleturpitt.com and she is also on Twitter and Instagram as @elleturpitt.

Tabatha Wood is an Australian Shadows award-winning author of weird, dark horror fiction and uplifting poetry from Aotearoa, New Zealand. A former English teacher and library manager, her first books were guides for professional educators. She now tutors from home while also working as a freelance writer and editor, usually under the influence of strong coffee. You can read more of her stories, essays and blog posts at www.tabathawood.com.

Stephanie M. Wytovich is an American poet, novelist, and essayist. Her work has been showcased in numerous venues such as Weird Tales, Nightmare Magazine, Year's Best Hardcore Horror: Volume 2, The Best Horror of the Year: Volume 8, as well as many others. Wytovich is the Poetry Editor for Raw Dog Screaming Press, an adjunct at Western Connecticut State University, Southern New Hampshire University, and Point Park University, and a mentor with Crystal Lake Publishing. She is a member of the Science Fiction Poetry Association, an active member of the Horror Writers Association, and a graduate of Seton Hill University's MFA program for Writing Popular Fiction. Her Bram Stoker Award-winning poetry collection, *Brothel*, earned a home with Raw Dog Screaming Press alongside *Hysteria: A Collection of Madness*, *Mourning Jewelry*, *An Exorcism of Angels*, *Sheet Music to My Acoustic Nightmare*, and most recently, *The Apocalyptic Mannequin*. Her debut novel, *The Eighth*, is published with Dark Regions Press. Follow Wytovich on Twitter as @SWytovich, and at her blog at stephaniewytovich.blogspot.com.

About the Illustrator

Elizabeth Leggett is a Hugo award-winning illustrator whose work focuses on soulful, human moments-in-time that combine ambiguous interpretation and curiosity with realism.

Much to her mother's dismay, she viewed her mother's white washed walls as perfectly good canvasses so she believes it is safe to say that she has been an artist her whole life! Her first published work was in the Halifax County Arts Council poetry and illustration collection. If she remembers correctly, she was not yet in double digits yet, but she might be wrong about that. Her first paying gig was painting other students' tennis shoes in high school.

In 2012, she ended a long fallow period by creating a full seventy-eight card tarot in a single year. From there, she transitioned into freelance illustration. Her clients represent a broad range of outlets, from multiple Hugo award winning Lightspeed Magazine to multiple Lambda Literary winner, Lethe Press. She was honored to be chosen to art direct both Women Destroy Fantasy and Queers Destroy Science Fiction, both under the Lightspeed banner.

Elizabeth, her husband, and their typically atypical cats, live in New Mexico. She suggests if you ever visit the state, look up. The skies are absolutely spectacular!

About the Editors

S.D. Vassallo is a co-founder and editor for Brigids Gate Press, LLC. He's also a writer who loves horror, fantasy, science fiction and crime fiction. He was born and raised in New Orleans, but currently lives in the Midwest with his wife, son, and two black cats who refuse to admit that coyotes exist. When not reading, writing or editing, he can be found gazing at the endless skies of the wide-open prairie. He often spends the night outdoors when the full moon is in sway.

Steven Long is an editor for Brigids Gate Press, LLC. Spending the last 20-plus years in publishing, he has worked for a handful of publishers, from small mom-and-pop concerns to major corporations such as Random House. In more recent years, he has returned to a passion that inspired him to pursue a career in publishing: writing. The founder of a blog that celebrates Maine small business owners, he is currently working on a master's degree from New England College. His first publication, a flash creative nonfiction piece, will be published *The Adirondack Review* during the winter of 2021–22.

Content Warnings

Refuge by Kev Harrison: sexual assault.

Y Ceffyl Dŵr (The Water Horse) by Catherine McCarthy: sexual assault and death.

Fight or Flight by Elle Turpitt: implied sexual assault.

Darkness Peering by Ben Monroe: domestic abuse.

The Travelers by Laurel Hightower: implied child death.

What the Night Swallows by Gabino Iglesias: implied sexual assault.

We hope you enjoyed this anthology. Please visit our website, brigidsgatepress.com, for news and future releases!

9 781957 537153